The Boy Friend

MIKA JOLIE

Publisher My Happy Chaos Publishing
www.mikajolie.com

Table of Contents

Explicitly Yours, Dean Conrad Morello. 5
Chapter 1 6
Chapter 2 14
Chapter 3 27
Chapter 4 37
Chapter 5 44
Chapter 6 50
Chapter 7 66
Chapter 8 72
Chapter 9 86
Chapter 10 95
Chapter 11 104
Chapter 12 111
Chapter 13 117
Chapter 14 129
Chapter 15 139
Chapter 16 151
Chapter 17 157
Chapter 18 166
Chapter 19 179
Chapter 20 183
Chapter 21 197
Chapter 22 207
Chapter 23 219
Chapter 24 233
Chapter 25 237
Chapter 26 244
Chapter 27 257
Chapter 28 265
Chapter 29 269
Chapter 30 279

Chapter 31...290
Chapter 32 298
Epilogue...308
Acknowledgments...315
Old-Fashioned Recipe..316
The Boy Friend Playlist..317
About Mika Jolie 320
Also by Mika Jolie 322

OKAY, HERE'S THE DEAL, I'm going to share my story with you. Let's get a few things out of the way. There's going to be sex. Some details might be a bit explicit. I curse like a motherfucker. The plot will be a little wonky and will not always follow some forced narrative. Sure, there will be conflict, climax, resolution . . . Bullshit, bullshit, bullshit. But don't expect me to be a fucking Prince Charming. I'm the tall, dark, and handsome Casanova the nuns warned you about. Hearts will be broken. Tears will be shed. Friendship will be tested. Eventually, I'll realize the mess I'm in isn't fictional, and I'm the motherfucking star of my own story.

With me so far?

Okay. Grab a Pinot Grigio, a warm fuzzy blanket, and join me on this wild ride.

EXPLICITLY YOURS,

Dean Conrad Morella

Chapter 1

"Friends buy you lunch. Best friends eat your lunch."

SEE THAT GUY SITTING BY the window inside the rustic-yet-trendy bar? The one with the broad shoulders filling out a half-zipped, blue plaid pullover and slim-fit, black cargos? He's dragging a hand through his short, dark hair, and his strong brows are pinched together in a mixture of confusion and disbelief as he stares at the attractive woman sitting on the other side of the round table. Yes, the pretty boy with the what-the-fuck look on his face—that's me, Dean Conrad Morello.

Why am I having difficulty breathing, you ask?

It's because of the woman sitting across from me, wearing the fitted gray bomber jacket, and the skinny jeans tucked into black leather knee boots with fuck-me heels. She's staring at me with eyes the color of the Laphroaig single-malt in my hand. Right now, they have a connotation of decadence and pleasure as she chews on a few truffle fries.

"So, what do you think?" She tosses her rich dark brown hair over her shoulder. Several streaks of indigo highlights, almost the same shade as her jeans, play with the light. And I can't help but notice how it shines, even in the dimness of the bar.

This is Cori—short for Coriander—Phillips. She hates her first name. I think it's cute. One wouldn't describe her as quirky, or ethereal, or alien, or any other condescending adjective used to depict women who are decidedly not "the girl next-door." Basically, what I mean is: she's undeniably beautiful in a not-quite atypical way. However, she's much more than a pretty face. She's smart as hell, deeply perceptive, unfailingly kind, witty, and happens to be my BFF—you know, best friend forever—so don't get any ideas.

She also just dropped a bombshell on me.

"I want a baby," she repeats.

Maybe she thinks I didn't hear her the first time. The noise level around us is amped—customers are talking, arguing over sports, complaining about work or spouses—it's Friday night, after all. But I have the eyes of a hawk and ears of an owl. We're at *Une Pression*—French for beer on tap—a popular restaurant in town. Make that the only restaurant in town. Our little town has three commercial establishments—*Une Pression*, a gas station, and a garden shop.

If you live in Alpine, New Jersey, your nights are either spent in Manhattan or here. Tonight, the place is jam-packed. Waiters are scurrying by, arms overloaded with trays of drinks and plates piled high with food.

Every Friday night, Cori and I meet here for our *non-date* date for a couple of hours, bullshit for a bit, and then go our separate ways.

"Why do you look like you're about to faint?" Amusement fills her voice. Cheeks, dappled with freckles as chaotic as the fall leaves, lift in a smile. When I don't answer, her chair scrapes the floor. She's ready to get to her feet and give me mouth-to-mouth resuscitation if necessary. "Are you okay?"

I press a finger to my eye before it twitches right out of my head. Surprise isn't an emotion I've ever expressed well. Generally, someone gets hurt, and it's never me. Almost robotically, I grab my scotch and swallow a big gulp, letting the oak flavor muscle its way down my throat as I process Cori's news.

My first thought is that this is her way of proposing one of those wacky *let's-make-a-baby-together* bullshit ideas. Women are crazy like that. I've heard plenty of "if neither of us is married by this age, then we should have a baby, or we should hook up." Seriously, that's insane.

Anyway, Cori is not like that. Thank goodness. She's a confident, straightforward chick. I like that about her. Which means, if she wanted me to be her baby daddy, she'd come right out and ask.

I'd say no, of course.

But she hasn't asked, so no need for any panic attack.

This knowledge offers no solace. My gut tells me, whatever she's thinking is not going to sit well. I arrange my face into something I hope is calm, cool, and collected. "Where the hell did that come from?" My mind still swirling, I mutter, "A baby."

"I know." Full lips, shimmering with pink gloss, rise into a smile. "Can you believe it?"

No. I can't fucking believe it.

One of her elbows is resting on the rough wood of the round table separating us. By the way her body tips forward, I know her delicate, floral, half-moon tattoo, with the words, 'Stay Wild Moonchild,' inscribed in thin italic font on the right side of her lower back, is revealed just enough to give a boner to most men within gawking distance. She also has a tiny anchor on her right inner ankle.

She takes a slow, deliberate sip of her Old Fashioned cocktail, lowers her gaze, and looks straight at me again. "I love children, you know that."

Yeah, I'm aware of her love for children. But loving other people's kids for eight hours twice a week and choosing to want one of your own are two different things. In any event, before I jump on the let's-get-Cori-pregnant bandwagon, I need to understand the drive behind this decision.

"A baby is a game changer. Lots of responsibilities," I point out. Friends are supposed to talk friends from walking off the ledge, right?

I mean, close friends are life's treasures. Cori falls in that category. Other than my mother and my sister, Katharine, any woman you see me with, I've either fucked, or I'm about to fuck. So I bet you're thinking the term I should be using to describe our closeness is BFFWB—best friends forever with benefits, of course.

That's a big presumption on your part. Let me assure you, I can have a platonic relationship with a woman.

Okay, you're not completely wrong.

But there's an exception to every rule. My friendship with the dark-haired beauty who is currently eating the fries off my plate, and who appears completely oblivious to every man checking her out, has been platonic for over two decades and shall always remain that way.

No fucking way!

Yeah, I know. But Coriander Phillips is the one woman who is permanently off-limits.

"I think . . . " She twirls the thin black straw from her drink between her fingers, then places it on the white paper napkin. "No, I know it's time."

"Your twice-a-week fill of snot-nosed six- and eight-year-olds is not enough for you?" My gaze roams around the packed bar on this wintery night. On my right, the beautiful brunette from the live band is singing her rendition of "Maneater." Prior to Cori's news, I was enjoying the vibe; now all of it has become white noise.

"They are not snot-nosed brats." She tilts her head back and laughs, exposing the long elegant stretch of her neck. "I love teaching those kids about art."

My Coriander Stay Wild Moonchild grew up to be an artist. A few years ago, she purchased an old farmhouse and converted it into her studio, gallery, and one of those trendy classrooms where women paint while sipping wine. She also teaches art twice a week at our former elementary school. While success didn't happen overnight, it's safe to say that she's one of those artists who is earning a living doing what she loves.

As for me, I grew up—somewhat—followed my dad's footsteps, and became a financial genius. I love my job. We'll get to that later.

My eyes drift to the wall of alcohol bottles and the upside-down stem glasses in racks above the bartender's head. "Kate didn't talk you out of this?" Kate is short for Katharine, my younger sister by twenty-two months. She's a replica of our mother—petite and blond—except, she inherited our dad's brown eyes, like me. I, on the other hand, am a full-blown version of my father—bronzed skin, dark-brown hair verging on black, chiseled jaw.

"She's supportive," Cori answers after taking another sip of her cocktail.

Of course, my sister is encouraging this absurdity. I should have known. Every female has a crazier female friend who will help them do the craziest shit. Needless to say, Cori and Kate are very close in a way only another woman can understand. They'd take a bullet for each other without any hesitation, not in the head, but the leg or something.

Flashback to twenty-one years ago, on the school playground at our super-exclusive private school. In strolled a scrawny little girl in an aqua T-shirt that read, 'Stay Wild, Moonchild,' and purple-blue hippie harem pants. I remember that day as if it happened yesterday. She couldn't be missed. She marched straight up to me and demanded I apologize to Katharine. After I pulled one of her two pigtails and dared her to make me, she punched me in the gut with her seven-year-old strength.

Why?

Because she thought my buddy Lucas and I were bullying Katharine.

Everyone knows everyone in our enclave, and our school was the size of a lunchbox—not cramped, but small. But that was apparently Cori's first day, and she had no clue Kate and I were siblings.

Anyhow, Cori and I have been inseparable ever since. We've never slept together, never been to first base, never kissed. We have a platonic friendship. Nothing more. We have no romantic interest in each other.

While I would fuck the majority of the female population, I have no interest in actively pursuing that goal with Cori. Don't get me wrong, this doesn't mean she doesn't enter my strictly sexual fantasies every once in a while. Perfect example, look at the way the tip of her tongue brushes against that cocktail cherry between her lips. I can't help but think I'm the lucky recipient of her tongue touching my flesh, licking down my chest or further south.

Of course, my dick stirs in my pants, that's a common physiological reaction.

But understand, these are occasional, fleeting thoughts. I've never jerked off to Cori. Nope. I have some scruples. My mind teetering out of Friendtopia into HornyTown, USA is beyond my control.

Look, that's just the way the mind of a man with a strong sexual appetite works, especially one with a hot woman as his best friend. I fantasize about having sex with a lot of women I see in my daily life, that doesn't mean I want to pursue or actually have something with them.

My point is, putting the time and energy into exploring whether sex is on the table between Cori and I, or making it happen, isn't worthwhile, too many obstacles. If shit goes bad, then what? Yeah, not worth it. We have a healthy, guy-girl friendship.

Trust me. Both of us are happy and comfortable with my role in her life. I'm the *boy friend*. Every woman should have a guy in her life she can go to when she needs help understanding the male species.

Chapter 2

"He's not my boyfriend."

"ANYHOW"—CORI LEANS back in her chair and runs her hands down the thighs of her jeans— "my mind is made up." There's a clear, calm, decisiveness in her voice.

No. No. No. I feel stuck in the same spiral staircase. No matter if I go upstairs or down, I'd keep coming back to the same spot.

Cori wants a baby.

Out of desperation, I say, "You're not married."

One of her perfectly trimmed eyebrows rises. That's Coriander's stop-being-a-moron face, saved just for me.

Yeah, I got the memo. This is the twenty-first century, pantsuit nation, a woman needs a man like a fish needs a bicycle.

Whatever.

I'm aware some women choose the single mother route and tackle life alone while chanting, 'I'm woman, hear me roar.'

Blah, blah, blah.

Seriously, please take a chill pill.

Call me sexist if you want. I don't really care. I've also witnessed my mom roughhoused by two terrors, and we had two nannies and a hands-on dad. More importantly, this is my Cori. She deserves the white picket fence, the big backyard, and the two-point-five kids, with a loving husband. The whole shebang.

"Why not start with a boyfriend?" I continue with my cross-examination. When your best friend decides to drop a bombshell on you, it's time for some third-degree. "You don't even have one."

She reaches onto my plate for a fry. "Whose fault is that?"

What the hell does that mean? I don't cock-block . . . ever. Or get jealous. Perhaps a bit protective, but this is Coriander we're talking about. She's . . . you know . . . a part of my universe, one of my best friends. I don't like to see her hurt, broken, or sad. We've been down that road twice. Her college boyfriend, Mike Dubois, and recently, Barry chicken-shit Clemens.

Miles away, I was able to break down the components of their relationship and determined pretty-boy Mike was an asshole. When I warned her he was a douche and not as in love as he had claimed to be, she trusted him with her virginity anyway.

They broke up by Christmas break. Katharine and I helped her recover. But it was me who weathered the storm with Cori the most. For a few months, I became her boat, kept her head above water.

If I'm not doing the happy dance, it's due to caution, nothing about cockblocking. "What brought this on?" I ask after a long minute.

"I'm turning twenty-eight." She snatches another fry from my plate and tosses it in her mouth.

"And I'm turning thirty," I remind her. My birthday is in two weeks. Hers is in April. Two months from now. "Your age isn't a reason to have a baby." I lean forward, holding her gaze. "A baby is a life changer—lots of responsibilities, dirty diapers, lots of crying." Most importantly, Cori would belong to someone else. Not the baby, I'm not worried about a fractious little person latching onto one of her nipples.

"I can handle a baby." She puts her hand over mine, her brown eyes serious. "I want this. Please support me."

Needing a moment, I swallow another gulp of my scotch. It's not the baby. My concern is the asshole who ends up planting his dipshit seed in her. They'd probably end up married or, worse, fall in love. Eventually, the dickhead would develop some sort of hostility toward my place in her life.

See where I'm going with this?

No, it's not all about me. I'm not egocentric, all wrapped up in myself. For the record, my friendship with Cori has been tested a few times on both sides. There was the girl I slept with on a regular basis in college. I think her name was Maribel or something, a hot Venezuelan with a body handmade by Jesus H. Christ himself; H is for Harry—picture Prince Harry. Not that I think they look alike, but I like Prince Harry. The guy is a prince and spends his time sleeping with gorgeous women or flying military jets. Total badass.

16

Maribel thought she was my girlfriend and demanded I cut all ties with Cori. For a nanosecond, I actually considered saying, "*Sayonara*, see you never," to my little Moonchild.

Then sanity kicked in—one of the rare times my dick and my brain were not in agreement.

On several occasions, we get the same shit from men filled with insecurities. They have this crazy notion that a man and a woman can't be friends.

My point is, I know it's coming. One day she'll no longer be the yin to my yang.

Something in my gut twists. I take another shot of the scotch. If it's my support Cori wants, then she shall get it. "You're serious about this baby thing?"

"Yeah."

"All right." I wipe my hands on the cloth napkin. "Your pussy doctor should be able to give you a list of sperm donors."

"They're called obstetricians or gynecologists or" –she looks down at me— "OB-GYNs, if the other words are out of your vocabulary range."

"I like pussy doctor better," I say, wiggling my eyebrows.

She cackles at that. "You're incorrigible." A slight flush touches her face. "I'm going to do it the natural way, goof."

"Natural . . . as in?"

She shocks me by letting loose an unrestrained laugh. "Yeah, like sex."

I down the rest of my scotch in one shot and signal the waitress for another round. Hell, by the end of the night, I'll be shitfaced.

"I don't just want to have a baby. I want the whole thing: to date, fall in love." A dreamy look I've never seen before settles on her face. "I want the fairy-tale ending."

"They are called fairy tales for a reason."

She gives me a don't-be-stupid-look. "Your parents found it."

No argument from me about that. Thirty-two years later, my parents still gush over one another. Get this—they still hold hands, kiss each other, and all that mushy stuff. It's really gross, said in my seven-year-old voice.

Cori steals another fry from my plate. By the way, she has a mound of fries on her own plate. "I want to start dating again."

She's been on a long hiatus since Barry, which worked in my favor. For the last year, I've had my buddy back. A new man in her life means she'll no longer be able to catch a movie or go bowling with me. The idea weighs heavily on my chest. "You want to fall in love?"

She takes another sip of her drink then meets my questioning gaze, hers serious. "I want the whole thing."

"The whole thing?"

She gives me a big white smile. "Lust, love, and a smidgen of romance."

Well, damn, what can I say about that? Cori has always believed in romance, and I can tell her mind is made up. Once she reaches that point, I can no more change her mind than I can persuade a snowstorm not to come. Any rationalization about why this is a bad idea is pointless right now. "All right," I concede. "I'll help you find the right guy."

Her eyes don't blink for at least forty seconds. "What?"

"We'll start a process."

"No," she says firmly. "I don't need a process."

Arms crossed over my chest, I lean back in my chair. "You have dates lined up?"

"Well, no. I was thinking of creating an online profile."

Oh, hell no. Those sites are filled with assholes who get off sending pics of their dicks to women. Seriously guys, stop doing that shit. I've never met a woman who finds a dick selfie sexy.

"No online dating."

She arches a brow. "Why not?"

"Those guys on those sites are perverts."

"That's right." She snaps the imaginary light bulb on. "You used to be on one, right?"

Silence.

"What was it again? Hook Up dot com or something like that."

"It was an experiment." A brief stint that passed with flying colors. Hooked up with a bunch of women, although, now I can't envision any of their faces. But let's stay focused on Cori. "I'm ruling out online dating based on experience."

"Whatever." She throws another fry in her mouth. "I'm still creating a profile."

I can feel the stubbornness rolling off her body. Knowing when to wave the white flag, I go back to another topic I have a chance of winning. "Then we come up with a process."

She groans. "Oh, boy."

"I'll come up with a list of questions." After chewing down another bite of my burger, I say, "We can meet for lunch and go over them."

"Oh. My. God. Not one of your processes."

"Hey, I'm a hedge fund manager. Assessing risk is what I'm good at."

"What does your job have to do with me setting up an online profile?"

"Want to know why we're successful at what we do?"

She raises a brow. "Other than your good looks?"

From any other woman, I'd take that as flirting, an invitation. But this is Cori. For as long as I've known her, she's never flirted with me. "You need a strategy." I take another sip of my drink. "I'm going to help you with all of that."

She rolls her eyes.

"Believe me," I say, fully confident I'm the man for the job . . . to help her find her . . . What did she call it? Her happily-ever-after, or some shit like that. "I'm the man for the job."

Cori drums her fingers on the table. "You're my happily-ever-after?"

Shit. I almost choke on my scotch. I shake my head. "No."

Something crosses her face, but is quickly covered with a smile.

"What I'm saying is, the hunt for a spouse is a process."

After a long stare, she says, "I feel like I'm in the Twilight Zone. Kate was right."

The mention of my sister makes me suddenly suspicious. "What exactly did she say?"

"That you'd want to take me on as a project."

"She doesn't know what she's talking about." For the record, I love my sister—she's a pain in the ass—but she's right, this is a project.

"Hey." She flashes a smile that lights up her whole face. "Don't bash my best friend."

Ouch. "What the hell am I? Chopped liver?"

"Well, both of you are," she quickly adds, catching her faux pas. "Anyway, I can find my own date or potential husband."

I shake my head. "Should I remind you of Mike?"

She gives me a blank look. He's not the kind of ex-boyfriend one can forget.

"College boyfriend." I've never fully accepted the fact he'd been her first. Not out of envy; Cori was too good for him. "He stole your virginity."

"Stolen implies it was against my will."

Which hadn't been the case. Point taken. "Okay, Mike, the guy who broke your hymen."

"You're disgusting."

Yeah, I know. The smile tugging on the corner of her lips is a clear indication she doesn't find me one bit nauseating.

"He turned out to be a jerk."

"Lesson learned." She lifts a shoulder. "No regrets."

"From what I remember, I did present a strong case for you not to sleep with him."

"Remind me again why."

"You were too young."

"I was nineteen, some consider that late." She tilts her head to one side. "Oh, in case you've forgotten, you were having sex at nineteen."

"I'm a guy."

Cori scoffs. "You're sexist."

I shrug.

"By the way," she says, a teasing tone in her voice, "whatever you can do, I can do . . . while wearing heels."

"If a fire were to break out, do you expect a fleet of women to show up?"

"Yes," she answers without a beat.

"They'll be in broken heels."

She throws her hands up in the air. "I give up."

"You still love me." Truth be told, I'm not sexist about anything. I believe in equal opportunity for everyone and everything, except, when it comes to Cori. No man will ever be good enough. Seriously, is any worthless-piece-of-shit man good enough for your daughter or sister?

What's that? No?

Exactly.

Cori steals another fry from my plate. "I'm beginning to wonder why you and I are still friends."

"Because I'm a good-looking SOB."

She snorts.

"And, I make you laugh."

"Oh, yeah, I almost forgot." She sighs as if this admission pains her. The dynamic between us is effortless. Easy. Fun.

"Then there was Barry, or something like that," I mention her last boyfriend for the first time in a long time.

"We dated for a year," she said in a nonchalant tone.

"He hurt you." This pains me to say, but I need to present my case. The douchebag broke her heart just when she started dreaming of wedding bells.

She straightens herself, shoulders squared, her gaze defiant. "I dumped him."

It's true, she dumped his ass. But that doesn't mean the breakup hadn't hurt. "He asked you to do the impossible."

"Dean Conrad Morello, ending our friendship is not impossible. However, if I ever cut all ties with you, it will be because you hand me the scissors, not because of a man. Do you get that?"

That makes me feel better. "Ditto, gorgeous." I lean forward and place a couple of fries in her mouth. She closes her eyes and chews with a look of ecstasy on her face. Two things put that look on Cori's face—fries and salted caramel brownies. Mine is the look of pleasure on a woman's face at the pinnacle of an orgasm.

"So, can we go back to normal now?" she asks, once back to earth from her *fry-gasm*.

"Only if you agree to let me screen your potential baby daddy."

"Baby daddy doesn't marry the woman," she says in all of her smartassery.

"You're missing the point."

She studies my face for a long minute before asking, "Why is that so important to you?"

Does that question even warrant an answer? She's one of the members of my universe. I take her hands in mine. "You need someone who's stable."

"Don't worry." She gives me a small smile. "I'm not going to abandon my children to travel the world with my husband."

The sadness in her voice pushes every emotion from my being. Technically, her observation is not too far off. Cori's mother is a wildflower, a former child star who married an artist. Between them, they produced Cori.

I can count the instances her parents have been around on one hand. Twenty-one years ago, with Cori's father by her side, Sage Foster Phillips dumped Cori at her mother's house and decided her destiny was to travel the world with her husband and help the less fortunate. The rest is history.

Unlike her parents, who were born to spread their wings, Cori was born to spread her roots. Because of that, I understand her desire to settle down. Don't get me wrong, she's not one of those chicks who has a fear of being alone. Quite the contrary, she finds solace in her own company. I'm not worried about that. However, when my Moonchild marries, it will be a one-time deal with someone who's willing to give her the world. Hell, she deserves the damn moon.

"I just want to help." I give her hands a light squeeze before releasing them, and reach for my scotch. "Let me at least do that."

"Fine." Her rich, golden brown eyes are sparkling again. "I'll consider your opinion."

Some of my underlying tension melts away. "Not consider, you'll take it into account."

"Isn't that the same thing?"

"Nope. You see—"

She raises a hand, stopping me mid-sentence. "I'm not an account you're closing in on." She extends her right pinky finger out to me. "It's a deal."

We pinky promise, pinky swear, something we've been doing since I was nine and she was seven years old. But this time, something doesn't feel right. I attribute it to one thing

25

only—anticipation, a nervous kind of energy. It tingles through me like electrical sparks on the way to the ground.

The day I've been dreading is here, and I can't halt the beginning of the end of Coriander Moonchild Phillips and Dean Conrad Morello.

Chapter 3

"Life was meant for good friends and great adventures."

POST-SEX CUDDLING IS all about emotional bonding and intimacy. I have no interest in any of that with a sex buddy. Leave it up to me, I'd say goodnight, go home, take a hot shower, and collapse into bed totally relaxed . . . and satisfied.

The body pressing against me is warm and soft. Red hair is spilled over my chest. I'm holding her in silence, but this is not an intimate embrace. The heat her body is projecting offers no solace. Instead, I feel trapped.

"What's on your mind?" she asks against my chest.

"Nothing." Through perfect teeth comes the lie, vibrating in the air, inconsequential to the medium through which it travels. Only I know the difference. Something is bugging me, for sure, and the culprit is Cori. I'm not sure why I'm bothered by her sudden need to settle down. I shouldn't be, yet I am.

A quick glance through the sheer curtain indicates the sky has long since darkened from bleak winter gray to familiar black. A clear evidence I've overstayed my welcome. Time for my exit. There's one problem with that. She's lying next to me, one of her legs locked with mine.

Cuddling after sex is one of her favorite things.

Pets are good for cuddling. Preferably a dog. They're furry and warm. I'm not a dog.

Touché.

My point is, I'm not a total dickhead. So, for at least ten minutes, I'm sucking up this need for physical intimacy that doesn't involve some sort of penetration.

By the way, we're at her place. Women don't spend nights at my house. Not even Cori.

Anyhow, for the next few minutes, I'm the good guy, the perfect lover, as I appear to give her my undivided attention. Truth is, I'm thinking about the other top two things on a man's list—sleep and food. I have no clue what the *after*-sex topic of choice is right now. But years of experience have trained me to say what every woman wants to hear: *Yeah, sure, we can do that. No, those jeans don't make your ass look fat.*

While we're on this topic, what's wrong with a nice, round ass in jeans? As a man, I can attest that I find nothing sexier than a tight, nice, round ass. Give me some meat on those bones, and I'm a happy boy.

"What do you think?" she asks.

I open my mouth, ready to regurgitate the usual, *Let's make it happen,* to Red when my Spidey sense cautions me not to open my mouth. I faintly caught her saying something about a weekend.

I wait. Women tend to repeat themselves.

"Can you come?" she asks, her voice is low and husky, filled with the aftermath of sex.

After another minute, hell yeah, I'll be ready again. Preferably, this time with her on top, riding me until we hit our high spot, while babbling insanities and nonsense. But I don't think we're discussing sex. "Come?"

"I have this event in New York in three weeks." Red is a lawyer. One of the good ones, whose mission is to save the environment. We met at a charity event a month ago. "Would you like to come?"

"I'm away." No lie. I'm actually not available.

Every year, the guys and I—Cori and Kate included—go on a ski trip right around my birthday. It's a tradition. The guys are Lucas and Cameron. You'll meet both of them later. This year, we picked Waterville Valley, one of the best ski resorts tucked away in the north-central White Mountains of New Hampshire.

Back to my current state, and for the sake of staying anonymous, let's call this woman Red. Okay, I can't remember her name; sue me. One of her fingers is circling the left side of my chest, right where my heart beats. I take her hand and move it south past my navel.

No, I'm not emotionally stunted. At some point in my life, I've experienced all the myriads of emotion. I love my family and close friends. I know joy and happiness so strong, I tingle right down to my bones. Watching my grandparents—Dad's side—fading in and out of reality with Alzheimer's was a fucker. So, you see, I'm not a cold asshole.

I just don't want her to think we are a possibility. We're not.

In case you're wondering, my heart has never been crushed by a woman at any point in my life. Not even during my transition from puberty, with braces and pimples, to a muscular, lean, cocky SOB. Relationships just aren't for me. At least not now.

"I'm going away with the boys," I remind Red.

"Oh, that's right." She wraps her hand around my cock and gives it a light squeeze. It stands erect, ready to go. "Your ski trip to Maine, is it?"

"New Hampshire." I mentioned my upcoming yearly ski trip earlier to Red. We can blame that moment of insanity on my BFF with her *I want a baby* shocker. Two days later, my mind is still reeling over the news.

"Yeah," Red whispered. "Ski trip with the fellas." She continues the slow and steady motion, sliding up and down my engorged flesh. "Your sister isn't one of the fellas; neither is your friend. What's her name again?" She tightens her grip. Seriously, this woman gives the best hand jobs.

"Coriander." She knows Cori's name. Why do women do that shit? If you feel threatened by a woman, just fucking say it. Jesus H. Fucking Christ!

For a moment, it crosses my mind to probe further, find out if she has a problem with my friendship with Cori. We all know how that would end. I'd say goodbye. The truth is, there's no woman in my life worth having that conversation with at the moment.

A little chuckle escapes her throat. "Such a weird name."

"I love her name. It suits her." Cori's smiling face pops into my mind's eye. *Not the time my little Stay Wild, Moonchild.* I shove thoughts of Cori into a far corner of my mind, reach for another condom on the nightstand.

"I want to come with you."

In a few minutes, both of us will be coming. "That's always the goal, baby."

For fuck's sake, I can't remember this woman's name.

And how hasn't she picked up on the fact I never call her by her name?

How is she listed in my contact list?

Red Head.

That's the name I used to enter her information in my contact list when we first hooked up. I kid you not.

Yes. I'm a fucker.

Ladies, if a guy keeps calling you honey or baby, flip him the bird and tell him to go stick it where the sun don't shine.

Wait. Don't tell him that. Some of us enjoy the backdoor very much.

A part of me is dying to lift her up and sit that delicious body on top of me. At this point, my cock is ready, but I also like the foreplay part of sex. The anticipation, there's a sexiness to it. After I finish protecting both of us, I roll to my side and catch one nipple between my teeth.

"I mean, I want to go to New Hampshire with you," Red says as her fingers skirt along my thighs. "The event is during the day. We can leave after."

My dick freezes. The impact of her announcement knocks all desire out of my system. Bracing my weight on my elbows, I force myself to concentrate and focus on Red. The moon drifting through the window has cast a soft glow on her face. She's gorgeous: dark-blue eyes like the ocean, strong cheekbones, with plump, medium-sized lips, and a small, pointy nose.

I take her hand in mine and sit her on the empty side of the bed; then I flick on the lamp on the nightstand.

"What are you doing?" Red asks with a frown.

"Going home." I'm on my feet, buck naked with a condom on my dick. With a swift tug, I pull the condom off, then start gathering my clothes. She's watching my every move. I don't really give a damn. I hang like a fucking elephant, and that's not bragging. My body isn't too bad, either. A little over six foot. About one hundred eighty-five pounds of lean muscle. Broad shoulders. Ripped abs. Little to no body fat from hours in the gym, playing basketball, football, and skiing. And she's done enjoying it, for now.

I find my black boxer briefs and slip them on.

"What the hell's your problem?"

There's a strange note in her voice, annoyance, irritation. I don't dwell on it. Instead, I say, "You knew the deal when we first started this."

"This? We've been sleeping together for a month."

Grabbing my jeans, I slip them on. *ESPN, here I come.* "We stay casual."

"Casual doesn't imply you and I can't do things together outside of fucking."

The problem is, even if you tell a woman it's only sex, eventually her emotions get the best of her.

A huge part of the solution lies in the understanding of the way we feel. Ladies, another piece of advice: if you want a relationship, establish that at the get-go. Stop fucking settling.

Really. It's because of your passive-aggressive ways that men like me exist. If you know you want more than the little bit a man is willing to give, don't waste your time trying to change him. That's not going to happen. Leave him and find someone else who will love you the way you should be loved.

My phone dings. Cori's name appears on the screen. Grabbing the device, I skim through the text.

Made two dates this week. Guess I just had to put myself out there, huh? BTW, need a rain-check for Wednesday night.

Two dates already? Today is fucking Sunday. Only two days since we met at *Une Pression*. What's the rush?

A chill runs through the house and in and out of the room. As much as I want to text Cori back, I bury the phone in my back pocket.

33

"What if I want more?" Red asks, snapping me back to reality. "That'd be the end of us, I take it?"

"Yes," I answer without any hesitation. Crossing the carpeted floor, I grab my button-down shirt and put it on. Hey, I never said I was one of those guys completely in touch with my feminine side. I just said I wasn't a total dickhead.

By the way, this is where she should be kicking me out of her house, but she's not going to. Remember, passive aggressive.

"It's because of her."

"Her?" I know who she means. I'm not dense.

"Coriander." A small sigh of annoyance leaps out of her mouth. "That's who texted you. Your face couldn't hide it."

This catches my attention. I let my gaze linger on Red, lying naked on the bed. She has a Coca-Cola bottle figure—large breasts with a tiny waist and enticing hips. "What's the problem?"

"Your Coriander. She's going to be there. You don't want us to meet."

Here we go again. She isn't completely wrong. But the fact that I never bring a woman on our yearly ski trip isn't about Cori. Cam and Lucas have brought a woman with them on occasion, and hey, more power to them. My hook-ups are temporary. If I start bringing the women I sleep with into my social life, I'm creating a connection, giving them hope.

In general, I don't mix my sex life with my personal life. The women in my life don't get to meet my friends, my family.

Never. Ever. Period.

"No, darling, Cori has nothing to do with me saying no. This is a guys' weekend."

"She's not a guy."

"Leave her out of this." There's steel in my voice, a silent warning. Without a word, she rolls on her back and focuses her baby blues on the ceiling. I can see I hurt her, and remember the part of me that's not a complete dickhead?

Well, this is where it downright screws me over.

"You want to come with me to New Hampshire?"

"Yes." She glances at me and smiles. "It'll be fun."

"Text me the time of your event." Ski, beer, and sex. Maybe she has a point. "I'll pick you up afterward." I stride over to her side of the bed, pull the comforter over her body, lean over, and brush my lips on her forehead. "Gotta go."

She wraps her arms around my neck and lifts her body off the bed just enough to tempt me. "Spend the night."

Did I mention I never spend nights at a woman's house? That leads to trouble. Lucas started spending nights at a woman's house. A year later, they were walking down the aisle. Three years later, divorced.

"Sorry, babe, got work in the morning." I unlock her arms from my neck. "I'll call you."

I'M BARELY INSIDE MY HOUSE, when I pull my phone out of my coat pocket and tap the screen. It lights up to Cori's message. Quickly, I compose a reply.

You're dumping me?

We have a standing date every Wednesday night, either at her place or mine. It's our hump day tradition. This week, she's the hostess. My phone lights up with Cori's response.

Never :) Tomorrow night? You. Me. Chicken cutlet. Netflix. Think about it.

Nothing to think about. I respond.

It's a date.

Cori confirms.

Perfect. See you tomorrow.

The chambers of my heart contract and relax.

"Friends are born, not made."

QUESTION 1: DO YOU enjoy sending dick selfies?

This is one of the most crucial subjects to cover early when getting to know a guy. My cock is pretty handsome, but I've never felt the need to text a picture of it to a woman. A dick picture requires an immediate *fuck you.*

The title of the document I've been working on for the last hour glares back at me: Questions to ask on a date.

Cori did agree to let me help her in this.

Stop rolling your eyes, and no, I'm not a control freak.

Okay, I am.

My point is, as a man, I have the innate ability to sniff out douchebags. More importantly, the world of dating—online or whatever—is full of faux pas and pitfalls. Some things can probably be negotiated, but dick selfies should never be one of them.

I know, I know, I don't date. So, who am I to talk?

While the concept of dating might be foreign to me, this isn't rocket science. I don't have to actually do something to know about it. We all know drugs are bad for us, right? Some of us do it anyway. Me, I never touch that shit, never been curious. So, trust me on this one. If I ever yearn for a committed relationship, I know how to woo a woman.

And this is why I've compiled this list of thought-provoking questions, to eliminate losers and make this experience as smooth as possible for my little Moonchild. This is a work-in-progress, but I'll share it with you.

Question 2: Have you ever kept a New Year's resolution?

If the answer is yes, dump him. No one keeps New Year's resolutions. One year, I toyed with the idea of starting to date, you know, taking my time getting to know a woman as a prelude to actually being a fully-fledged couple. That lasted a day. Fine, thirty minutes. Any chance of keeping that resolution went out the window right after the woman next to me kissed me at the stroke of midnight.

Question 3: Do you have any special dishes that you cook?

All men should have a secret dish to use as a weapon to knock a woman's panties off. No need to doubt my culinary skills. I'm only second-generation Italian-Danish American. My first two words were *manicotti* and *frikadeller*. Needless to say, I can cook my ass off. I have great culinary skills.

Question 4: What is in your fridge right now?

If a man says *beer,* or *I don't know*, dump his ass. Sure, I believe in bachelorhood and enjoy a nice meal out at a fancy restaurant. I'm also a health nut, and home cooking is essential. No, I don't believe a woman's place is in the kitchen, unless it involves the kitchen counter or the floor, and me between her thighs. Or behind her. You get the picture.

Question 5: Are you a big fan of any major pro sports team?

That should be a given, right? Wrong. There are men who actually don't watch sports. Cori loves sports. Most of the time, you can find her at the bar, squeezed in between my male buddies and me, drinking beer and screaming at the television screen.

Question 6: When did you last sing to yourself? To someone else?

One of the kicks I get in life is when Cori and I sing karaoke to "Summer Nights." She loves *Grease* for some reason. We can thank her grandmother for introducing the movie to her. We've watched it a couple of times. For a total chick flick, it's not bad.

Question 7: What does friendship mean to you?

My office phone buzzes. This is a decisive question, but we have to put the list on pause for now. After clicking "Save" on my desktop, I press the speaker button and greet our favorite office manager. "Are you calling to tell me your granddaughter is here to treat me to lunch?" A little background about Nora. She's our office manager and Cori's grandmother.

"Unfortunately, not today," she says on a laugh.

I release a heavy sigh for drama.

"Greg Armstrong confirmed for four o'clock this evening," she says over the tip tap of her typing.

Under the Dogbert stress ball, I eyeball the stack of folders that contains a proposed acquisition of a start-up alternative to Uber and Lyft. This is a huge opportunity for my client to capitalize on the car-for-hire service market. "Perfect."

"Oh, your mom is on line two."

I love my mom; we have a great relationship. But lately, she's been on a let's-get-you-married quest. "Got it." Tapping the blinking red light, I greet my mom. "You have any more of that chocolate pie?" The other night, Kate and I had dinner with our parents. For dessert, Mom surprised us with one of our favorites—white chocolate pie with berries and licorice. That required an extra hour at the gym, but so worth it. That shit is delicious as fuck.

"Any other guests I need to include at your birthday party?" my mom asks.

Okay, no more chocolate pie. Got it. Back to my mother's question, what she's not saying is, do you have a girlfriend? I love the fact my parents are one of the few who have found that elusive everlasting love. But marriage is the last thing on my mind.

I stretch my arms above my head, cracking my shoulder blades, allowing my mind and body to relax for a second. "Nope, I'm flying solo."

She sighs. "Dean Conrad Morello."

Uh oh. Whenever my mother uses my full name, she means business.

"Your father and I want grandbabies."

Dad, too. Well, I'll be damned. "Dad wants grandbabies," I say after a long beat. To summarize my relationship with my father, when I was a kid and had to write about someone I admired, I wrote a ten-page essay about my dad.

"Yes," my mom confirms.

Well, damn. That's news to me. My father, Dean Martin Morello—yes, his parents cursed him and named the guy after their favorite crooner from the legendary Rat Pack. Like old Dino Paul Crocetti—that's Dean Martin's real name—my father is the eternal essence of cool and success. I take after him.

As the legend goes, my dad is what the Italians called a *menefreghista*—one who simply does not give a fuck. For most of his life, he lived without rules or consequences and embodied the glorious excess of the world—women, women, women.

See the similarity?

The apple didn't fall too far from the tree.

Needless to say, the big guy eventually fell from grace and became completely pussy-whipped when he met my mom, Ana. Let's not dwell on the fact I just said pussy and my mother's name in the same sentence. Moving on.

I see you smiling. I know what you're thinking. One day, that'll be me.

Don't bet your last dollar on that one. You'd lose.

"What about Katharine?" I ask, desperately trying to bounce the pressure off my shoulders.

My mother sighs. "Your sister is a lost cause."

A little background about Kate. My sister was once engaged for two hours to the world's biggest bag of shit. The evening of their engagement dinner, she walked in on him screwing one of her closest friends in the coat room. That night, Cam and I had a field day with the asswhipe. Luckily, Lucas had some common sense and stopped us from committing murder.

"Can't blame her," I say, cracking my knuckles.

There's a slight pause. I already know where she's going with this. My gaze swivels to the framed diplomas from Columbia and Wharton Business School nailed on the wall, right next to the framed poster of LeBron James dunking over some dude. These are my prized possessions in my office. Check them out if you want.

Let's just put it this way. FINRA ain't got nothing on me.

"What about Coriander?" My mother finally asks.

And there you have it. Ever since I graduated college, my mother has made no attempt to conceal her desire for Cori and I to transition from friends to more.

"Cori and I are just friends," I say for the millionth time.

"She's a nice girl and single."

Not for long. She already has two dates this week. Rubbing the back of my neck, I stare at the list of questions on my computer screen, and say, "Cori wants to get married and start a family."

"What's wrong with that?"

"Nothing."

"I wish you'd want the same thing."

It's like I'm ten years old again, listening to my mother explaining nocturnal emissions: That's why they're called wet dreams, they happen when you're sleeping, and your underwear or the bed might be a little wet when you wake up. Nothing to be ashamed of.

"Why won't you date Cori? What's wrong with her?"

"Nothing," I answer. "We're just . . . not into each other that way."

My mother laughs softly. "Of course, love."

Sensing sarcasm, I ask, "Hey, what does that mean?"

"Nothing. See you soon."

I release a deep breath after ending the call. How do I explain to my mother that ninety-nine percent of men view relationships the same way we regard our favorite car. Take my toy du jour, for example, the Ferrari California T in sleek black. This rolling art piece encapsulates my priorities—sophistication, elegance, and versatility.

Just like my women.

I'll drive it until I simply get bored, then I'll either buy the latest model or invest in a different look altogether. No emotional ties. Just a fun ride. That's where I am in life right now. No expectation. No disappointment.

Chapter 5

"Friends come in all shapes and sizes"

MINUTES AFTER I END THE call with my mother, Cam and Lucas stroll into my office with smug looks on their faces. Something tells me I'm the butt of their joke.

"What's so funny?"

"Dude, I heard you're officially off the market?" Cam teases. "Or should I be asking if you've lost your mind?" The fucker has a way of not mincing his words. He's leaning on the bookshelf, arms folded over his charcoal wool sport coat, while he observes me with casual assessment.

Other than Cori, these two are my partners in crime. Together, the three of us are a formidable force. Lucas has that tall, dark, and badass thing going for him. Cam, on the other hand, has the all-American boy good looks and charms.

Yes, you're right on point. We are legendary. We exude power and confidence. We are Adonises among men. One look, and women are swooning at the sight of us. The second a single word passes from our lips, pussies are running to us.

Women wanna fuck us. We love fucking. It's a mutual love affair.

44

Alright, before we continue any further, let's get one thing out of the way. Stop rolling your eyes every time I drop the P word. Would you rather I use another arguable-yet-hilarious slang word like the pink taco, twat, or beaver?

No, I'm not going to use the word vagina. Last I checked, this is not an anatomy or physiology class.

"Should we be planning a bachelor party?" Lucas drops his big frame on the leather couch across from my desk.

I swivel in my chair to face Lucas. I've known this guy all of my life. Many moons ago, my dad, along with Lucas' dad, Juan Manuel Bernal, left Wall Street and started a small investing company catering to sophisticated investors. Seven years ago, Cameron's father, Ryan Daniels, joined the awesome duo to become the fearsome threesome. Together they created Morello, Bernal, and Daniels. This is where the three of us work as hedge fund managers. About two years ago, the founding fathers made us partners, passing the baton. Now, they spend most of their time golfing, while we run the place.

You guessed it, brains and brawn. My mind is a machine. I can process cryptic crosswords in mere minutes. Surprised my noggin upstairs actually works, too? Let's put it this way, I earned my MBA with the second-highest GPA at Wharton. Lucas earned the top spot by a small margin. Cam is the Stanford guy.

"From what I remember, you're the crazy one who took the plunge once upon a time and got married."

Lucas rubs his chin as he nods in agreement. Once upon a time, my buddy was married to the biggest bitch to have ever walked the earth. Eventually he regained his common sense and joined us back in Manwhoreville. No hard feelings toward her though. Together they managed to have the most beautiful daughter. At least one good thing came out of that mayhem.

"And I'll never do it again," Lucas says with serious conviction. "By the way, she still hates you guys."

Cam and I nod, point noted. Since we're on the topic of Lucas' ex-wife, her animosity towards us is not completely unwarranted. We planned Lucas' bachelor party . . . in Zermatt, Switzerland.

Before any judgment is passed, let me say this. If you're over the age of twelve, you know that the traditional bachelor party involves strippers, booze, and then more strippers. Yawn. That's all fine. And I'd never discourage lap dances and liquor.

Believe me when I say this, there are better options. Get more creative. In addition to the ho-hum routine of pole dancing and beer, consider mixing it up a bit. For Lucas' plunge into marriage, Cam and I incorporated both rugged outdoors and drunken revelry. Skiing fits the bill—a few runs on the slopes, a few bourbons in the lodge. Bonus? Ski bunnies.

For the record, Lucas didn't participate in any of the après—ski activities with the snow bunnies. The guy is loyal as fuck when he's committed to a woman. "You were a good boy."

Lucas circles an imaginary halo on top of his head. Trust me, he's no angel.

"Seriously, what are you thinking?" Cam says with a slight shake of his head, his green eyes fixed on me. "Committing to a woman whose name you don't even know."

"I'm not committed to anyone."

Lucas and Cam snicker.

"You're bringing her along on our trip," Lucas points out. "Sounds like—"

"Commitment," Cam finishes.

Lucas shrugs. "I was going to say hope, but yeah, that, too."

I glance over my computer screen, and quickly skim over an incoming email. Grabbing a notepad, I jot down a reminder to contact a client after these two knuckleheads leave my office, then say, "Unlike you assholes, I don't mind riding the same roller coaster twice."

Cam shakes his head, the idea of sleeping with the same woman twice appalls the guy. "Yeah, I don't get that."

"It's not like you've never brought a woman with you on our trip, so shut the fuck up." I shoot Lucas a death stare. He's the only one I've confided in about my momentary lapse of sanity. It's a given my brother from another mother spilled the beans to Cam. *Fucker.*

Lucas chuckles. "You don't even know her name."

I grab Dogbert and give the squishy, pliable polyfoam a squeeze. "So?" The truth is, the thought has crossed my mind, and I have about two weeks to resolve that little glitch.

Lucas' dark eyes study my face for a minute, then a *you're so fucked* smile spills on his lips. "When are you going to tell the others?"

"Cori," Cam adds.

"Why should it matter to her?" I ask to no one in particular.

The assholes look at each other and shake their heads. "Let's put it this way," Cam answers as he snatches a *kopiko* from the jar on my desk. Anyone who has been to Thailand or Indonesia will know what that is. "The two of you act like a couple. Frankly, I don't know why you're not fucking yet."

"Ra ra ra. Funny, asshole." I flip Cam my middle finger.

"You're an idiot," Cam says. "Just tell her."

"Don't see the big deal." I shrug. "But to get both of you off my back, I'll tell her tonight."

Lucas stands up and glances at his Rolex. "Lunch?"

"Yeah, meet you at Larry's in ten."

After the two stooges leave my office, I pick up my phone, scroll down my contact list to Cori, and press SEND. I know her schedule. Today, she's teaching. This is when her group of seven-year-olds goes to the cafeteria for lunch.

She answers on the first ring. "What's up, stranger?"

Immediately, I smile. My gaze shifts to the list of questions I've compiled on the computer screen. "Our usual time?"

"You got it. I need to go to bed a bit early tonight."

"I'm sending you something." Already, I'm composing the email. *Subject: Cori's Quest for Love.* I type a short note: *Read them. I love you! Dean,* then hit SEND. "It's a work-in-progress."

"What is it?"

"You'll see. Gotta go. See you tonight."

"See you later. I'm still making your fave."

A small smile plays on my lips. "Ah, a girl after my own heart."

Cori laughs. "Your heart is not available, remember?"

"True. True," I confirm. "I'll bring the wine, Cakebread Merlot." That's Cori's favorite wine.

"Perfect. See you in a bit."

Chapter 6

"Good friends. Good food. Good times."

A SCENT THAT HAS ALWAYS comforted me is the smell of breadcrumbs sizzling. It reminds me of my childhood, with my father preparing one of his favorite dishes for my mother.

The aroma of hot oil floods the air and teases my nostrils the minute I step inside Cori's modest Cape Cod-style house. My stomach immediately rumbles in response, beckoning me down the hall toward the kitchen. Chicken cutlets signify, to me, the ultimate home-cooked dinner. No one is going to go out to a restaurant and order something so simple, but when cooking at home, it's an evergreen.

Other than making pizza together as a family, chicken cutlet was the first complete meal my dad taught me how to make. The first official meal I ever prepared for a woman, even if the woman was Cori, it's one of those eighteen-year-old moments that will always have a special place in my heart.

I can't resist the delightful sensations that whip up inside my memory. The pride in my chest that night, as we sat on the kitchen floor of my dorm with our plates of the chicken cutlets I'd prepared, a loaf of bread, and salad, is still recognizable today. The look of delight on her face, as she delved her teeth deep and fast into one of my favorite meals, has always stayed with me.

With a small smile on my lips, I enter the galley-style kitchen, brightened with white paint. Cori is moving around from one end of the granite counter to another. Her hair is in a messy bun. Fitted jeans, with holes in the knees, cover her legs, an old faded Metallica tank clads her torso. Her casual beauty, as always, catches me off guard, switching on my brain circuit, as if all this time, I am a machine not fully powered up until I'm in her presence.

A smile of delight lights up her face when she sees me. "Howdy!" she greets over the whir of the fan over the stove top.

"Have I told you how hot you look when you cook for me?" I step in front of her long enough to brush my lips across her forehead, before placing the wine on the counter by the wooden salad bowl. Then I amble over behind her, and grab two wineglasses from the top cabinet. As I do so, my chest touches her back. The light friction causes heat to pool in my gut and spread.

This isn't the first time my body betrays me around Cori. But it's not something I ever dwell on. Brushing my reaction aside, I move to the other side of the room, unscrew the cork, and pour us each a glass of wine.

"Thanks," she says as she takes her glass from me.

For no reason, my gaze follows her lips as they curl around the glass. I stare at them, wanting to trace my finger along the sweet outline where skin meets mouth. Before I know it, my mind is sliding down the slippery slope, where we're kissing, soft and sweet at first, before switching gears to hard and passionate.

Desire prickles my skin. My nerve endings tingle. My dick stirs.

Whoa!

I step on the mental brake and pull myself back into Friendtopia. This sexual urge towards my best friend is uncharted territory. I've seen Cori in bed in a pair of too-short shorts and a tank top. We've gone away together. Never been tempted.

Okay, time to confess. Once in a while, my mind does skitter to the no-fly zone and wonder what it would be like if Cori and I were to blur the line and fuck for, say, a night or two. But those thoughts never linger for too long. Eventually, logic wrests control.

Nothing to dwell on. That's just the way a healthy heterosexual male's mind works, especially one with a hot-as-fuck woman for a friend.

Just to be safe, I drag my gaze away and clear my throat. "What can I do?"

"Wanna make the salad?"

"You got it." I unfasten the cuffs of my black button down, roll the sleeves to my elbows, and wash my hands. With a few long strides, I am in front of the refrigerator, pulling out the necessary vegetables for our salad.

Cori's kitchen is a unique blend of eclectic farmhouse that gives the space a modern-vintage style. Nothing superfluous—

The Boy Friend by Mika Jolie

minimalist and uncluttered. The chalkboard framed on the wall above where she keeps her coffeemaker is covered with one of her drawings. The flowers are white and the yellow nectar looks sweet. The petals fan widely over the canvas, and as I slide the drawer open for the wine opener, I think I can almost detect a fragrance.

"Smells good," I say, motioning to the chicken cutlets draining on a paper towel-lined plate as I chop the romaine lettuce.

"The one thing I can cook." She places two breaded cutlets in the frying pan after dipping them in the shallow white bowls, which hold the key to perfect chicken cutlets: beaten eggs in one, breadcrumbs, oregano, basil, red pepper flakes, salt, and pepper in the other.

"You have something on . . . " I swipe my thumb over her cheek. "Flour." Our gazes meet and hold. And, for the first time in a long time around Cori, I feel a different kind of warmth spreading through me.

My hormones are going crazy.

God help me. If I don't control myself, there's going to be a tent in my pants. Talk about awkward.

In desperate need to fight these urges, I refocus my attention to the assorted vegetables in front of me and mentally recite the Periodic Table of Elements—Be. Beryllium. I've never been a fan of chemistry, and my chemistry teacher's kind, timeworn face calms my dick down.

Definitely need to whack one off later tonight. It's a healthy thing to do. I just can't think about the woman standing a few feet away from me while yanking one out.

She starts to reach for the pair of stainless steel tongs. Since I'm closer, I grab them and pass them to her. She mouths a 'thank you' as she flips the cutlets to brown the other side.

"We forgot to make a toast." She picks up her wineglass, tucks a few errant strands of hair behind her ear, and smiles at me. "What should we toast to?"

Toasting is an expression of honor and goodwill that Cori takes seriously. "How about to you?"

She arches a brow. "Me?"

"For perfecting my favorite meal?"

"Of course." Her lips spread into a smile. "That's my *secret dish*."

"Here. Here." We raise our glasses and clink to a toast. Our gazes meet and hold for a second too long. The connection sends a startling jolt through my limbs and inspires an excruciating desire to kiss her until we are both panting for more.

What the hell is that about?

Twice, in the span of ten minutes, my mind has swerved out of Friendtopia into HornyTown, USA. Cooking for each other is nothing new. Once a week, we fall into this domesticated routine. Maybe it's because she's referencing the list of questions I sent to her earlier. Question number three is the one about how every man should have a secret dish to cook for a woman. While Cori can bake anything, she's not a fan of cooking. But she does make one hell of a chicken cutlet.

Well, shit, that makes sense.

That has to be the reason for this intense ache spreading to every corner of my body. Nothing worth losing sleep over. Nothing to dwell upon. Friends or not, I'm still a man, and I still have an ego. It's flattering and sexy as fuck that a hot chick has perfected the one dish that fills my stomach with joy.

Relieved to know my mind hasn't wandered too far down the path, I take a sip of my wine and put my wineglass on the counter.

"Dean."

"Yeah?"

"I like when we cook together."

"Ditto." I grab three heirloom tomatoes from the mango bark bowl and slice them. "So you read my list?"

She nods. "I'll be sure to ask Trevor what's in his fridge."

I freeze. "As in Trevor Bendover?" I ask, praying she's referring to another Trevor.

She removes the remaining cutlets from the frying pan onto the plate, turns off the stove, then takes a sip of her wine. "The one and only," she confirms.

A heavy feeling, which can be described as an elephant, sits on my chest. The dude is a slime ball. "He has no respect for women."

"The pot calling the kettle black."

"I respect women."

Cori lets out a low laugh.

"For fuck's sake, his name is Bendover." No way am I going to let her become Trevor's latest conquest or have little Bendover babies. Nope. Not as long as I'm alive.

She shakes her head in disbelief. "It's just a date."

"Trevor is a prick." We live in a small town, she's familiar with his game, which is, he doesn't fuck a woman more than once.

Don't even fucking go there. I said I don't mind riding the same roller coaster twice. Especially if it's a fucking toe curling, mind-blowing ride. Take Red for example.

Shit. I'm supposed to tell Cori about Red joining us for our ski trip. My stomach flips, and not in a good way.

Not yet, I tell myself. We have all night.

"That's the prick you dumped me for." I add the diced vegetables to the wooden salad bowl. I open the pantry, filled to the brim with her home-canned preserves, pickles, and vegetables, all prepared by Cori. Grabbing one of the canned pickles, I pour it into a small bowl. We're standing side by side, finishing the last touch of our meal. "Trevor is a player, only after one thing."

She juts out a hip and gives me a gentle bump. "Don't be the overly protective big brother."

That's the thing. As close as we are, I've never put Cori in the un-biological sister category. To me, she's always been a woman with the sweet ass body who just happens to be one of my closest friends.

"What time is your date?" The unspoken questions were location, what are you wearing, don't let him touch you. But even I know that would be a bit much.

"Seven thirty."

"Why so late?"

"Seven-thirty is not late." She shocks me by letting loose an unrestrained, blissful laugh. "By the way, last I checked, I'm an adult without a curfew."

Right, an attractive woman on the prowl for love. "I don't like this."

"Do you do this to Katharine?"

Since Kate called off the engagement, she hasn't dated much. As far as I know she's a born-again virgin. "Katharine doesn't date."

That garners a soft chuckle from Cori as if she knows all of Katharine's little dirty secrets. Yeah, let's not go there.

"His name is Bendover," I say. "You're not having little Bendover babies with him."

"First date, remember?" She opens a cabinet, tiptoes and pulls out two dinner plates. She heads over to the dining area adjacent to her kitchen and sets the table.

"I thought you were going to do the internet dating thing?" I ask when she re-enters the kitchen.

"I did. He was my first contact." She picks up her phone from the counter, taps in her code, and hands it to me. "What do you think of my profile?"

The first thing I notice is Coriander's profile picture. A picture I've taken of her from my cell phone—wavy dark-brown hair, feather dusting of freckles against her honey skin. The corners of her eyes are crinkling, her soft, full lips upturn. I remember exactly when the picture was taken. The night we saw *Hamilton* and stopped at one of our favorite restaurants for dinner. We were both stoked about seeing the play.

Her eyes, her lips, and her spirit all at once smiling at me. She looked so stunning that night, I couldn't tear my eyes away, had to grab my phone and freeze that moment forever.

Something pinches in my heart. For some reason, I'm not happy she used a picture of how I view her to attract men.

You're jealous, man.

No fucking way. She's dated and has had boyfriends in the past, never bothered me one bit. Okay, maybe just a little tiny bit. But that's only because, out of respect to her relationship, nights like this always come to a halt.

Totally not jealous in that *me man, you woman* sort of thing. Shoving the notion out of my brain, I read Cori's description of herself.

Birth place: Earth.

Race: Human

Politics: Freedom

Religion: Love

I'm an artist who'd rather wear flowers on my head than diamonds around my neck. I make a mean chicken cutlet, and I'm a firm believer of handwritten notes.

To understand this description of herself is to know Cori is of mixed race. Her mother is white and her father is African-American. Her skin is a pale brown that strays from light to golden, depending on the season, giving her a look of an indiscernible background. And as much as society attempts to label her, she never picks a box. In her view, that would be choosing one parent over another and disregarding the fact she's a fluid product of many influences, like all of us.

If someone were to ask me to describe Coriander, I'd say, she's an artist, a flower child with a rock and roll soul.

"By the way, I hope I didn't cause any problems by texting you so late last night," Cori says as she enters the kitchen.

The fact that I have a healthy sex life is no secret, but going into explicit details with the only woman I can call a friend has never been part of our rapport.

"You can text me anytime, Coriander," I say and mean every word. Cori's place is right next to my mother and Katharine on my *drop-whatever-you're-doing-and-go-to-her* list. At least until her need for me is replaced by someone who can also give her babies.

My stomach constricts into a tight knot. I shove all wariness to the side. My friendship with Cori encompasses all sorts of forms. We can discuss politics, scream in frustration, then hug each other goodnight. We laugh at each other's jokes. She's one of my squad I chill with—perfect example is tonight—Wine, Netflix, and chicken cutlet. No one can take these moments away from us.

A comfortable silence settles between us, as it does with true friendship. By the way, this is where I should tell her about Red joining us in New Hampshire.

At every moment, we have two choices in life, whereby we can ignore the big elephant in the room, or face it head on and risk being poked in the ass by their big ivory tusks. Tonight, my spirit is torn between dealing with the now and getting stuck in that moment when I disappoint Cori.

My jaw ticks below my ear.

Bringing a woman with me shouldn't bother Cori one bit. We've been in a non-sexual boyfriend/girlfriend relationship forever, for fuck's sake. And now she's on a husband quest. So why the heavy feeling in my stomach over the idea of seeing any disappointment in her eyes if I do come clean?

Deep down, I know the answer. No matter how I slice it, our yearly ski trip has always been about us. Our friendship.

Guilt gnaws at my chest. I should tell her, but coming clean doesn't feel right. Not tonight, not when she just prepared my favorite food. I straighten myself militarily and swallow, but the gigantic lump doesn't go down easily.

"So stiff." One of her hands squeezes my tense shoulder, and I nearly jump. "You okay?"

"Yeah." I carry the salad bowl and the plate with the cutlets to the dining area. Cori follows. "What are you in the mood for? Romantic comedy, horror, or drama?" I ask, pushing aside my pang of conscience.

"How about your all-time favorite Tom Cruise movie?" she asks, as we sit facing each other at the round dinner table.

60

A girl after my own heart. Already, I'm grinning. She needs to say no more. I discovered *Top Gun* during one of our family movie nights, and ever since, I've been in love with the best bromance movie ever made.

"I can kiss you right now."

Her gaze darts to my lips, lingers for a bit before looking away. But not quick enough for me not to catch the blush that crept across her cheeks.

Wait. Let's stop here for a moment.

Does that mean Cori has thought about kissing me? I want to ask, push a little, but the logical part of me knows better than to even entertain the idea.

"I don't think I can get tired of watching *Top Gun*," I say in the silence. Say what you want about *Top Gun*, call it cheesy, you can say it's overly homoerotic, but it's a hell of a film. Elite fighter pilots. Male camaraderie. Kelly McGillis as the fierce flight instructor. The first time I watched that movie with my Dad, I admit, I jacked off to Charlotte 'Charlie' Blackwood later that night.

Yeah, I think Kelly McGillis came out as a lesbian a couple of years ago. Doesn't bother me one bit. I've had the gratification of being sandwiched by two women, then watched them pleasure each other.

"Dreaming of Charlie Blackwood again?" she asks with a knowing glint in her eyes. Listen ladies, no matter how close you are to someone of the opposite sex, don't ever tell them your jack off stories. I made that mistake only once. Cori teases me about it every chance she gets.

"My lips are sealed when it comes to my sexual fantasies." Some of them include Cori, but that has already been established. Nothing crazy. Usually, the thought is along the lines of, "Oooo, I bet this one thing would be fun with her," or "dang, she looks good enough in that outfit that I want to rip it off her," or "she's really sexy after she works out."

She puts some salad on her plate then passes the bowl over to me. "How many times have you watched this movie?"

"I've lost count." I know what she's thinking. The first time I watched *Top Gun*, I yanked it three times, picturing Charlotte walking in those black stilettos. I couldn't be more than fourteen. The perfect age. "But not to jack off."

She laughs. "I didn't say that, but . . . "

"Just say it."

"Say what?" Her eyes sparkle with amusement.

"I'm a guy. My favorite activity is sex." I think about sex morning, noon, and night—and every second in between.

She shrugs. "You said it, I didn't."

I cut a piece of my cutlet, chew it down then speak again. "You were thinking it."

Ladies, let me clue you in on a little secret. Men think about sex a lot. Every second might be a gross exaggeration, but it's not too far off. If we were dying and had one wish, we'd ask for our favorite meal—mine is chicken cutlet—and then sex. If a guy tells you otherwise, dump him. He's lying.

She laughs. "Are you thinking about sex now?"

The question throws me off balance. I put up my index finger, chew down my food then answer. "Yes, but not because of *Top Gun*." Tonight the object of my sexual desire is my best friend. A thought I don't even dare entertain.

She stares at me for a long time, clearly mulling over my answer. I wait, hoping she'll push. Instead, she says, "Then why do you watch the movie?"

"Are you kidding me?" I ask in an incredulous tone, both relieved and a little disappointed the topic has moved to a safer territory. "The love between these characters, even two as contentious as Maverick and Iceman, is genuine. And the film celebrates masculinity, while simultaneously embracing the more sensitive aspects of friendships." My voice takes a softer tone. "Like our friendship."

"I see." She pulls the elastic band from her messy bun. Her hair falls softly around her shoulders.

For a split second I am filled with the desire to walk over to her side of the table and slide my hand into her hair. I shift in my chair, willing myself to focus on why I am at Cori's house tonight.

We're friends.

Two heterosexual people of the opposite sex who love spending time with each other without complicating it with sex. We have a platonic love. You know, love from the neck up.

I need to get a grip on my thoughts. "What exactly do you see?"

"You say the male friendship in *Top Gun* reminds you of our friendship."

I nod.

Her gaze drops to her handful of perky breasts for a brief second, before meeting mine. By the way, I love a nice set of tits. And I bet you naked, Cori's are magnificent.

"Except I'm not a dude," she says, looking amused.

The stiffness in my pants agrees wholeheartedly. "Believe me, I've never mistaken you for a guy, Coriander."

Another splash of red races across her cheeks. This time, she doesn't hide her face or look away. Instead, she says, "Be careful, Dean Conrad Morello, you're going to make me think you've checked me out once or twice."

This is a new territory in our friendship, this flirtatious banter. A part of me likes it. A part of me doesn't know what to make of it. Should I reach over and snog her, eat her out?

Probably not a good idea. Shit might get awkward.

"While you're safely tucked in the friend zone compartment, I'm still a man." By the way she's biting the edge of a smile, a vain attempt to keep her creeping grin at bay tells me she's enjoying this banter, just as I am. But before this goes too far, and my boner gets out of control, I steer the conversation back to our neutral ground. "Tell me about your day."

And for the next hour, we discuss safe topics, like her classroom of crazy seven-year-olds. I tell her about work. We drink wine, move over to the couch, where we drink more wine and watch *Top Gun*.

Because it's a school night, I don't linger after the movie ends. At her door, I bury a hand in the back of her hair and tug her close for a quick kiss on her forehead. Ignoring the butterflies wanting to come alive inside my stomach, I whisper, "Thanks for tonight."

"Ditto," she says with a wide smile, then closes the door behind her.

Hands stuffed in my coat pocket, I head to my car. Outside is silence, peppered only with my footsteps on the moon-bleached stone path and the wind whistling through the bare branches of the trees that line the sidewalk. I glance up into the night sky, a blanket of black velvet with scattered stars, flickering. My eyes catch one of the stars, and it twinkles, just for me, it seems.

Guilt rolls over me. My steps halt. I need to go back there and come clean about Red. My gaze swivels to Cori's house which is now pitch black. The frigid night air slithers up and down my body. I let out a long exhale, my breath shows as a stream of white steam in front of me.

Tomorrow. I'll tell Cori about Red tomorrow.

Chapter 7

"My guy friend tells me the truth."

TWO DAYS LATER, I'M sitting in my office with my face buried in the computer screen, when my phone buzzes. My initial instinct is to ignore it, but I have a date with this hot chick I met last night. We texted this morning and confirmed. My dick is ready for a few rounds. There's nothing else to discuss. But let's be real, women love to talk about shit.

My phone dings again. I peek at the screen. There are two selfies from Cori in two different outfits. My stomach lurches, adrenaline pumps. If she were here, I'd be screaming to her how fucking gorgeous she looks.

Picking up the phone, I study the images a little closer. In one picture, she's in a brown embroidery sweater dress with over-the-knee fuck-me boots. The second picture, she's still in the same fuck-me boots and a chambray dress with peekaboo holes on her shoulders. For the briefest second, my mind ventures there . . . again. Cori bending over in front of me wearing nothing but the fuck-me boots, my hands on her ass as I thrust my hips and sink into the cleft between her legs.

My cock springs forth, rock hard.

Ignoring the aching bulge in my pants, I headbutt the hot desire thrumming through my veins and read her text.

This or that?

One thing is certain. No matter which dress she picks for her date with Bendover, she's wearing the boots. My fingers hover over the keyboard of my phone for a moment. My mind debating if I should talk her out of wearing the boots. Slowly, I type my answer.

Brown with flowers.

She looks radiant in both dresses, but at least the sweater dress has a turtle neck and thick long sleeves. Trevor is not only a prick, he's also very touchy. My phone dings again.

Think it's sexy enough?

Cori would look sexy wrapped in a brown bag. Bendover knows that. He's had his eye on her since high school. My insides curdle like milk with lemon. I text her back.

Definitely sexy. Behave Moonchild.

Her answer comes quick.

Always. Talk later.

SOMETIME IN THE MIDDLE OF the night, I'm awakened by the rattling of my cell phone. Half asleep, I pick it up, tap the screen awake, and read the text from Cori.

Date #1—major fail. Men are assholes.

Immediately, my gaze shifts to the time. It's a little past eleven thirty, an early night to end a date. Then again, my date ended about one hour ago, right after she asked the three dreaded questions:

Do you want to get married?

How many children do you want?

How much money do you make?

My answers:

Live in Alpine. Marriage, not on my radar. Neither are children.

My stance on marriage and children turned out to be deal-breakers. We still banged.

Back to Cori. My mind darts to the worst-case scenario, which involves Bendover's slimy hands on her. I know where the asshole lives. It's easy to pay him a visit and smash my fist into his nose. Holding my breath, I send Cori a text.

Did he try anything?

She responds.

No. But he doesn't understand first date does not always include sex.

The tension slowly leaves my body. I rub my eyes and read the text again. You know, just to be sure I'm not dreaming. Because deep down, I was praying the date with Bendover didn't work out. Why, I'm not sure. Nonetheless, I'm relieved and grinning like a fool as I text her back.

Not all men.

Another text arrives seconds later.

Tell me one who's not?

Without a second thought I respond.

Me.

It's the truth. I'm fucking nice as hell—family-oriented, quick-witted, personable, and easy going. Those qualities make me a nice guy. In case you're wondering, there's no rhyme or reason for my response to Cori either. I'm not looking to get out of the friend zone and start banging my best friend.

My phone dings with another text from Cori.

We're friends.

Something roots in my chest. Wishful thinking maybe. I shove the thought aside and write back.

I'm glad you're not going to have babies named Bendover.

Another message from Cori pops up.

LOL. Funny. Thanks Dean.

Smiling, I type back.

Anytime, Moonchild.

After the screen of my phone goes dark, I lumber to the bathroom, take a piss, wash my hands, stroll back into my room. The light on my phone is blinking, indicating a message. I flop on my bed, key in my code to unlock the phone, and see a flurry of smiley faces, along with the sweetest goodnight note.

Every girl needs a guy friend. Thanks for being mine. :) :) :) :) :)

My text is short and one hundred percent from my heart.

Forever.

Chapter 8

"A friend is always good to have,
but a lover's kiss is better than angels raining down on me."

DID YOU KNOW KARAOKE MEANS empty orchestra?

A brief history of the word that means sing-along to us. The word Karaoke is a blend of two words—*kara*, which means empty, and *oke,* which is short for orchestra. There you have it, a quick, painless, lesson on one of Cori's favorites pastimes.

Tonight, we are letting loose at Sepia—Cori's most cherished Karaoke bar in lower Manhattan. The whole place looks like a big garage. We're sitting in a booth, not too far away from the stage. A large plate of nachos is in the middle of the table. One bottle of wine already consumed between Cori and Kate, another popped open ready to go. Lucas and I are nursing our beer slowly. On the stage, two girls with NYU jerseys and skintight jeans are singing their worst impression of "Elastic Heart." Next to me, Cori is rocking side to side, softly singing along to the lyrics.

The corners of my lips twitch with amusement. I'm glad we're here. I love it. For one, Cori seems happy. Second, Sepia carries the best beer selection. The crowd is a bit young for my taste, students from NYU for the most part. If the female selection was a little riper, I'd be here pickin' every weekend.

No need to question my intelligence. I don't think riper is a word but...ah hell, you know what I mean. Anyhow, tonight I'm not chasing tails. The reason we're here, on this blistering cold Friday night, is to take Cori's mind off the dating game.

"Dating is like riding a bike," Cori says over the hundreds of conversations told in loud voices, all of them competing with the rock music that dominates the atmosphere.

"But the bikes are on fire," Katharine adds with a nod.

Tonight marks Cori's first week back in the dating scene. She's been kissing a few frogs in her pursuit to find her prince. Her mood the last few days is what you can best describe as 'meh.' After one too many late-night text messages of 'major fail,' or 'joining a convent tomorrow,' I decided my Moonchild needed a break.

"And . . . oh—" Cori snaps her fingers. "—the ground is on fire." Her words are stumbling over one another.

Katharine tips back the last of her drink. "Everything is on fire."

Lucas rubs the left side of his temple. I swallow another swig of my beer, quietly listening to the man bashing. Cam got lucky tonight. He has a date.

"Because" –Cori breaks into a giggle in the middle on her sentence— "oh, yeah, dating is hell," she mumbles before she and Kate belt lyrics to "Wagon Wheel," along with Darius

Rucker. We have enough drinks in us to pretend we love country music.

Plain and simple, they are plastered. This is their 'dating is hell' pity party. I shoot Lucas a look across the table—a silent request to drive my inebriated sister back to Alpine, since she took the train to the city. He nods in understanding. My worry eases. Kate is in good hands. As for Cori, I'm her guardian angel tonight.

"First of all, Kate, you're not dating anyone," I point out to my sister. "Second, you're drunk."

She narrows her brown eyes at me. "How do you know I'm not dating?"

"She would have told me." I point to Cori sitting next to me.

"Never." Cori hiccups. She takes a bite of a cheese-covered nacho and moans. "I'd never . . . err . . . discuss . . . your sister's love life, or lack thereof."

Kate snickers. Lucas gives her shoulder a sympathetic squeeze.

Cori, drunk, has always been cute. Tonight is no exception. Her body is relaxed. When she smiles, it's at its widest and brightens the room.

"Good," I say to my sister. "I don't want to know."

"I date," Kate slurs. "Tell him, Cori." She pokes Lucas in the ribs. He grimaces, feigning pain. Gotta love a guy who's willing to get beat up by my drunk sister.

"Umm, I'm Lucas." He leans back and casually drapes one arm along the back of Kate's chair. "Cori is sitting next to your brother."

Kate giggles, and hiccups, making a little wet sound. "Ooh, your body is hard."

"One hundred percent male, baby," Lucas beams.

Kate bats her lashes, and then murmurs, "I like it."

Everyone, this is where I vomit.

Lucas shifts his weight, so that they are facing each other. The fucker smiles, as if Kate's words are fucking golden, and then says, in a voice rippling with a seductive, Spanish accent, "I like yours too, gorgeous."

Whoa!

Slow. The. Fuck. Down.

"Dude," I warn. That's all I had to say. The underlying message is clear—save the charms for another woman. This is my sister.

"We should stop flirting." The asshole, who up until now was also known as my best friend, chuckles. "Your brother is getting into his overly-protective mode."

Well, at least he got the message that I'm itching to swing out and put a dent in his pretty face.

"Oops," Kate says then giggles.

Lucas pulls her into one of those side hugs. Just when I'm ready to leap over the table and kick some serious ass, he releases Kate and focuses his attention on Cori. "So, you haven't met Mr. Right?"

The Boy Friend by Mika Jolie

"Let's see." Cori's voice wheels me back in. I glance over at her. Her left index finger is ready for a countdown. "So far, I've met Mr. Asshole, Mr. Douchebag, and Mr. Liar."

Lucas laughs then repeats the name. "Mr. Asshole."

Cori nods. "That's Trevor."

I sit back and glug down another mouthful of my beer, while Lucas continues with his grilling. "As in Bendover?"

Cori pops a nacho into her mouth, chews then answers. "Mr. Bendover himself."

Lucas shoots me a 'How could you let her make that mistake' look. I shrug. The type that silently says, I tried, but my warning fell on deaf ears. For as long as I've known Cori, she's always been too positive to be doubtful, and too optimistic not to give someone a chance.

"Bendover is scum," Lucas says, echoing my sentiments.

The corners of Cori's mouth quirk up slightly. "Hence, the appropriate name, Mr. Asshole. I think he'll screw anything."

Sadly, many of us on this planet—myself included—would jam their idiot-stick into anything, as long as it doesn't electrocute them. Although, I'm not sure if that's entirely true. If you put a DYSON upright vacuum cleaner in a pair of black fishnets, I'm sure some man would screw it. Not to brag, but I only fuck women and my right hand.

"Mr. Douchebag?" Lucas asks.

"He's an actor with an over-inflated sense of self-worth."

"Compounded by a low level of intelligence," Kate adds.

"How do you know this?" Lucas asks, his gaze shifting to Kate's face.

"I was there." Kate takes another swig of her drink and lets out a satisfactory *ahh,* before finishing her sentence. "We double date."

"Say no more." Lucas puts up a hand, his attention back on Cori. "And Mr. Liar?"

"The tan around his ring finger gave him away. As it turns out, he's married, expecting his second child."

Lucas winces. "Ouch."

And this is why women view men as dirtbags. Hell, I'm one of those dirtbags, except I don't mislead my women. I give no declaration of undying love, or any promises of forever or faithfulness. No pretense.

Guys, I don't care if your appearance is a ten. If your personality is a three, guess what? You're a three. Don't lie to women.

"Oh, well." Cori straightens her shoulders. "I've decided I'm going to whoogle my next date."

"Whoogle," I say, arching a brow, then glance over at drunk and disorderly, also known as Cori and Kate.

Cori gives me a playful nudge. "Look them up online."

"Thanks for the clarification." I take another swig of my beer. Before Cori explained whoogle, I never heard of the term or the meaning of it.

"I think it's a brilliant idea, Cori," Kate encourages her partner in crime. "We need to make sure they aren't married."

"Or serial killers," I point out.

"I just want to be elusive," Cori says while drumming her fingers on the table.

I guess the possibility of meeting serial killers doesn't bother her much. Hey, if I were a woman dating online, my number one fear would be if I were going to be murdered. "Do you mean exclusive?"

Cori glances at me, brows creased together. "That's what I said." Flipping her hair, she looks at Kate for confirmation, to which my sister nods. "In any case, I'll find my lobster."

"Your lobster?" Lucas asks quietly.

"It's a known fact lobsters mate for life," Cori points out.

"According to what theory?" I ask, amused.

"Monica and Chandler," Kate says with one hundred percent Moreno stubbornness.

"Ross and Rachel," Cori adds.

"Contrary to . . . what's her name?" I glance over at Lucas for help.

"Phoebe," Lucas answers.

I lift my beer in a silent toast. "Thanks, bro."

"Anytime."

"As I was saying, Phoebe was wrong," I continue, my eyes never leaving Cori's face. "These arthropods mate once, then never see each other again. As a matter of fact, when a female lobster is ready to become a mother, she seeks out the region's reigning male lobster and pays a call to his burrow for some lobster lovin'."

"Also, the female wafts urine into the male lobster's home," Lucas adds, smiling.

"The golden shower." Lucas and I laugh and high-five each other across the table.

Cori rolls her eyes. "You're a buzz kill."

"I aim to please, gorgeous." I mime a dagger to the heart.

Cori laughs good-naturedly. "It doesn't matter what you say, I'm going to find my lobster."

Lucas and I swallow another long mouthful of our beers.

"I got it," Kate announces, her face bright with excitement. "Why don't you date my brother?"

The question throws me off, causing me to almost choke on my beer. Kate's words hang over the table for a beat. A thrill of anticipation skitters down my spine. I tell myself, whatever she says doesn't matter, will not affect me. We have a long-term connection. She gets along with my family and friends. I can bring her around my parents without worrying about them painting my spare bedroom yellow or blue. Dating has never been an option.

Yet, my curiosity is piqued.

Her body shifts toward mine, close enough that our knees touch. Close enough that I can see every single gold spec in her whiskey eyes. Slowly, her gaze rakes over my face, like she's buying a new car, and I'm the model.

"How would you treat me if we were dating, Dean?" she asks in a low voice laced with wine.

For some strange reason, the idea of Cori and I together causes countless butterflies to fly wild in my stomach. This is where my moral compass usually kicks in full force and wheels me back in into Friendtopia. I can feel my sister and Lucas watching us with interest, but right now, I don't care. Every inch of me is, instead, conscious of the bare length of Cori's thigh brushing against my jean-clad legs.

I stare into her face for a long, speculative moment, contemplating the depth of her curiosity, then say, "If we were dating, I'd woo you the right way."

She smiles, clearly amused. "How?"

After taking another swallow of my beer, I say, "I'd hold the door open for you." Whether it's the building door, elevator door, car door, or even the revolving door, I'd hold it. "I'd put my strong, firm, man hands on that door, back up my cute, toned ass, and instruct you to enter, by saying, 'after you,' or, 'you may enter, sexy sugar mama.'"

Cori laughs. "You already do that."

I nod. "True, but it'd be more intimate."

Cori tilts her head. Her gaze still on me. "Do explain."

With pleasure. I'm enjoying this exchange. "I'd stand there, look at you, and smile like I wouldn't rather be doing anything else but standing there, looking at you, and smiling while holding that door open for you." I lean into her, and lower my voice. "At that moment, I'd make you feel as if you're the most sublime creature on earth."

Cori swallows hard and shakes her head. "I'd feel all of that just by you holding the door for me."

I can tell when Cori is thrown off her axis a bit. The idea that my words have affected her, surprisingly, makes me want to give in to the cocktail of lust burning a fiery path through my veins.

I reach and stroke a few strands of long, silky, brown hair, before letting my finger skim down to the throbbing pulse at the base of her neck. "There's more. Want to find out?"

Her rich golden eyes darken and wrap around me like a blanket, engulfing me in their warmth, and making me feel at home. The air is taut with sexual tension. My gaze drops to her lips. They part and then the tip of her tongue touches her lower lip.

My brain stutters and twitches. My dick twitches too.

And then Cori crinkles her nose and laughs. Talk about boner killer . . . not that I have one but . . . Never mind. She grabs my biceps, leans into it in that affectionate way friends do with each other. A silent reminder of our status.

"Dean loves playing the field," Cori finally says, the heat of her breath fanning over my face.

I nod, confirming my status. Mr. Player. That's me. One hundred percent.

"Just like you and Cam," Kate adds, her attention on Lucas. "By the way, where is Cam tonight?"

"He has a date," Lucas answers.

"You mean, he's screwing a woman as we speak." Cori rolls her eyes. "See what I mean? Men are rats."

"Worse than that, they're fleas on rats," Kate adds.

Here we go again. "Hey." I immediately go in defensive mode, because us men must stick together. "We always make it clear we're not the marrying type, right brother?"

Lucas raises his beer in my direction in a toast. "Here. Here. Been there. Done that. Never again."

"Well, enough of that pity party for me tonight." Cori stands up and extends one hand to me. "Wanna karaoke?"

Moonchild loves to karaoke, and she always drags me with her. The truth is, I enjoy getting silly with her. Karaoke is our thing. I drink the last quarter of my beer, rise to my feet, and take her hand in mine. "Let's do this."

Lucas coughs and mutters sucker under his breath. Kate scoffs and elbows him. Ignoring the bastard, I place a hand at the small of Cori's back as we head to the stage.

"How about "Summer Nights"?" she asks while flipping through the playlist.

Leaning over her, I scan through the playlist from *Grease* and point my index finger to "You're the One That I Want."

She turns to me, smiles, and says, "Tell me about it, stud," in such a husky voice that, for a split second, I am speechless.

These momentary lapses really must stop. I puff out my chest and say, "Let's do it."

A few minutes later, the catchy tune fills the room. And I swear, it's as if it's every woman's favorite song just came on.

No, not their *fave* song at the moment, or the one they like to wax poetic about once they've had too many glasses of their favorite wine. This is the song that reminds every woman who has seen the movie about the expression on Danny's face when Sandy appears in those black, skin-tight, leather pants. That's how every woman wants a guy or a woman to look at them someday.

I am singing about having chills, and how they are multiplying, in my best Danny Zuko voice. When Cori joins me, a hush falls over the room. Her voice is smooth, clear and quiet, yet powerful. Lost in the moment, I wrap my arm around her waist and pull her against me. As I continue belting out the lyrics, the bar comes to life. Before I know it, every woman is passionately singing the lyrics along with us. We play to the crowd, encouraging them.

The scene is swimming through my cerebral cortex like a wakeful dream. I'm transformed, losing all sense, except the music. I'm Danny Zuko, on my knees in front of Sandy—AKA Cori—singing about how I better shape up, because she needs a man.

The crowd goes wild. When we're done, a cacophony of applause bursts forth, praising and raising the roof a few inches. In a state of blissful euphoria, I pull Cori in my arms and place a kiss on her forehead.

CORI SHIVERS NEXT TO ME the minute we step out of the bar. Lucas and Kate left about half hour ago, in order for him to relieve Emma's sitter.

"You're okay?" I ask Cori.

She nods, and pulls her coat more tightly around her, in an attempt to stop the freezing air from slithering up and down her body. Around us, the snow is falling like white confetti. We are moving slowly down the sidewalk to the crosswalk. I remove my peacoat and wrap it over her shaking shoulders.

"You don't have to do that."

"A gentleman always puts the needs of the woman in his arms ahead of his." I slide my hand into hers, linking our fingers. With a gentle tug, I guide her to the right, away from the small group of college students leaving the bar. We continue in perfect harmony, fingers laced tightly.

"Not because she's helpless or unable," she says as we reach the corner.

"Definitely not." I release her hand and focus my attention on the entertainment flyers papering the light pole, while we wait for the green light to switch to red.

"Why, then?" Cori rummages through her purse and produces a lip balm, which she swipes across her lips.

A taxicab slows in front of us, honks its horn. I wave it away, then turn to Cori. Her eyes are still a bit glassy from alcohol. "Because," I start, my voice an octave lower than before. "A gentleman always wants to show a woman that she's valuable and worthy of respect."

"Thanks for tonight."

I brush a snowflake off her cheek. "Anything for you, Moonchild."

She tips her head, looks up at me, and flashes a smile that suddenly makes my heart feel way too big to fit in my ribcage. Before I realize what is happening, Cori wraps her hands around my neck, tiptoes, and presses her lips to mine.

Chapter 9

"Friends don't kiss friends."

THE FEEL OF CORI'S LIPS sends my mind into a sensual state of intoxication. My eyes immediately drift shut. Every nerve in my body is vibrating, and my heart . . . Well, it's going bonkers.

Cori is kissing me.

On the streets of New York.

I am completely unprepared.

Common sense tells me to stop. Don't engage. Pull away. But I can't seem to find the strength.

I can't think straight.

My head is spinning.

Holy shit.

The kiss. It's wrecking my equilibrium, transporting me somewhere heavenly.

Her lips are soft, succulent, and fine as they linger against mine. The warmth of her mouth sends a current running through my body. Chills run over my skin, and fire burns inside me.

I feel dizzy.

Drunk.

High.

My senses have been seduced by the rapid beat of my heart, the sweetness of the raspberry lip balm she swiped on a few minutes ago, the snow falling on our faces to where our lips meet, each one of us tasting the cold drops.

I'm brought to new heights. I need to suppress my shock, what's going through my head. Act normal. Relax. Think: lead actor in a black-and white film.

When Cori makes one of those soft mewling sounds from the back of her throat, I wind my hand into the softness of her slightly damp hair. Placing my other hand on the small of her back, I pull her against the wall of my chest.

Control shifts. I take over and kiss her with all the pent-up longing buried deep inside me. She moves with me, meeting me toe to toe, our tongues battling in an erotic collision. Our lips are eager, testing, exploring, until we finally break for air, breathless.

There's a delicious moment, where her face is washed blank with confusion, as if her brain cogs couldn't turn fast enough to take in that we've just kissed.

"Wow." She's the first one to speak. Her voice comes out hoarse, barely audible. "That was . . . amazing."

"Out of this world," I agree, and clear my throat. Her lips are swollen strawberry pink. My heart is still hammering in my chest as if I just climbed the Eiffel Tower.

"Your lips . . ." Her voice trails.

There's a pregnant pause. Words seeming to have failed her. No judgment here. My mind is still in a fog. Her gaze drops to my mouth. Mine lowers to hers for a moment, before our eyes meet again.

"They're so soft," she whispers, her voice fills with such longing that it makes my skin heats up, completely oblivious to the frigid winter air.

"So are yours, Moonchild."

"I've always wondered what it would be like to kiss you."

This admission surprises me. In a good way. I don't need my ego stroked, but this is Cori—the hottest woman on earth—confessing to being curious about the two of us kissing. "And?"

"It was magic."

Jesus. Fucking. Christ. She can't say shit like that and not expect me to want more. We're still standing inches apart with one of my arms roped around her waist. I run the pad of my thumb where a snowflake has kissed her cheek and melted. "Are you drunk?"

She shakes her head and lets out a low laugh. "Why do you ask?"

"Because I'm going to kiss you again, and I want to make sure you're not three sheets to the wind." I search her gaze.

Her eyes are no longer glassy, instead they are dazed with desire.

"This isn't a drunken mistake." Her voice is subtly sensual and smooth, a velvety whisper. And then she licks her bottom lip.

A fresh bolt of desire thrums through my veins. I am consumed by desire to mark her as mine and possess her. A need I never knew I'd feel for a woman. A need that is so intense, it wrenches a deep, rough male groan from me as I pull her, caveman-style, into me.

Hungry for the connection, I slam my lips to hers. We are kissing again, so deep and hard that our lungs are breathing each other's essence. And I can't think, because Coriander is the most amazing kisser. Ever.

Sparks are flying all around me. I am still lost in the fabric of time, floating on waves of pleasure, when she places her palms on my chest and steps from my reach. Only then do I fully become aware of our surroundings. The sound of yellow taxicabs rattling over potholes and speed bumps. The happy, chattering crowd has long since dissipated.

"We should stop," she says, voice wobbly. "Friends and all."

She's right, of course. Friends don't kiss each other like we just did. And yet, I can't help thinking, this is what it must feel like waking up on Christmas morning, running into the living room . . . and getting kicked in the balls by Santa Claus.

"I mean—" Cori's gaze is searching mine, her face clouded with concern. "—we were curious and . . ."

"Now we know, it's safe to say our curiosity has been satisfied." I swallow the pang in my chest and smile at her in hope to ease some of her concern. She's worried about any possible damage done to what we have. More so, Cori is looking for a commitment, someone to have two point five kids with. None of those things are in my horizon.

There's an awkward silence while we stand there, staring at each other. A force greater than I've ever known can't shake off what just happened. The ping of the crosswalk light saves us. On the almost-deserted sidewalk, I reach for her hand, thread our fingers together, and cross the street to the parking lot.

"Dean." She says my name as I open the car door for her.

"Yeah."

"Tonight. The kiss."

"Stop worrying." I give her another reassuring smile, even though I want nothing more right now than her lips on mine. I've kissed many women in my lifetime, and no one else has burned me alive. But ultimately, what is most important is our friendship. "Nothing will change between us," I reassure her.

She lets out a long breath of relief. "Friends forever."

"Until the end of time and after."

AS SOON AS I ENTER my house, I strip off my clothes and head straight for the shower. My brain is filled with all sorts of dirty, wicked things I'd like to do to Cori. Blame the fucking kiss. The kiss she initiated and went with me again the second time around, until common sense kicked in. On her part.

Problem is, it ignited something inside me. Lust. Need. And something else I can't explain. My mind is in shreds, a surging perplexity. The kiss. The sweetest, hottest fucking kiss I've ever experienced in my life. Now, I want to breach that invisible line long established between us and fuck her until neither of us can move.

Can't think about it.

A nice shower should do the trick. Time to rinse this madness from my system. I step into the shower, toes flinching as they touch the chilled ceramic floor. I turn the metallic dial, releasing thousands of lukewarm drops to wet my hair and trickle down my back.

Images of Cori and I kissing continue to flood my mind. My senses are overpowered by how perfect she felt in my arms, the sweetness of her lips against mine.

One hour later, I can still feel the imprint of her lips—soft and warm—against mine as we explore each other, the butterflies coming alive in the pit of my stomach. And that thing my heart did—the way it slowed down and skipped at the same time.

For fuck's sake, I'm still turned on. If Cori were here, I'd bend her over and do her right here, with the warm water raining down our bodies.

A crazy thought of course. Because . . . well, she's on the do-not-touch list.

I grab the soap, scrub my neck, my chest, and drag it over my body. The action soothes my skin, but fails to alleviate my desire or aching bulge. Instead, I'm transported back into HornyTown, USA, with Cori's lips running along my torso.

My right hand palms my throbbing dick.

A wave of guilt washes over me. Can't whack one off to Cori.

Can't go there. I have no business wanting her. She's my best friend. That makes her forbidden.

I'm also a fan of casual sex, no strings attached. My definition of dating is going to a girl's house, banging her, then going home. Cori loves romance. She deserves the two point five kids, a loving husband, a dog named Fido, and the picket fence.

We'd never work. In the far back recesses of my mind, I acknowledge the danger and dreadfulness of lusting after her.

But that kiss . . . the blast of passion and heat it revved up inside me. Who knew a kiss could make a grown man feel so much? And now, I want to do wicked things to her sweet little body that I have no business wanting. Things that can only lead to a tangled mess.

And yet, need and hunger continues to roll through me. Desperate to numb everything inside, I turn the knob, setting the temperature as warm as my body can handle, and hiss.

The raging hard-on I've been sporting should go down any minute. Clenching my jaw, I release my dick and reach for the shampoo, wash my hair, and rinse off the suds. The ache continues to claw at my limbs, making my muscles tight with desire. This is what I call *la douleur exquise*—a heart wrenching pain of wanting someone who is unattainable

Mind over matter, I repeat in my head over and over.

I can do this. But I feel myself slipping. I'm losing this battle. Moving on its own accord, my hand clasps around my dick again. My eyes drift shut, and I give into the temptation of fucking my best friend.

She's on her knees in front of me, wearing nothing but a lace black thong, tits jiggling while she works my dick in her mouth from the base to the tip.

She looks so fucking hot.

The hair on the back of my neck prickles. Goosebumps slither up my arms and legs. The slow burn of desire crackles. My dick throbs in my palm. Grunting, I squeeze my shaft, then continue the slow and steady motion, sliding up and down.

I want Cori, I'm hungry for her. The realization makes my head spin and scorches my body from the inside out. My heart beats faster, blood rushes to my face.

She's now on her back. Spreading her thighs open, I step into the vee of her legs and fill her to capacity in one, long stroke.

My eyes drift shut.

My head falls back.

My hand moves faster around my dick.

I am thrusting inside her, deep and borderline rough. With each stroke, I imagine the walls of her body crushing down, until she's able to accommodate every inch of my cock.

I groan with pleasure.

My gut constricts. My balls tighten.

My breath hitches.

Pressure builds, rising higher and higher. Electricity shoots down my legs, feet, all over my body.

"Fuck." I grunt, pumping faster as pleasure wracks my body in thick, ropy, satisfying spurts.

I draw a shaky breath as a shudder races through me. For a long minute, I stand in the shower, hands flat on the tile wall in front of me, my head bent low, so that the hot water beats down my shoulders.

I'm so screwed.

Chapter 10

"A strong friendship doesn't need daily conversations . . ."

"YOU SHOULD DATE CORIANDER," I say to Lucas. We are in the boardroom for our monthly pow wow with the big guys, AKA our dads. We're the first ones to arrive. Good timing. It gives me a chance to convince one of my best friends to date another close friend—the one I've jacked off to all weekend.

Fucking pathetic.

Lucas sorts through some meeting materials. His brows are furrowed as his fingers slide over one smooth sheet of paper. Then he lifts his gaze and meets mine. "You're asking me to date Cori."

I nod and glance over the cream walls decorated with pictures of our staff, logos, awards, plaques, and other markers of company pride and prosperity. A blue folder, a pen, and a glass sits in front of each chair, perfectly square and spaced—a sure sign that Nora's OCD-like tendencies were in full force when she set up the room.

A powerful jolt of pride surges through me. This is our company—Cam, Lucas, me. Our fathers created it, but we're prepared to carry on the legacy whenever they're ready to pass the baton.

Lucas walks around the oblong table and plops his weight on one of the comfortable black leather chairs. "Why?"

Adjusting my gray tie, I turn to the window. Outside is a perfect winter day. Sunny and clear. The two inches of snow from the other night has since melted. The glare of the morning sun shines straight into my eyes. I squint and focus on the pretty blonde in black yoga tights and a waist length brown jacket as she takes a sip of her coffee.

"You're not answering," Lucas says smoothly. "So, either you've gone off the deep end, or something happened between you and Cori. I'm going with the latter."

I turn to face him. "Or maybe I just think you can make her happy." By the way, I can see the expression on your face. No, I'm not an idiot. My gut pinches at the thought of sweet, beautiful Cori dating one of my closest friends. But it makes sense, doesn't it? Set her up with Lucas and that will put a lid on my desire for my best friend.

Lucas' dark eyes linger on me for a long minute. Then the fucker laughs so hard he can't stop. To make things worse, he's laughing at me, not with me. I lean on the wall, hands in my pants pockets, eyebrows lifted, waiting.

He waves his hands in the air, his flag of apology. But the waves of laughter keep coming. "You slept with her, didn't you?" Lucas asks when he finally regains his composure.

A second passes, I say nothing.

"Shit, you kissed her," Lucas says. Captain Obvious.

Technically, Cori kissed me first. She started the whole thing. I simply took over. But no need for minute details.

"Why won't you date her?" I dodge his question with my own.

"You've kissed her, and now you want to be a real *boyfriend*," he says, air quoting the word boyfriend.

"No," I reply, mostly to myself. The truth is, after one kiss, I am totally hooked. Addicted. Desperate for another hit. That realization has my world spinning, throwing me off my axis. "I want Cori to be happy." That's partially true. I also want her under me, on top of me.

Lucas takes a sip of the water in front of him, then swivels his chair in my direction, face serious. Dark eyes assess me. "You can make her happy."

"Sounds like I'm missing some fun." Cam casually strolls into the room with a fresh cup of coffee in hand. He examines my face for a long moment, then sits next to Lucas. "What the hell happened to him?" he asks, pointing his coffee cup in my direction.

"He kissed Cori," Lucas volunteers.

Cam arches a brow, the equivalent of a question, but says nothing.

"And now our crazy friend thinks I should date her." Lucas swivels his chair to face Cam. "What do you think? Should I take her out?"

Cam strokes his chin, seeming to give Lucas' question serious thought. "Yeah, I think you should definitely take her on a date."

"Both of you are assholes," I mutter.

Lucas shrugs. "Your idea."

Cam laughs. "I thought Cori was in the market for a husband," Cam says. "This guy here" —he tilts his chin in Lucas' direction— "is never gonna marry again."

"It's true," Lucas agrees.

"I'm a little insulted you didn't ask me." For a fraction of a second, the corners of Cam's mouth twitch upwards. "I mean, I'm a good-looking guy." He flexes his former wide-receiver college football biceps. "Body of a Greek god."

"You're also a dog," I remind Cam.

"The pot calling the kettle black," Cam says with no hint of being insulted.

Lucas coughs. "Are you implying my days as a beast are over?"

"You have a daughter." I'm reaching low here, but the level of a man's desperation can drive him to many things. "Figure eventually, you'll realize there's something called Karma."

"Ouch." Lucas takes a long sip of his coffee, studies the cup for a moment before looking back at me. "While I'm flattered by this proposal, the truth is, you already know why I've never thought of Cori as more than a friend. And it's not because I don't think she has a hot little body on her. Because I do. So does Cam." He smiles.

I shift my weight to my right leg, not liking the fact that they've checked out Cori's anything.

"Perhaps," Lucas continues, his voice calm and controlled. "It's time you start thinking about why the idea of us jerking off to Cori bothers you."

Oh, God. My friends whacking one off. To Cori. Shit, I thought they meant they checked out her ass or something. And I get my first real sense of doom. It starts deep in my gut and ends up dead center between my eyes as a tension headache. "You went too far."

"Man to man, that's the only way we understand each other," Lucas says, showing no sign of remorse for the unnecessary mental image. "For the record, I don't jerk off to Cori."

But I have. Now that I've mentally fucked Cori, I can't stop. Even squeezed one in before coming to work this morning.

"But you have to admit, she's a walking boner," Cam chimes in.

My jaw clenches. Not feeling at all steady, or calm, for that matter, I tilt my head to one side and study the expression on Cam's face. He raises his hand in that 'hey, chill dude' manner. Relief floods through me, good to know Cori isn't a regular player in their wet dreams. Just mine.

"Have you talked to her since the kiss?" Lucas asks.

"Better yet, how was it?" Cam probes.

Sighing, I rake a hand through my hair. Yes, men are pigs. However, there's one thing men and women have in common. We both love to provide graphic details about our sexual experiences, but we never share information when we care about the other person.

"We haven't talked," I finally answer. It's been two days, nothing unusual, yet I'm aching to spend more time with her. "We texted briefly about an art event, but that was it." I cast my eyes on Cam and flip him the bird. "You're scum."

"Hey, the inquiring mind wants to know." Cam stands up, fixes the cuffs of his blue-striped shirt. "Two things." He pauses, takes another sip of his coffee. "During this exchange, did you happen to mention you're bringing a woman with you to New Hampshire?"

Fuck. I've completely forgotten about Red. A sick feeling washes over me. "I'm going to tell her." Liar, liar, pants on fire. I've had plenty of opportunity to come forward. Chicken shit, I'm officially a chicken shit.

"What happens now?" Cam continues, his tone serious.

"Nothing," I answer way too quickly, just as my father and the other fathers enter the room. Being the three good sons that we are, we head over to our dads. Handshakes and man-to-man hugs are exchanged. "What's going on, old man?" I say to my dad. By the way, if you want to know what I'm going to look like when I'm in my fifties, take a gander at this guy. Tall. Lean. Square jaw. Clean shaven. Strong shoulders. Stomach flat from all the yoga that he does. I even inherited his chin dimple. My dad is not only handsome as fuck, he also projects a level of confidence and easy manner. Our staff loves him.

"Your mom wants grandbabies."

"Apparently, so do you."

My dad laughs. "It's true. We're hoping they're with Cori."

I groan. "Cori and I are friends."

"Yeah, well, you know your mom and I started out as friends."

I nod. I've heard the story a million times. Friends to lovers.

"And then, one day, we kissed," my dad continues.

My heart trips so hard, I have to close my eyes and take a deep breath. "I know the story, Dad."

"Of course you do. But it's a great story, worth retelling." He claps me on the shoulder, just as the blonde I spotted outside enters the boardroom with the rest of the staff. Our eyes meet. Her lips curve into a small smile as she removes her coat.

"Who's that?" I ask my dad.

"That's Lorraine, she's a yoga instructor."

I cross my hands over my chest. Shit, had I known my dad's yoga instructor was this hot, I would have taken him up on his offer a long time ago. "A yoga instructor at our board meeting?"

"Yoga is a great way to meditate. I asked Lorraine to do some breathing techniques with us."

I look her over, full lips, bright green eyes, perky tits, sweet round ass. Nice. "Um, yeah, of course." With that I walk over to my chair and busy myself with some notes, giving my dad and his partners a chance for their usual rounds. After a few handshakes and cordial conversation, the meeting starts.

"Everyone, this is Lorraine, my yoga instructor. I'd like to start this meeting with some breathing techniques and sequences."

My gaze follows Lorraine as she saunters over to the head of the table. For a nanosecond we make eye contact. When she smiles, I smile back. This is too easy.

"Pranayama is the formal practice of controlling the breath, which is the source of our prana, or vital life force," she says in a Zen-like voice. For the next fifteen minutes, we practice breathing techniques, before switching into a brainstorming session.

When the meeting ends, I head to my office, three doors down the hall, with Lorraine's phone number tucked into my pocket. Once there, I unlock my laptop and focus on my work. Immediately, thoughts of Cori's lips on mine resurfaces. The truth is, they were poking around during the whole meeting, but I managed to keep them under control, for the most part. Who wants an inconvenient boner during a staff meeting?

Anyway, I click the mouse to a report. It takes all of my willpower to focus, but I manage to shut down the part of my brain that keeps thinking of my lips trailing along Cori's neck, sucking on her breasts, kissing across her belly.

We're friends.

I don't do relationships.

She's looking for one.

I need to accept things for what they are. No need for the over-analysis. It's pointless to even entertain or give life to these dirty-as-fuck daydreams. Our friendship is more important than our out-of-this-world kiss.

On my desk, my phone dings. I grab it and read Cori's text.

Hey, stranger. Guess what? I met a guy.

Chapter 11

"Finding a friend is as hard as finding a true lover."

THE TEXT ROCKS MY HEART, leaving it moving in foreign ways, to which I am not accustomed in all my years of living. I sit, suffocating like a fish out of water—wide eyed, heart in my mouth, my leaden lungs suppressing any efforts I make to inhale.

Needing a few minutes to compose my thoughts, I set the phone on my desk and shift my gaze to the computer screen. Everything is a blur. Any attempt to focus is a moot point. I'm caught between opposing needs—ignore Cori's text or be the friend that I've been for the last two plus decades.

Yes, the first option makes me the ultimate asshole. I'm well aware of that. But shit, bear with me here; my thoughts are more tangled than my headphones. I don't know where I want to stand with her. All I know is, now that we've kissed, there's this part of me that wants . . . more. And that scares me.

Sucking in a sharp breath, I check the time. Today is her day to teach. She should be in class. I'll call and leave a message. Easy.

I pick up my cell, scroll to her name, and tap TALK, dialing her number. To my surprise, she answers on the first ring.

"Home today?" I ask.

"No. I had a doctor's appointment, heading to work now."

I can hear the distinctive click of her heels hitting the pavement. It's not hard to imagine Cori in her usual fitted black jeans, long black coat, the winter sunshine reflecting off her dark-brown hair.

"Sick?"

"Routine check-up," she answers. "What's up?"

"Just got your text." Might as well go straight to the point.

"Oh." She laughs. "Yeah, I just met him."

At the doctor's office? Please don't let it be her OB-GYN. She can't start dating him. The asshole already gets a view of her snatch at least once a year. What the fuck?

Irrational jealousy knots in my stomach. Yeah, calm the fuck down big guy. A few jerking off incidents while fantasizing about banging my best friend does not make her mine. I grab the Dogbert stress ball and give it a good squeeze.

"What does he look like?" I ask. "What does he do?" Don't worry, I'm not being intrusive. The barrage of questions comes with being the *boy friend*.

She laughs. "He's a lawyer."

Relief washes over me. At least we've learned the douchebag is not her doctor.

"He's pretty hot," she's saying on the other end of the phone. "Tall, light brown hair, and built like he should be a Calvin Klein underwear model."

Automatically, I think of the Justin Bieber Calvin Klein skits on Saturday Night Live. Classic.

"So he's built like a sixteen-year-old boy." I'm lower than dirt, I know. A total sign of immaturity on my part. I'm supposed to be in my best friend behavior, I get it. But I'm still a man. "When's the date?"

"Tonight, at eight. Stopping at my Gram's for a few."

I stroke my chin, pondering whether or not I can ask Nora for the biggest favor of my life—play sick so Cori can cancel her date. "Is everything okay?"

"Yeah," Cori responds. "She's going away with Tim." Tim is Nora's *friend*. He's been her friend for the last fifteen years. She's not big on labels. "I may have to house-sit for a few days. Want to join me?"

All the blood rushes to my dick. Cori has house sat for her grandmother before. At times, I've stopped by for a couple of hours, along with Katharine or by myself. Those instances were before our kiss. Now, the idea of being alone with her has my mind reeling with dirty thoughts—one pebbled nipple between my teeth, my mouth on the bare flesh between her thighs.

I clear my throat. "Did you invite Katharine?"

"No." A car door closes. I listen to the jiggling of keys then an engine revs up. "But," Cori continues, "if you think you . . . um . . . you might be uncomfortable around me—"

"I'm not." The fact that my dick is as hard as wood right now is a pure indication I'm feeling a lot of things. Uncomfortable is not one of them. This leads me to think, perhaps the kiss has occupied as much space in her head as it has in mine. "Should I be asking you the same question?"

"Do you know what I love about having a guy as one of my closest friends?"

Let's pause for a minute.

Do you notice she didn't answer my question?

Ladies, let me give you a little bit of advice. If your intent is to avoid conflicts and keep the peace, you're only starting a war within yourself. There are some thoughts we can't avoid, and some feelings we can't deny.

With that said, typically, I'd push a little more to get the truth from her. We've been down that road before, with Barry. At the beginning, she didn't want to divulge the reason they broke up. Eventually, she confessed that it came down to our friendship or Barry.

She chose us.

Me.

My heart still trips over itself every time I think about that. No matter what, there will always be Cori and Dean.

Because of this, I tell myself to let everything go, for now. The fact that I've never gotten lost in a kiss before is inconsequential. What transpired between us was . . . well, a slip to be never repeated again.

Best to back off, lighten up the mood a bit. "What do you love about having a guy for a close friend?" I repeat her question. "Let's see . . ." I tap my index finger against my temple. "You love having a hot guy as your wingman?" I can feel her smiling on the other end, and the corners of my lips quirk up in response.

"Okay, two things," she responds, her voice more relaxed. "The first is definitely having a hot guy as a wingman. The second is, you're one guy I can always count on."

A valid statement. Her parents rarely check in, and when they do, it's always to bring her up to date about their latest adventure.

"Always," I confirm and mean it with every inch of me. "I gave you my word before. We're good."

She lets out a breath in obvious relief. "Thank you."

It's pretty clear, as hot as the kiss was, Cori has no desire to test the waters any further. I'm okay with that. My mind is still having trouble wrapping itself around the fact that we actually kissed anyway. "Text me after your date."

"Will do."

And just like that, we're settled into our normal routine. She'll go on a date. When she gets home, she'll text me that all men are dogs.

THE COOL WIND HITS MY FACE as I open the stainless-steel refrigerator. The inside is well-stocked with local produce, but I can't seem to decide what I want. Tonight, I'm insomnia's bitch.

I grab a beer, twist the cap off, and glance at the stove clock. Eleven o'clock has morphed into twelve and now one.

Cory has yet to call.

I head over to my living room. The chill from the hardwood floor clings to my bare feet, a small discomfort against the ache the rest of my body is suffering. Flopping onto the sofa, I twist off the cap of the beer bottle and take a swig.

My mind is blank; where there should be dreams of a threesome, or whatever, lays a heavy blackness. I'm worried about Cori. What if this asshole is a killer?

Okay, it can happen. I've heard about those Lifetime movies.

A distraction. I need sports. Grabbing the remote, I click on the television and let my fingers guide me directly to ESPN. Highlights of a college basketball game plays on the screen. I gulp down another mouthful of my beer, check my phone again, annoyed with its silence.

Nothing.

Fifteen minutes later, as I'm reaching for my phone, it pings. I swipe the screen and read Cori's text.

Tonight was great. Details to follow. Tired. XO, Cori.

Remember that feeling of trepidation I experienced when Cori first announced her need to find love?

It creeps over me like an icy chill, numbing my brain. In this frozen state, my mind offers me only one thought. Today, the end of Cori and Dean begins.

Chapter 12

"Just friends."

HAVE YOU EVER HAD A pure bullshit of a week, when you wish you could press that 'Do Over' red button for a second chance?

Well, I have an empty spot on the couch right here for you. Come join me.

My day started with the wonderful news that one of my clients has asked his wife for a divorce. Get this, at the age of fifty-eight, he's found happiness with a twenty-two-year-old. I can't stop singing, 'She ain't nothing but a gold-digger,' in my best Jamie Foxx voice.

I know. I know. I'm being a cynic. There's no proof she's really in love with his millions and looking for a daddy figure. And according to the latest hype, fifty is the old age of youth.

Anyway, that means it's time for me to come up with a plan on how to divide their assets and ship that baby to their lawyers. Believe me, it's never that easy. One of them will treat any proposal I've put together as unworthy of serious consideration and demand I provide a new, perfect plan that will make everyone happy. Seriously, people think it's fun to be a super genius, but they don't realize how hard it is to put up with all the idiots in the world.

Stocks also took a tumble, as third-quarter earnings season kicked off on a sour note. Both the Dow Jones Industrial Average and the S&P 500 indexes dropped by more than a percentage point. Shit like this has made my week tension-filled. On top of that, Cori has gone AWOL.

Instead of focusing on the mountain of work that awaits me, I fall into my seat in my office and swivel the chair toward the main view from my window. All around the sun is sharp and glinting, slowly removing all trace of the fresh layer of snow that had fallen in the middle of the night. My gaze stays on the winter trees lining the road. Their denuded forms stand stark, almost like charcoal outlines stretched by a passing artist.

Too poetic for you?

Blame it on my mother. You'll meet her soon. Growing up, we used to have family movie night every Friday. I can go on and on about whether *Pretty Woman* is better than *Annie Hall*. Can *Out of Africa* compete with *Breakfast at Tiffany's*? How the Civil War pales next to the tempestuous love-hate-love union of Clark Gable and Vivien Leigh.

Like it or not, I watched *The Notebook*, *Bridget Jones Diary*, and a slew of others I don't even want to name. I can recite every line of *Sense and Sensibility* and *Casablanca*. I'm not proud of that talent, but Cori loves my impression of Rick Blaine. At least Humphrey Bogart was the epitome of a man back then.

Cori again. You're dying to hear about her date with what's-his-name, aren't you?

So am I.

She and I have exchanged text messages here and there. Nothing. For fuck's sake, I don't even know his name.

But, let's be fair, if you were getting busy for the first time in a long time, would you really be texting your guy friend?

See, I understand.

To be clear, that nagging feeling in the pit of my stomach is not jealousy. Take a step closer and look at our history. Friends since seven, remember? She's the yin to my yang. My feeling comes from one friend caring for the other.

Okay, there's a slight attraction on my part. But nothing I can't handle.

My phone rattles again. This time, it's my sister, Kate, on a group text, confirming our plans for tomorrow night.

Paragon at 7. I reserved a table for 5. See ya!

Paragon is a premiere, Mediterranean restaurant, located in the heart of Manhattan. It's my birthday tomorrow. I'm turning the big 3-0. The big milestone. The goal is to drink and eat until our hearts' content. We get to do it all over again on Saturday, with my parents and fifty of their closest friends. The following weekend, we head to New Hampshire.

Other than the fact that Cori has gone AWOL, and one of my clients is letting his dick do the talking, life isn't too bad.

I pick up my phone and respond.

Got it. See you then.

My phone buzzes again. This time it's Cori.

Can we add one more person? I might bring a date. Hope that's okay.

When Cori was ten, a punk kid—who was twice my size, if not more—used to pick on her. I walked up to him and got in his face like the scrawny twelve-year-old that I was. He punched me in my stomach, knocking every wisp of air from my lungs. I lay on the concrete in a fetal position, struggling to breathe.

That's how I feel now, trying to inhale, to exhale, totally stunned as the text bounces around inside my skull.

Let's get something straight. Tomorrow night's celebration has always been the five of us. We did let Barry in because the douche was Cori's boyfriend. Other than that, *just a date* does not gain access to our group outings. No, I'm not a fucking crybaby, for Pete's sake. Besides, everyone knows men never really grow up, we only learn how to act in public.

I press the heels of my hands into my eyes, draw a sharp breath, and then type,

First round on me.

But in my head, I'm screaming: No, you can't bring a fucking date. Six is a crowd.

Tomorrow night should be fun. At least my inner psycho has the last word.

EVERY HETEROSEXUAL MAN SHOULD HAVE a hot yoga instructor in their speed dial. Lorraine and I never made it out of her apartment. We fucked the night away. No need to vomit, and you over there, please stop rolling your eyes. First, I think I made it pretty clear, this isn't a romance novel. Second, sex is a remedy necessary to allow for free and clear thinking.

No joke.

Third, have you been paying attention to this developing story? Cori is dating, bringing her pretty boy with her the night of my fucking birthday. Talk about sending a crystal signal to me. Well, I got the memo.

Fourth, my dick is awesome. Women flock to me, and I love women. One last vital piece of information I should reveal to you.

Ready?

A man can have sex without any form of emotional attachment.

Gasp.

Stunned? I hope this isn't unexpected news. Ask any man to choose between sex or oxygen, guess which he'd pick?

Yes, we'd all be dead.

Let me put it this way, the expression of "blue balls" is not simply a reference of being deprived of sex. It is the culmination of days, weeks or months of not being able achieve release and rid oneself of this suffocating and aching feeling.

Seriously, sex for us is a physiological need to get off.

I know, I know. For most women, this just doesn't compute. Well, here it is, one of the most fundamental differences in the wiring of male and female sexuality, that men can separate sex from a relationship, while for a woman, the two are usually intertwined.

This explains Cori's stance. She knows me like the back of her hand. Right now, my dick rules my world.

Too bad, in the quiet moments of the night, Cori's face is the last thing which dominates my brain.

Chapter 13

"No, we're not dating, but she's still mine."

WHEN I TURNED TWO, I was really anxious. Because I'd doubled my age in a year, I thought, if this keeps up, by the time I'm six, I'll be ninety.

Obviously, my calculation was off.

Happy Birthday to me!

The big fucking 3-0! A fucking milestone. And I love it. We can't help getting older, but we don't have to get old. My parents are living proof; you'll see on Saturday. Youth is a gift from nature, and age is a work of art.

"Hey, old man." Cori wraps her slender arms around my neck and pulls me close. Her body presses against mine, soft and warm. "Did you get your birthday gift?"

Earlier today, a package containing a scrapbook was delivered to my house. Going through thousands of vacation photos can seem like a mind-numbing vortex and a bit overwhelming, but not for Cori. She assembled a ton of pictures, snapped over the course of a year, of me with our family and friends. The pictures are all from different things we've done this year, and each page has a different theme—

camping, tailgating at the Giants game, concerts. Name the moment, it was captured. One of my favorites is a picture of Cori and me, wrapped in an orange plaid blanket during one of our camping trips. She's leaning on me, her head on my shoulder as I pretend to know how to play the guitar.

I think it's adorable and thoughtful that she took the time to arrange a great collection of memories into such a beautiful display.

"It's now sitting on my coffee table." I draw in a breath, inhaling sexy, subtle notes of berries and vanilla. She smells satisfyingly sweet, like how it smells when one walks into their favorite candy store.

Her full, glossy, pink lips curl into a mischievous grin. Pink lips—she's not wearing her red, official-date lipstick. Clearly, she's not serious about Abercrombie. Either that, or he didn't come. Good.

"It's my role in life to make sure you stay in touch with your feminine side," she teases.

"You get an A for effort." I step behind her, help her slip out of her coat then hand it to the Maître D. Noticing a thin strap of Cori's red camisole dangling from one of her shoulders, I hook it with my index finger and drag it over her honey skin into place. The touch lasts less than a second, but the feel of her smooth skin sends a rush of scorching heat through my body.

I swallow the big gulp of lust and try to focus. I mean, look at her. She's looks hot as hell tonight. And her eyes . . . they're bright and liquid warm, sprinkled with light brown specks, framed by beautiful thick lashes. They remind me of *Sbiten*—the hot winter Russian drink.

"Where's your date?" I ask.

"His name is Brandon. He had to answer a call for work." A smile spreads across her face. She waves at someone over my shoulder. "Oh, he's right here."

I turn and my gaze collides with the man who is obviously Cori's date. He's about my height, lean with tousled dark-brown hair, blue, serious-but-friendly eyes, distinct cheekbones, and an angular, clean-shaven jaw. Cori was right. He's a pretty boy, the type you see on billboards for Abercrombie and Fitch.

Releasing my grip on Cori's waist, I stand to my full six-two frame and exchange a firm handshake with the Ken doll lookalike. "Hey, man, I'm Dean."

"Brandon." He places a hand over Cori's shoulder, marking his territory. "I've heard quite a bit about you."

His tone doesn't reveal much. But his eyes, they are assessing me as if I'm his competition. A small smile plays on my lips, as my gaze shifts back to Cori's pretty face. "Yeah, all good things, right, Coriander?"

"Some." She hooks her arm through Brandon's and holds on to him.

Do you notice how she bats her eyes and makes that cute little girly laugh? That's my Cori flirting.

Not with me.

We don't do stuff like that, but I've been around her long enough to know her mannerisms.

Goddamn it if I don't feel a zing of envy. For so long, I've been the guy she leans on for the good and bad times. Not that this guy is the one, but I'm a man, and I recognize right away, this dude is in it to win her over. Even when Barry existed, I never felt he'd taken my spot as the one who holds her steady in place.

I shove down the resentful longing and wave toward the private room where the rest of our party is waiting. "Let's join the party."

Cori starts to walk ahead of us, stops, and looks us over. "You're coming?"

"Yeah, in a sec," I answer and watch her sashay her way to the private room. Neither Brandon nor I move. He cocks his head in a way that speaks of a fighter appraising his opponent.

Rolling the cuffs of my black fitted shirt, I let him size me up.

Men don't intimidate me. It's the opposite. But Brandon is giving me the vibe that we're equals. Instead of feeling bothered, I find his cockiness quite amusing.

Neither of us speaks. Words are not needed. My message is clear—break her heart, you're fucked.

The smirk on Brandon's face relays what's going on inside his head: Move over, big guy, there's a new man in Cori's life.

Dinner will be fun.

CONTRARY TO WHAT YOU'RE THINKING, we survived dinner. I can sing "We are the World" during a feast with anyone. But let's establish one thing. Although Brandon was bearable during dinner, his presence buzzes around me like a fly I could not swat. I don't care much for the prick. He's too touchy. For two hours, his arm remained draped over Cori's shoulder.

Seriously, I get it. He's into her.

Who wouldn't be?

She's fucking beautiful. My admiration for her is deep-seated and long-lasting.

On the flip side, she's also my friend, who is feeling a bit vulnerable right now. While I'm around, no man is going to take advantage of her. At any rate, it's fair to say, Brandon and I have already made up our minds. We are enemies.

Nonetheless, he's Cori's date, potential future husband and father to her children. I have to play nice.

We left Paragon about one hour ago. After we ate and drank, we decided to keep the celebration going. We headed to a club for late-night revelry, with dancing, cocktails, and tequila slammers.

The club is electric tonight. Lights are pulsing in time with the blaring bass of the music. Dancing bodies tangled together. Neon signs aligning the walls. Good vibes are flowing like a virus . . . a good one.

I spot Lucas and Kate. They are moving as if their limbs are made of spaghetti. The chick who managed to catch Cam's attention has her tongue down his throat. They push through dancing bodies tangled together towards the exit. In the midst of the chaos, he manages to wave goodbye. God, I love that man.

Where am I? Why am I not part of the shenanigans, with my hands up in the air, jumping in a huddled group like Tic-Tacs being shaken in a box?

On any other night, that would be me. But I'm right here, leaning against the bar, white-knuckling my scotch. My heart is keeping time with the heavy bass, pumping the music through my veins. The Latin music should be cranking my joy right up, hijacking my brain. Nerves are trying to take over my body.

With my glass of scotch clutched tight in my hand, I look through the crowd. She's still dancing with Brandon. About a half hour ago, I slipped through the crowd and made a bee line for the bar. I'm still here. My gaze lowers to my drink. What is this, my third now? I can't remember. The alcohol isn't doing its job. I'm not numb.

A smile is painted on my face as I listen to the pretty brunette, with the fuck-me rack, going on and on about her strong social media presence. Apparently, she's one of those Instagram stars who gets paid to travel and post pictures while on location.

Over the roar of the music, she's telling me about her most recent trip to Brazil. I can barely make out anything she's saying, so I lower my head closer to her lips. In the process, I catch a glimpse of her black lace bra and luscious scoop of flesh.

My dick doesn't even stir.

What the hell is that about?

Sometime soon, I'll call a car service and let the chauffeur drive us around while we go at it. *So wake up, buddy.*

"You should follow me on Instagram."

For the record, I don't do social media much. I have a Facebook page and a Twitter account. Both are sitting there collecting dust. I have no desire to post every single thing I do in my life. "Not a social media guy."

"You can't take your eyes off her," the brunette observes and she's not talking about her twin towers.

In the dark of the room, my attention is glued to the dance floor, but not on the fast dancing of the crowd. If a single pearl had the power to hypnotize, imagine just what the effect would be if hundreds of luminescent beads were meticulously sewn into one of the most seductive shapes ever.

That's Cori.

A force larger than myself holds me hypnotized to the movement of her body, bathing in the dim, purple glow of the club, the sway of her hips enough to tempt any man.

I'm not impervious to her effect. My aesthetic senses seem to have awakened. My eyes are eating her up like a child feasting on his birthday cake.

A remix of Rhianna's "Work" is playing. Cori is moving in her sexy, wide-legged, black pants to the crazy beat as if her hips were made to rock to the rhythm. The bass seems to thump in time with her heartbeat as though they are one, filling her from head to toe.

My skin tingles, and my lungs feel like mush.

I like RiRI. I liked this song . . . until now.

She does a butt jiggle-wiggle combination. The sequins of her pink camisole catch the glittering disco ball that illuminates the sunken dance floor. The legs of her pants move one millisecond later than her body, then continue moving one millisecond after she stops. Brandon's head tilts back, bliss on his face. He wraps his hand around her waist and pulls her against him close enough to feel his junk.

She's fluid, sensual, elegant, and bold.

This is where the Cori I know and love would politely establish some distance between her and the asshole. Instead she looks up at him. Asswipe lowers his mouth to her ear. Whatever he said must have been like winning the fucking lottery, because her lips curve into a smile. An odd feeling cranks over my chest.

Protectiveness, I decide.

"When are we leaving?" the brunette purrs.

I tear my attention from the dance floor and focus on the pretty brunette. Her curves are pressed against me, all hyped and ready for a good time. "I'm here with friends."

Did I just turn down sex? Who is this person talking?

Sadly, it's me.

I can't believe I just turned down sex. What the fuck is wrong with me? The only logical thing I can think of is, I'm looking out for Cori. Friends don't let friends go home with a total stranger. Do they?

Technically, Brandon isn't a stranger. As I've learned during dinner, this is the douchebag she went out with the other night. You know, the one we're still trying to get an update on. This is date number three. From what I've heard, that's typically scoring night, right?

A pain stabs my chest like a knife piercing my skin.

The brunette motions to the bartender and mouths her drink of choice. Then she follows where my gaze was glued seconds ago. "She looks to be having a good time." She takes a sip of her drink that has just arrived. It's one of those fruity things with both a fruit skewer and a paper umbrella. "I bet you he scores tonight."

A muscle ticks in my jaw. "No one is scoring." Sadly not even me, especially on my fucking thirtieth birthday. My heart betrays me and lugs my attention back to the dance floor where Cori is living it up with Brandon. "Listen, babe, I have your number. We'll get together." I down the last drop of my scotch. It tastes more like anguish than a twenty-three-year old scotch. Setting the empty glass on the counter, I say, "Gotta go."

Immediately I head for the dance floor. Wedging my way through sweaty bodies rubbing against each other, I head straight toward Miss Happy Feet and Sir-Touch-A-Lot. Time to break up their little foreplay. The music switches to a remix of Robyn's "Dancing On My Own." The fucker—AKA Brandon—now has his hands on her lower back. A look of pure bliss on his face.

My pace picks up.

Halfway there, my sister grabs my wrist and drags me off the dance floor, back to the bar, where Lucas is watching us with an amused expression on his face. The brunette is no longer there. I guess she moved on to her next prey.

"What's that about?" I ask.

"You look pissed off," Lucas notes. What a genius he is.

"You can't put her in a glass and expect no one to break through. She has needs, just like you and me." In case you're wondering who is talking, that's my sister.

"And me," Lucas reminds us.

"What the hell are you talking about?" I ask, brows glued together.

Kate smiles in that I-know-it-all way she does when she's sure of herself. Lack of self-confidence does not exist in my sister's vocab. She's classy, sassy, and a bit bad-assy. "You want Cori. It's obvious."

I drag a hand through my hair. "You've lost it." For confirmation, I glance over at Lucas. The mofo shrugs.

"You're jealous. That's not a bad thing," Kate continues.

"What have you done to my sister?"

"I agree with Kate," says Lucas. And I always thought he was smarter than me. That theory is now up for reconsideration.

"Hey." Kate picks up where Lucas left off. "A little jealousy in a relationship is good."

Jealousy is a one-stop word for all the roots of evil in the brains of humans. I've never been jealous of anyone in my life. I glance back to where Cori and Brandon are dancing. The dude is still copping a feel. That's when I am finally forced to acknowledge the green flowing through my veins . . . at least to myself. "I'm not in a relationship with Cori."

"Not yet." She brushes her blond bangs from her eyes. "It's nice to know there's one woman you don't want to lose." Kate wedges her way between Lucas and me. "Who's driving me home?"

Lucas tips his imaginary fedora, and then extends his arm in her direction. "At your service, m'lady."

"By the way, I don't care if we're siblings." Kate pokes me in the shoulder and narrows her eyes at me. "There's a lot at stake here. Before you go on your quest, make sure you're serious. Otherwise, I'll get someone to kill you. I know people."

"I'm not going to make a play for Cori," I argue, but I don't even convince myself.

"Right." She tiptoes and places a kiss on my cheek. "Just remember, she's my friend too. And if you hurt her—"

"Again, I don't want Cori."

Lucas says nothing.

"Right," Kate says. "Happy Birthday."

After Lucas and Kate make their exit, I contemplate my next move . . . staying or leaving. In the end, I pad over to the dance floor, shake Brandon's hand and hug Cori goodnight.

"You're leaving?" Her voice is a whisper in my ear. It's intoxicating.

Something unfurls in my gut, and I'm pretty sure it's desire. "Yeah," I answer, voice low and filled with gravel. "Work in the morning."

A part of me waits for her to tell Brandon she's leaving with me. Instead, she smiles. "I'll see you on Saturday," she says, referring to my parents' dinner extravaganza in my honor.

Jesus, she's staying behind with what's-his-face. A wave of disappointment hits me, and it's ridiculous, because Cori and I are friends. She's the type of friend when, after we die, I hope we stay ghost friends and scare the hell out of people.

That's all we are.

And I've never *not* been okay with our situation or wanted more . . . and then the kiss happened.

I release Cori and establish a bit of space between us. As I turn on my heels to walk away, Cori grabs my wrist and pulls me to the side. Her eyes—a sweet combination of innocent and wild—search my face with gentle concern. "You look morose."

I don't care how grounded you are, everyone needs one friend who understands what we're not saying. Her concern tugs my heartstrings. I thumb her cheek and give her an 'I'm-okay' smile. "Be safe, and be good."

She leans into me, climbs on her toes, and places a kiss on my cheek. "Always."

After a nod, I find the exit. As tempting as it is, I don't look back. Cori can dance the night away with whomever she wants. I have no claim on her.

Chapter 14

"Friends are connected heart to heart."

FATE HAS A THOUSAND WILES. Lust is one of them. It's manipulating my senses, making me yearn for the one person who isn't available.

Two days after my birthday night, the disappointment that slammed my chest, from watching Cori with Brandon continues to gnaw at me. You'd think that would knock some common sense into me.

On the contrary, whatever this thing is that I'm feeling has intensified. Everything in me is saying, screw the what-ifs and go for it.

I want her. I want her bad.

Blame it on the kiss. In that moment the world stopped, where everything melted away, leaving us alone in our own little world.

Pure fucking bliss.

I want to do it again. Every hour. Every minute. Every day.

The idea gives me an adrenaline rush, makes my heart beat faster.

My dick stirs in my pants.

Jesus H. Christ, I'm this excited over a far-fetched possibility.

I'm fucked.

Exhaling, I scrub a hand over my face. This is just a little glitch, a natural course in our friendship. Cori and I came of age side by side—acne breakouts, braces—and through all other growing pains, we've remained friends. This reaction is par for the course.

I mean, at some point in an opposite-sex friendship, one person usually develops some sort of feelings for the other, right?

A small obstacle.

All I have to do is maintain the appropriate boundaries. First, stop mentally fucking her. Second, get my dick to stop thinking about her.

Control of both heads at once. A difficult task, but it can be done.

The idea of risking our friendship, just to turn all the things I've done to her in my deep dark secret fantasies into reality, isn't worth investing any effort. The romantic comedy section of Netflix might say yes, but we all know reality's a little more complex and totally unscripted.

Is she fuckable?

Fuck yeah!

If there were a perfect world, where I could hook up with my only female friend and it wouldn't jeopardize our friendship, I would totally do it. With that said, a best friend with benefits relationship is not an option. That comes with a boatload of complications.

What if she were to come to me and beg?

Okay, I'd consider the proposal, but warily. Anyway, that will never happen. Let's face it, relationship-wise, we're on different paths. Cori loves romance; she's the happily-ever-after type. On top of that, it's common knowledge, no one ever transitions well from friends to dating, let alone remaining friends after a hook-up.

My point, my friendship with Cori overpowers hotness. Anything that may negatively affect the closeness we share is a deterrent and needs to be locked up. Even the possibility of mind-blowing sex is not worth losing everything . . . a girlfriend. I mean a *girl friend*.

Girlfriend? I shake my head dismissing the idea. We'd never work. Based on my track record, the attraction factor eventually fades. What then?

A lot of awkwardness.

It's not as if we can go our separate ways and never see each other again. As my sister pointed out, our world is a never-ending continuum. Everything I am is woven into everything she is. My parents are friends with Nora. We share mutual friends. She's my sister's best friend. No point beating a dead horse and go on about how much I value our friendship.

Somewhere, in the back of my mind, I know the possibility of hooking up with Cori has all the makings of a complete clusterfuck. And yet, I can't stop contemplating—to pursue

132

Cori or not to pursue? You've got to admit, this question requires some serious thought.

Enough of this self-actualization. Back to work. In thirty minutes, I have a meeting with one of my clients. Yeah, the one divorcing his wife of thirty years. Fun.

I take a sip of my bulletproof coffee—Cori's favorite way to drink it. My gaze swivels to the vintage ruby desktop clock beside the stack of folders. A smile tugs on my lips. The clock clashes with the rest of the room's executive motif, but it's a present from Cori. A little trinket she picked up at an antique shop and gave to me after I graduated from Wharton. What the timepiece lacks in elegance, it makes up in sentimental value.

Dragging a hand through my dark hair, I stare at the computer screen that's mocking me with appointments, trades to be made, emails waiting to be answered. And yet, all I want is to hold Cori, press my face into her hair, or better yet, her neck, so I can inhale her like she's my own salted caramel cupcake.

Jesus H. Christ. I'm fucking surrounded by her.

I power down my computer, grab my messenger bag, and dash out of my office for my appointment. Cori has me twisted in knots and all sorts of fucked up.

TWO HOURS LATER, I'M SITTING at a trendy restaurant, listening to my client boasting about how he's feeling rejuvenated, full of life, while his new chick plays footsy with my leg. I guess twenty-something pussies are the fountain of youth. As expected, my plan how to divide assets was returned with a hell no.

From him.

The asshole wants to hand his fortune to Ms. Golddigger on a silver platter. My gut tells me to let him fuck himself and just do as he says. I don't get paid to be anyone's morality police. But in some ways, it's my job to steer my clients off the cliff.

"If you want to remarry, I strongly suggest you draw up a tight as a virgin's ass prenuptial." I flash future Mrs. Donner a small smile and move my leg out of reach. "No offense, sweetheart."

She arches her back, pushing her false knockers front and center. "None taken."

Perhaps this is where she expected me to flirt with her. Not happening for so many reasons. Respect for my client and shit . . . oh, my dick—well, not even a slight twinge from the dude. Can't blame him. We don't dip into another man's goods.

Speaking of goods. Come to think of it, I haven't slept with anyone since Lorraine. I've become a regular at rubbing one out while thinking about Cori. Now, this is pathetic.

My phone vibrates on the table. I glance at the flashing screen. The temptress herself. Perfect timing.

"Excuse me." I pick up my phone and read her text.

Need your help. Model canceled. Tonight's class=Male physique. Say yes.

Cori to my rescue. I swear we are connected, heart to heart. It takes all of my strength not to smile.

Once a week, Cori runs one of those popular wine and paint classes. Every so often, she brings in an actual model and teaches techniques how to draw the human body. Throughout our friendship, she's never asked me to pose for one of her assignments or anything else. Looks like my Moonchild is in a bind.

For the record, she has files of models she can call anytime. But it's obvious she doesn't want one of them. It's me she wants in that room when she teaches these women how to capture the male physique. Talk about stroking my ego.

"Need to answer this. Work," I lie, already typing my response.

Be there in one hour.

"I'll make some of the changes you've asked for," I say to Mark Donner, after sliding my phone in my suit jacket. "But as your financial advisor, I think you should know that the woman you've dumped your wife for has been playing footsy with me."

The way her jaw drops is priceless.

Fifteen minutes later, while the future Mrs. is making a desperate plea for forgiveness, I pay the bill and walk out with a shitload of work to do. But first, a stop at Cori's studio.

A LITTLE OVER AN HOUR later, I am standing in the middle of the refurbished farmhouse that Cori uses as her art studio and gallery, with nothing on but a pair of black boxer briefs. Every so often, I catch one of them staring at my package while Cori explains tonight's painting class—the male physique.

"The serratus anterior muscle may be the sexiest muscle on the male physique," Cori says to the crowd. She's standing behind me, her chest pressing on my back as her fingers skate across my sides. "This is the muscle group on the side of the rib cage."

My body is on fire. My hands are aching to touch her as much as she's touching me. When she reaches my waist, the touch lingers, and I swear my dick—the treacherous prick—spills my secret to the gaggle of women sipping on their wine.

I shift my weight, adjusting my junk. A few of the women smile. One mouths *call-me*. She's cute, too. But aw, hell, it's obvious who is causing this effect on me. Our sexy art instructor.

Think chemistry class. Desperate, I force myself to mentally recite the periodic table. That always does the trick. True enough, the bastard's excitement goes down a notch.

"Class, what are some words you'd use to describe our model's chest?" Cori asks the group of women. My gaze follows her as she moves around the room. She's in skinny jeans, a gray T-shirt that reads *I arted* across her breasts with a hand-held palette underneath the black printed words. My mouth quirks at the saying. She has a thing for funny T-shirts and art.

"Broad and powerful," one woman says.

My eyes flicker between unfamiliar faces.

"Immaculately sculpted," a pretty, caramel-complexioned woman says. Warm chocolate eyes examine every inch of my body. "Chiseled, V-cut abs, bulging triceps, and—."

"Can I touch?" a pretty brunette interjects, holding my gaze.

My lips twitch in amusement. I feel like a gazelle, in the middle of the savannah, who wandered off from the rest of the herd, and suddenly realized that those nice striped things in the distance are, in fact, a pack of hungry, hungry tigers. For the record, I'm not too confident that the tiger is the natural predator of the gazelle, in case anyone reading this is trying to learn about ecosystems.

"Touching is not an option," Cori says, her voice filled with amusement. She returns her focus to me. Her eyes skim over my face, shoulders, rest on the black ink of the Maori tattoo on the left side of my chest, before meeting my gaze. "I'm sure, at some point, each one of you have seen a beautiful male body before."

A bolt of heat surges through me. Cori thinks my body is easy on the eyes. This is a first. In all of our years of friendship, she's never once said anything about my physique. When she turns on her heels ahead of me, I can't help myself. I stare at her ass as her heels *click click* across the hardwood floor.

"Yeah, but my goodness." The cute brunette fans herself.

"And he's just a friend?" Another asks, voice fills with doubt.

Once I got there, Cori explained to the class I am a last-minute stand-in doing a friend a favor.

Another woman adjusts her red framed glasses, winks at me, and says, "If you don't want him, I'll take him."

Cori raises to the toes of her black heels and reaches for a blank canvas. Her tattoo plays peekaboo with my eyes. Like any perverted man, an image of her on her knees, ass up in the air, tat in full view, flashes in my head.

I groan and peel my gaze away.

"In tonight's class, we'll be creating a beautiful male torso that is ripped," Cori clears her throat. "Drawing the male figure can appear challenging at first sight, but once you master the step-by-step technique we'll go over tonight, it will be nothing but fun. You will learn how to draw the basic runway pose, and how to represent the proportions of the male figure."

"From where I'm looking, his proportions are um . . . perfect," one chimes in.

Someone snorts. Women are ruthless. I smile. Shit like this doesn't bother me.

"Your friend has a nice package," says the lady with the red glasses.

As human beings, we are all connected to everything and everyone around us. This is a fact. Not a concept or a dream. So, if someone is staring at you, and thinking and feeling strongly about you, then it is very possible that you could feel it in your body or mind.

Yep, Cori is checking out my package. While I don't have a full-on erection—not because my dick isn't trying, but mind over matter—I'm also not suffering from shrinkage. When Cori finally looks up past my waist and meets my stare, I smile. And I swear, she blushes.

"Okay everyone." She claps her hands together. "It's time to get creative."

Chapter 15

"There's a natural chemistry between us as friends."

THE REST OF THE WEEK turned into a blur. One day was spent driving to the Hamptons and back home. By Friday, I needed a break from the daily grind, which explains why I'm in Hackensack at Riverside Mall tonight.

I'm leaning against the wall at Burberry. The designer store smells like heaven in a handbasket, and the floor shines like the surface of a lake at sunrise. A white, quilted, puffer jacket hooked over my arm, my attention is fixated on my cell phone. Through invisible speakers, the latest hits fill the air without effort. Down to my right, a pretty employee, with blond-tipped dreadlocks, is quietly folding a shirt into a neat square shape. She raises her head, we make eye contact for a few seconds, long enough for her to know I think she's hot. She smiles.

My phone pings, drawing my attention to the text message. It's Lucas, reminding me that I need to make a move. We are tangled in an intense battle of *Words with Friends*. I study the board, then send him over the game-winning word with a silly, satisfied smile wrinkling my face.

As expected, my phone lights up with a text from Lucas.

Define oxyphenbutazone.

With a big-ass grin on my face, I key in my response.

A phenylbutazone derivative C19H20N2O3 having anti-inflammatory, analgesic, and antipyretic effects.

An emoticon middle finger follows. I laugh and type.

Be my bitch.

Bite me. Brunette or Red 2nite?

My gaze automatically settles on the off-white, closed door. Cori is in the fitting room, trying her third dress for an event with Brandon.

Life is a cruel irony, isn't it? I'm officially the guy who is lusting after his best friend and helping her pick out a dress for a date.

LOSER!

All caps for emphasis. I'm so deep in the friend zone, next thing I know, she'll be asking me to meet Brandon's fucking parents.

The same pretty employee strolls by and openly gives me a once over. I return the admiration until she disappears somewhere in the back of the store, probably in their inventory room. I once fucked a girl in one of those. Good times.

I text Lucas back.

Hanging with Cori.

In less than two seconds Lucas sends another text.

Should I still ask her out?

I respond.

Fuck off.

The fitting room door opens. Cori steps out with the biggest smile on her face. "So, what do you think?" she asks, her hands on slim hips jutted to one side.

I bury my phone in my pocket and focus on Cori. She's wearing a sleek, fitted, black dress that skims her body in the most sensual way. Today, her lips are almost nude, covered only with her signature, pale pink gloss, which reminds me of a rosebud. She looks more beautiful than the winter sun above pristine snow.

My heart rate kicks up a notch, and my skin prickles. A host of scenes plays in my head. My fingers sliding the oversized ruffle covering her one toned shoulder, as my lips linger on her bare skin, her mouth. A hand cupping one of her breasts.

My dick raises its head, ready for action.

I am still staring at Cori as if she's a puzzle, and I'm the missing piece, when she speaks. "Is it a no?"

Is she kidding me? She's fucking stunning. I clear my throat. "It's gorgeous. You're gorgeous."

"I agree with your boyfriend," a freakishly thin waif says.

A faint flush of pink blooms on Cori's cheeks. One of the things I love about Cori is the way she reacts to the simplest thing, the sincerity in everything she does.

"Oh, we're not together," Cori explains.

The woman eyes me with open interest. "Well, darling," she says to Cori, "if you don't want him, then, sugar, I'm free tonight."

As much as I'm enjoying the admiration, I've never been one to dump Cori for a quick lay. Besides, size double-zero and no tits has never been my thing.

"Sorry," I say directly to the woman. "She may not want me, but I'm all hers tonight." I catch the slightest curve at the corner of Cori's mouth.

The woman smiles. "Enjoy him. He's yummy. When you're done, feel free to send him my way." With that, she struts toward the cash register.

Once alone again, Cori turns to me and asks, "You really think so?"

Do I think I'm yummy? Hell yeah. She can take a lick if she wants. But the way she's chewing the bottom of her lip tells me she's not thinking about licking my popsicle. "What are you worried about, Moonchild?"

"The dress," she answers. "Do you think I should buy it?" She twirls around in front of me, her dark hair moves with her, hiding her face until she stops and flicks it back over her shoulder.

"Am I known for sugarcoating shit?"

"You're not Willy Wonka," Cori responds and we laugh together.

Don't look too deep into this about compatibility. It's a giant cliché. We've been friends for over two decades, remember? I've said that exact line to her at least a million times in our lifetime.

"You got it." I place one hand on her bare shoulder and gently turn her toward the fitting room. "Now go change. Dinner's on me."

"Dinner." She looks up at me and raises a brow. "No hot date tonight?"

"What's that?" I ask, playfully evasive.

"That's right, the great Dean Conrad Morello only fucks his women."

"It's a mutual understanding." I give her a gentle nudge toward the fitting room.

She pauses, tilts her head and twiddles her hair in a seemingly absent-minded way before saying, "One day you'll fall in love."

My heart trips. Ignoring the reaction, I tap my rock hard flat stomach. "Don't bet on that. Now go. I'm starving."

A few minutes later, she joins me in her usual jeans and an oversized tee. She pays for her outfit, then we head to Oceanaire—a seafood restaurant at the mall. The environment is sophisticated and lively.

After we place our order, she leans forward and searches my face. "Do you think the dress is too fashion-forward?"

"Oh, hell, woman. The dress is hot. Abercrombie boy will be putty in your hands."

"I'm serious, Dean," she says with a smile.

"Okay, maybe a little, but that's a part of who you are." She's a beautiful mixture of teacher, hippy, and sophistication. "If Mr. Lawyer thinks it's too much, he should be dumped."

She laughs, her shoulders easing back in her chair. "We're not exclusive."

I ignore the clench in my stomach and take a long draft of my beer, before asking the one-million-dollar question. "Do you want it to be?"

"I'm not sure. We've only been on a few dates," she says with a shake of her head.

Four dates. They were together last night. "He's inviting you to a company function. He wants serious."

Her smile fades, replaced by a thoughtful frown. It's a look Cori gets when she's troubled by doubts. "We'll see."

There's uncertainty in her voice. Before I can question it, my phone buzzes. It's Red, asking to meet at her place at ten. It's been two weeks since I've seen her. Shit, next week, she's coming to New Hampshire with me. Must tell Cori. But not tonight. We're having dinner. I helped her pick out a fucking dress for her date with Brandon. Can't ruin such a bonding moment.

Without taking my eyes off the screen, my fingers move swiftly across the keyboard and typed

Got a thing.

"Need to leave?" Cori asks.

"No, we're fine."

My phone buzzes again with another text from Red.

Striking out? Still on next Friday?

This is my window of opportunity to say no. Call the whole thing off. But I can't. Not over a text message. I'm a lot of things, but never a coward.

Cori's gaze is on me, watching me. In the past, her scrutiny never bothered me, but tonight, as I sit across from her reading the text, I feel . . . exposed.

With my stomach coiled in knots, I answer.

Will touch base later.

Afterward, I bury the phone in my jacket. Sometime between tonight and next Friday, I'll come clean. Technically, I'm not doing anything wrong. Last time I checked, my relationship status said available, which means, I'm free to do as I please.

Still, a pang of guilt niggles at me.

"You know, we don't have to have a drink," Cori says while opening the menu. "I'm well versed on our Friday night routine."

I raise a silent brow and meet her gaze. The soft warmness of her eyes wraps around me like a blanket and makes me feel at home. "Please explain our routine to me."

"We meet. We catch up, then you go be with your flavor of the week," she says, her expression angelic, her voice pure devil, no hint of resentment.

I glance around the room. Under the delicate lighting. The tables are close, but the wine crate stacks help to keep a little privacy. The intimacy gives the vibe of two people on a date. I don't want the moment to end. "I want to be here. Unless you have plans."

"None. I'm all yours."

My heart hammers upon hearing the words. I remind myself, the heart is a lonely hunter. The bastard needs to keep doing its job . . . pump blood.

"Your dress? Wear it tomorrow."

Cori nearly chokes on her drink. "At your parents' dinner?"

I nod.

Go ahead, call me 'selfish,' but I see it more as 'honest.' I don't need that 'good person' badge. I've tried to squelch my desire for Cori, to no avail. It's a losing battle.

"It's for a date with Brandon."

"Wear it." *For me.*

She stares as if I'd just produced a rhinoceros from my pocket. I can just imagine the sparks in her brain, desperately trying to connect the dots, and instead, just causing a short circuit.

"What's in it for me?" she finally asks.

Me. My lips on your bare shoulder, kissing your skin until you melt. "It'll make me happy."

This has her arching a brow. "Is this an ego thing?"

As always, our conversation has a natural rhythm. No long, drawn-out, awkward pauses, or one person dominating the other. "What do Jay Gatsby and I have in common?" I ask, referring to one of my favorite literary characters ever written.

"You're both obsessed with a woman you can't have," she mocks, her voice filled with amusement. "You must tell me who it is."

All of my wickedly dirty thoughts have been about this woman. But I can't tell her that. Not yet. Not until I decide if whatever is going on inside me is worth pursuing.

I laugh, shoving any possibility of Cori and Dean aside for now. "Not even close. Gatsby walked into rooms wearing a shirt with no collar. Even a little thing like that made people talk. I bet you they still do, in today's society."

"Your point?" she asks after a forkful of her Caesar salad.

"Personal wattage. Some people are lucky enough to win it in the biological lottery. I like to think of it as a matter of attitude. And the right clothes don't hurt."

"Got it, Morello, I should never question your ego." She laughs again. "Can I ask you a question?"

"Anything."

"Do you like Brandon?"

Between you and me, the answer is no, that's already established. You think I'm going to lie here, don't you? Well, sit back and learn. "Does it matter?" It's called answering a question with a question.

"You know it does."

The truth is, under different circumstances I might actually like the guy. "It's about how you feel Cori. Do you like him?" This is a crucial piece of the puzzle. My next move hinges on her answer. If she's into the guy, I'll quietly bow out. Not that I'm officially in a race for Cori's attention.

She shrugs. "He's nice."

"Just nice?" Any woman who describes a man as 'nice' never turns out to be into the guy.

"I don't know. Feels like something is missing."

Hope kicks hard in my heart, wanting to come out. Hope. "Like what?"

"Chemistry."

"You can't force chemistry to exist where it doesn't." I can't help but wonder if she can feel the sexual tension crackling in the air. "The same way you can't deny it when it does."

"Like us."

She's right. The chemistry between us can set this place on fire. Not trusting myself to speak, I lean back and let her words soak into my system.

"We clicked the moment we met." She takes a sip of her wine then asks, "How old was I?"

"Seven," I answer, voice low.

A smile touches her face. "That was twenty-years ago."

I nod and take another swig of my beer. A barrage of memories hit me. The day we climbed the large oak tree at our local elementary school and spent hours discussing *Toy Story*. The framed photo in my office, of Kate, Cori, and me in midair in our black graduation gowns, celebrating our last day of high school. The time she jumped on my back during a flag football game, and my mother snapped a picture of us with our tongues sticking out.

Over the years, we've shared laughter, secrets, even tears.

My heart squeezes hard. "We've known each other for a long time."

"There aren't that many men I click with." Cori leans forward and holds my gaze. "But you and I . . . God, our energies just flow, you know. Nothing between us is forced or coerced. We're just . . ."

"Present," I add.

"Yes, we're present." She answers with an expression on her face I can't quite read. A weird silence stretches before she says, "Thanks so much for standing in your underwear for over one hour while a bunch of women drooled over you."

"The pleasure was all mine."

"How can I repay you?" she asks, face bright, seeming back to her regular self.

"You owe me a dance."

She blinks. "A dance?"

"We didn't dance on my birthday. That's the reason why I'm asking you to wear the dress tomorrow. I want my birthday dance." I put down my beer, look her in the eye and say very seriously, "Wear the dress for me tomorrow, Cori."

For a minute, she says nothing and gives me a long calculating look, as if she's waiting for me to retract my request. When that doesn't happen, she takes a sip of her wine, then says, "You're right, I do owe you a dance."

Ladies and gentlemen, this is why Cori is my Nemo. If she gets lost in the great big ocean called life, I'll find her.

"Men and women can be friends."

TWENTY-ONE PILOTS IS BLARING in my car. I'm spitting out the lyrics to "Stressed" along with the alternative duo as I pull my car in front of my parents' estate. Quickly, I tap the security panel and watch the impressive wrought-iron gate swing open.

I steer the car down the long, well-lit driveway. My parents' manor, partly covered with creeping ivy, epitomizes sophistication. The architecture is classic, timeless—red brick exterior, slate roof, pool, spa, and an illuminated tennis court. From the outside, your first thought is, this place is stunning, and you'd think inside must be pristine—which it is—and rigid—which it has never been. At our craziest, Katharine and I have wrecked every wall with crayons. We called it art, and our parents let us.

I maneuver my car along the long driveway, passing a large, grassy lawn, manicured hedges and shrubs, and park beside a dark-blue Ferrari. "Caught the game last night?" I ask Paul casually while handing my car key over. He's one of my parents' permanent staff members and is working the valet parking for the evening.

"Think Cavs will repeat?"

"Need defense." I answer. We exchange a firm handshake. "See you later." Before I can reach for the hand-carved, wooden, double-doors, they swing open.

Oliver—also known as Chief—stands before me in his sixty-seven-year-old British grandeur, upright and rigid like a sergeant major, except he's our family butler. Yes, Kate and I grew up with a butler. I mentioned before, we were born with a silver spoon in our mouths, and I've never felt guilty for it. If anything, it's a drive for me to work as hard as my dad, so I can pass on the same mindset to future little Deans. That's if I ever have children. Right now, it's not on my radar as I step onto the limestone floor inside the impressive double-story entry foyer.

"Hi, old chap," I greet Oliver.

He's been running our household since Katharine and I were tiny little knuckleheads.

"Your coat, sir?" Oliver's familiar English lilt asks over Dean Martin's warbling voice crooning "Volare" from hidden speakers strategically placed throughout the house.

I slip off my navy peacoat and hand it to Oliver. Don't roll your eyes. I can hang my own coat, but doing so would be an atrocity in Oliver's guide on 'how to run the home and other royal etiquette.'

"I see we have a full house." I glace over at the few guests parading by the crackling fireplace in the lounge area.

"Fifty of your closest friends."

My lips twitch in amusement. When it comes to friends, my motto has always been less people, less bullshit. Sure, I know half of the town, but other than my family, there's only three other individuals I'd consider getting shot for. My parents are deeply ingrained in this town, and by the magic of genes, so are their children.

"How long have you been with us, Chief?"

"Twenty years, sir," Oliver answers after hanging my coat in the large closet.

He's witnessed our stages of terror, our struggles with puberty, when my sister became a drama queen, and I turned into a zombie. The geezer even caught me sneaking girls to my room on several occasions. Instead of scolding or ratting me out to my parents, he walked into my room one morning with a box of condoms, gave me a pep talk about safe sex, diseases, and unwanted baby mama drama. That morning, after he left my room, I added the box to my collection.

Fun times.

I clap his shoulder. "It's time to drop that pretentious British accent."

"Women love accents," Oliver points out.

I chuckle. "Good to see you haven't lost your wit, old man." I enjoy a good banter. Oliver and I always bounce remarks between each other like a kid's rubber ball. "See you in a bit, Chief."

"Behave, Sir."

"When you stop calling me sir, I'll behave."

"Never, Sir," I hear Oliver say as I head down the hall.

Welcome to my parents' humble palace, a little piece of paradise, nestled on two acres of land, secluded among old oak trees. The house where Katharine and I grew up is a prestigious, six-bedroom, grand, stone manor. The walls are smiles and cheekiness, decorated with the pictures of the people who have shaped my life.

A grin tugs the corner of my lips. It's always good to be back here. I love my three-story house. I love my freedom. I love sleeping in my own bed. But this house is always going to hold a place in my heart. This is home. It is much more than the sum of its parts, and for that, I have to thank my parents, the glue of my existence.

I pass the cozy library, the over-sized state-of-the-art gourmet kitchen complete with a pizza oven—my dad's passion is making homemade pizza. This culinary area is a chef's delight and is the center of the house. In this kitchen, we've spent many Friday nights rolling fresh dough, laughing while Katharine and I play helpers.

Entering the formal living room, I skim over the crowd. People are moving, smiles are emerging, glasses are clinking in celebratory toast, but it's Cori my gaze is instantly drawn to, looking too gorgeous to be real. My heart—my biggest muscle lately—slams a vicious cycle of beats inside my chest. Her back is to me; she's circled by three men about my age. Each one staring at her with a look of bestial lust. All of those fuckers would gladly cut off one of their nuts to get in her pants.

You're wondering whether or not our little Moonchild is enjoying the attention. For as long as I've known her, she seems oblivious to the open-mouthed stares. However, the jaded male in me is saying bullshit. Come on ladies, you don't notice when a guy is wondering if you're into shrimping or tea-bagging?

Seriously, you can't tell?

Let me give you a clue. Take the hipster with the man bun, for instance. Yes, the one in the dark-blue velvet jacket and tan slacks. His eyes are resting a little too long on her face. I bet you he's looking at her lips and imagining the dunking motion of a tea bag when making tea. Now, instead of a cup, he's picturing Cori's mouth, and instead of a tea bag, he's picturing his balls. Trust me, they're all manwhores. It takes one to know one.

Anyway, she's enjoying herself. When you know someone like I know Cori, you don't have to see the other person's facial expression to know their mood. Look at her posture. Her shoulders are relaxed. Do you see the easy way she touches each one of those pricks?

I bet you her face is sparkling like the glass of Moet in her hand right now. No, make that more so. My guess is, right now, she's talking about the French countryside mural she painted for my parents.

Cori has two professional passions, teaching and art. Yes, those assholes know she's the artist behind it. They've been to the house many times.

Fucking idiots.

Instead of marching up to her and pulling her away from those lecherous jerks, I let my eyes linger over her appearance. She's wearing the little black dress as I asked, her hair is pulled in a bun, and the only jewelry she's sporting are the turquoise dropped earrings I gave to her last year for her birthday.

My dick begins to harden in my charcoal gray slacks with approval.

Down boy.

My words fall on deaf ears. My heart flips-flops, skips a beat. Desire pulses through my veins. I want to taste her like my first cup of coffee in the morning; slowly, yet eagerly.

As I look at her, transfixed by her presence, she turns and pierces me with her gleaming, sugar-brown stare. Then she smiles, throwing me a half-wave as she keeps chatting. I take the wave to mean she'll be over in a minute, after the three horn balls stop drooling over her.

Soon enough, she says something to her admirers, then heads over to where I'm standing.

Chapter 17

"Friends yearn to stay connected."

"HAPPY BIRTHDAY, AGAIN." Cori leans forward, parks one hand on my bicep as she places a kiss on my cheek, heating my skin with her touch. "I bought you a gift."

My gaze automatically drops to her lips. All I want to do is take her in my arms and slam my mouth on hers.

Dazed with lust, I reach for her hand and hold on before the urge to kiss her takes over. "You already gave me a gift. It's sitting on my coffee table. And . . . ." I let my voice trail off, making sure she's looking me in the eyes, as I finish, "You look beautiful."

For a split second, her eyes darken, then she lowers her head to her drink, breaking our connection. When she looks back at me, all trace of being affected by my words have receded from her face. "It's nothing big."

I frown in confusion, lost for a second.

"The gift," she reminds me, her eyes twinkling with humor.

Oh. Right. "Where is it?" Other than the champagne glass she's holding, her hands are empty.

"In the library."

A vision of Cori's back against the wall, her legs wrapped around my waist, our lips devouring each other, rattles in my head. One more kiss. That should cure this madness. "No time like the present." I clasp her hand in mine and start toward the doorway.

My sister appears from nowhere and stands in front of us. "There you are." She hooks one arm in Cori's. "Can I talk to you for a quick minute?"

"Oh." Cori glances at me, a slight frown on her forehead. "Dean and I—"

"The night is young." My sister waves a dismissive hand. "There's someone I'd like to introduce you to." Kate holds my gaze, silently telling me whatever I have planned when it comes to Cori is not going to happen on her watch. "He's the relationship type," she adds, sealing the deal.

Have I mentioned that my sister is the biggest cockblocker ever? In high school, all of her friends wanted me. Instead of hooking me up, she went above and beyond to obliterate any chance of getting close to her friends. I give her an A for effort. No need to tell her I made out with most of them.

"What about Brandon?" I ask directly at Cori. Just yesterday she asks me to give Abercrombie kid a chance. She also expressed doubt about anything developing between them.

"Status quo. Nothing serious." She holds my gaze captive, giving me a glimpse of her private thoughts. Moonchild isn't a casual dater, has never been. Nothing serious is her way of telling me they haven't made it past first base.

Call me selfish, but that makes me happy. "So, you're still open to meeting other men?"

"Oh, look." Kate tilts her head toward the bar, where Lucas and Cameron are talking to Cori's grandmother and her life partner—aka friend. "Your buddies are calling you." Before I can argue, she's dragging Cori away into the crowd.

Every bit of me wants to go after them and get an answer, but I remind myself, while patience is bitter, its fruit is sweet. For now, I stay in my corner and watch Cori until she disappears into the crowd.

Needing a distraction, I continue scanning the filled room. Nora is leaning on the bar, her purple dyed hair laying over one shoulder of her bright, Boho dress. Her friend, Tim—who is about twelve years her junior—as always, is by her side. Both of them are engrossed in a conversation with Lucas. I walk over and join them. "What are we drinking?"

In the office, it's all formality with Nora. Outside . . . Well, we're friends, family. She throws her arms around my neck into the kind of hug one saves for their favorite son. "Happy Birthday!" She fixes the collar of my gray button-down shirt as if I'm a snot-nosed ten-year-old. "When are you going to make an honest woman out of my granddaughter?"

By the way, she says this to me every time we see each other. Whether Cori is around or not.

"Cori is like a sister to me. You know that." In case you're making the *ewww* face, I don't want to fuck my sister.

Seriously.

Shit.

This is me holding to the last bit of control when it comes to this attraction developing towards Cori.

Lucas coughs something that sounds very close to bullshit in his hand. I ignore the asshole.

"How about a shot?" Nora signals the bartender. In less than a minute, four shot glasses, filled with what I guess to be Belvedere Vodka, are placed in front of us. "To getting the girl." She raises her glass in a celebratory toast.

I can note that I'm not chasing the girl, but what's the point? It's been said a few times, and my words have fallen on deaf ears. I clink my glass with theirs in a celebratory toast, and then throw the liquor down the back of my throat. Ripe peaches with hints of almond and apricot burst in my mouth. Good stuff.

Nora places a kiss on my cheek, then lightly smacks the other. "I love you like the son I never had. Cori is in a quest to find a husband. You're the one. Now wake up and make it happen."

"Gonna say hello to my mother." I place a kiss on Nora's cheek, grab a beverage from one of the waiters moving through the crowd with trays of appetizers and drinks, then stroll over to where my Scandinavian side of the family is huddled—light hair and skin, blue eyes, a narrow nose, and slender body type. A complete opposite of my dad and I.

"Here you are." My grandmother, Monika—my mother's mother—pinches off the flow of blood from my cheek. I smile into the blue eyes that belie her seventy-four years. She has laughter lines from her gift for smiling easily, her personality is all there to read in those creases.

"Your girl is here." My grandfather, Palmer, slaps my back with all of his Scandinavian strength.

"My girl?" I glance over where Cori is still talking.

"Son, wipe your mouth." My grandmother elbows my side. "You're drooling."

I laugh. No point denying that part. My grandparents have always been keen on what's happening in our lives. For example, the minute they met Kate's ex, they labeled him a dud. They were right.

"What are we drinking?" My grandmother's Christmas eggnog is always overly spiked, but indescribably delicious. She also has a passion for a nice port once in a while. God bless her, she can still enjoy a nice port.

"My usual."

"So, forty-year-old Tawny port?"

"Don't get my mother drunk, Dean," my mother chides. "And I need grandbabies. You're thirty now."

I glance over at Cori again. She's the quiet and confusion of my heart. My brain and dick are still at war with each other. The one south of my waist says fuck it, go for it and risk our friendship. The logical side of me repeats over and over to stick with the status quo.

My gaze lowers to the neat scotch in my hand breathing in a fragrance that only years in an oak barrel can achieve before meeting my mother's gaze. "Does that mean it's time for me to get married and grow a belly?"

"Hey, I still have a six pack," my dad says behind me as he comes to stand next to my mother, he runs a hand over his flat stomach with pride. "Okay, maybe a four pack."

"Three," my mother corrects him, "You're still the sexiest man in the room." She leans over and kisses him. Side note—no matter how old I am, I don't like seeing my parents making out.

Grandma smiles and hooks her arm in the crook of mine. "Do you have the girl, yet?"

"Trying to tie me down too, Gram?" I ask, not one bit irritated by this endless barrage of nosy family.

"Not as much as your mother. She's ready to play grandma, and I'm ready to play great-grandma. My days are numbered, you know."

Right. She's been saying this every week, every month, every year for the last fifteen years. "You know, I'm not the only child." I wave a hand where my sister is introducing some chick to Cam. This is a rarity. She never introduces one of her friends to my friends or me for that matter. Her reason? We are too dirty for her friends.

Ouch.

Although, in my eyes, dirty is good. Relationships always need a little kink, whether it is already spicy or requires a little nudge.

"We already had this discussion," my mother says in a solemn tone. "What's wrong with you Dean? We raised you both to be grounded."

"I am grounded." I take a sip of my drink for the first time and let the amber fluid sit in my mouth a while before swallowing. "That's exactly why I don't feel the need to be married." I lean down and place a kiss on her forehead. "See, you all did an excellent job. Maybe too good of a job."

"How's the office?" my dad asks.

"Great. We're holding down the fort."

"Donner called."

"He's a dick."

"Imbecile," my mother gently corrects me. She's never liked cursing.

"What's going on with his account?" my father continues.

"Nothing. He suffered a momentary lapse of old age and convinced himself he was in love with a twenty-something with fake boobs."

"Oomph." My grandmother snorts.

"Exactly, Grandma." I smile at her. "He's a dickhead."

"Dean!" My mother shakes her head.

"Oh, Ana." My grandmother narrows her eyes on my mom. "Your son is thirty-three years old. The boy can curse."

"Thirty, Grandma." And I haven't been a boy since Tina Bennett gave me my first blowjob when I was fifteen. But no need to go there.

"Thirty, thirty-three . . . whatever." My grandmother waves her dainty wrinkled seventy-year-old arm. "You can say dickhead if you want."

"Mom!" My mother's face is now as red as a tomato.

"Fine, no more cursing," I agree. See, I love my mom. From my peripheral, I catch one of the assholes guiding Cori toward the terrace. A bolt of possessiveness slams through me. "It's time for me to mingle."

"With Cori," my mother says, hope in her voice. She always had this thing, where the two of us would eventually fall in love and live happily ever after.

"Friends, Mom," I gently remind her. Although lately, my dick would say otherwise.

"Men and women can't be friends," my father points out. "Your mother and I started as friends."

Oh, boy. Here we go. Another trip down memory lane about how they went from friends to lovers. I've heard this story a million times. They met in college, became friends, got drunk one night, got naked (vomit) and the rest is history. Their version is a little different. The naked part is always zapped, but we all know that's how their happily ever after happened.

"The two of you would make very cute babies," my mom continues.

I shake my head, turn on my heels until my grandmother grabs my wrist, leans forward and whispers. "Kiss the girl, let her know you want her. Otherwise, you'll lose her to someone else."

"You're a wise woman." I wink at her and head to where Cori is now talking to Kate. Her eyes meet mine and hold for a few seconds. I stare, willing myself not to look away, willing the connection to hold.

Let's pause here for a second. Eye contact is a dangerous, dangerous thing, but oh, so lovely when a discovery is made. Do you see the hint of desire in her eyes? The way her lips part the slightest bit? They are screaming, *kiss the hell out of me, please.*

This is the moment it hits me. Cori is just as intrigued about the fire the kiss has ignited as I am, the possibility of us. She may be more reluctant to pursue it, you know, our friendship and all, but the attraction is not one-sided and is worth exploring.

My pulse races with excitement as the focus on our friendship falls to the wayside. There's that moment between action and consequence, eternal and fleeting. Good judgment tries to seize control and loses.

I can't let this realization slip through my fingers.

Thinking *fuck it*, I finish my drink, place the empty glass on the nearby table, then maneuver my way across the room through the mingling party guests, stopping here and there for a quick greeting. As I close the space between us, I catch my sister's gaze shooting daggers at me from all the way across the room. Her jaw is set in that *you're a dickhead* way. Her eyes are spitting fire at me, a reminder that Cori is completely off-limits. Pursuing anything can easily ruin our dynamic. My heart knows that. My dick knows that. She's my best friend, my human diary. She means the world to me.

And I want her.

"More than friends, less than lovers."

BY THE TIME THE TIME I reach Cori and my sister, hipster guy, AKA Brian, has managed to finagle his way exactly between the two women.

"In art our spirits rise, in stories, we are enthralled and elevated," Cori is saying as I position myself across from her. Our eyes meet, and her lips curve into a smile that matches mine. "With creativity, we make connections between disparate people, we learn that, through our many lenses, we are seeing the same whole, only the path before our feet is still blurred. Life should never be art versus science, but a beautiful marriage of the two."

Cori is naturally gorgeous, but in her element, she shines and is sexy as fuck. Pride fills my chest. That's my girl. I'm so turned on.

"What are we talking about?" I'm interested to know what brought so much passion out of Cori.

"Brian was telling us about the Maquoketa caves. And somehow, the conversation shifted to art and science," Cori says, her gaze going from Brian's to mine.

"I'm planning on going there again this spring," Brian says with enthusiasm. The guy is practically begging Cori to come along.

Did I mention the poor guy has no game? Let's put it this way, if the dude falls into a barrel full of tits, he'll come up sucking his thumb. Cool guy though.

"Sounds great, man," I say encouragingly. Truthfully, I don't give two cents where Brian travels, but I've never been a rude guy. Everyone deserves at least one second of the day. I turn my attention on Cori. "Can I talk to you for minute?"

"Sure," Cori answers rather quickly. She turns to Brian, who is still vying for her attention. "Thanks for the information. I'll be sure to look up everything. See you in a bit, Kate."

Oh, yeah, this whole time my sister is glaring at me. Unconcerned, I tilt my chin towards the bar, and say, "Lucas and Cam are flirting with two of your friends."

Kate spins around. True enough, Cam and Lucas are doing shots with two gorgeous brunettes. She shakes her head then places a hand on Cori's arm. "Don't leave until we finalize our plans for next weekend."

"Sure," Cori answers.

"Be back," Kate says, then disappears into the crowd. Poor girl and her need to keep us away from her friends.

"Cori." Brian clears his throat. "You should join us on the next trip."

Yeah, over my dead fucking body. This is one of those moments when I quickly pull deep and find my center;

otherwise, I might apply some pressure to his face . . . by means of my fist.

"It's worth thinking about," Cori responds.

Is she kidding me? Why is she entertaining this guy? She should have said hell fucking no, I'm not going away with you. Because you see, I'll be busy getting naked with Dean.

Zen. Center. Breathe.

Cori tilts her head in my direction. "You want to ask me something?"

I want to do more, and I intend to tell her as much, but not here. Instead, I say, "Come with me." And I swear, her eyes darken at my words.

As we wedge our way through the crowd and out of the room, my brain is only aware of my hand on Cori's lower back. The material covering her skin is soft and clings to her curves. My mind, once again, bolts to that place where I watch her undo her zipper, let the one-shoulder dress slide down her hips and onto the floor. Then she's in my arms naked, and we are kissing.

My dick twitches, anxious to be buried balls deep inside Cori's most guarded place. At the rate I'm going, I swear, I'm on the verge of setting a world record for the most frequent boners in a day.

"What's on your mind, big guy?" she asks, snapping me back to reality.

You. Lately day and night. "You have something for me."

"Oh. Right. The library."

Once we are out of the room, I remove my hand from her back as we head down the hall. "Are you going on a date with Brian?"

"No. Why do you ask?"

We make a right, our footsteps clacking in perfect harmony. "He's interested, and you're looking for a baby daddy."

"A baby daddy doesn't marry the woman." Her mouth twists in a teasing smile. "You do know that, right?"

"Oh, yeah, you're looking for a husband. Brian is a decent catch."

She laughs. "I'm not fishing."

"I thought you were looking for your lobster."

"True," she says after a long pause. "But I don't think he's the one."

"Why not?" I mean, he's a little weird, but one of the good ones. I push open the heavy-arched door and let her enter the room before me. My eyes follow her slender frame as she heads over to the desk I've often used when I need somewhere to bury myself in my work.

"This is for you." She picks up something wrapped in a simple brown paper and hands it to me. "It's a book."

With a few quick strides, I close the space between us, take the book, and unwrap it. It's one of my favorite books, *1984* by George Orwell. A few months ago, I lent her my copy. After she told me how much she enjoyed the novel, I insisted she keep it. "I would have picked up another copy."

"Now you don't have to." A smile spreads across her face. "Besides, I owe you for coming to my rescue the other night."

A feeling heats up my chest. This is my window of opportunity. "There's other ways to repay me."

"Oh." Her gaze appraises my chest, then roams down my narrow waist, to the front of my pants, before moving back to my face.

I place the book on the mahogany desk. Leaning on the desk, I cross my arms over my chest, my eyes on her the whole time. What I see in her face—a hint of desire, a subtle hesitation. A blush.

"What do you have in mind?" she asks in a whisper. "Monetary?"

My heart stops for one beat, then lurches to my throat. Hunger rips through me, pulling every muscle in my body.

I peel away from the desk to my full height, obliterating any space between us. Cupping her cheeks, I gently tip her face toward mine. My gaze falls on her lips and stays there for a long moment, before I say, "Definitely not monetary."

A heavy silence surrounds us. Not the uncomfortable kind, but the kind that makes the air crackle and snap with sexual tension.

Cori licks her lips. "Then how would you like to be paid?"

From invisible speakers, the lyrics of "Sway" softly play in the room. I let my hands fall to her shoulders, down to her bare arms, where goosebumps rise under my touch. "Let's start with a dance." I had every intention of letting her know how I feel, but shit, Dean Martin is crooning in the speakers. The desire to hold her in my arms overwhelms me.

A nervous chuckle slips from of her mouth. "Here?"

No better place, in my eyes. "Right here, Coriander."

She catches her lower lip between her teeth, seeming to ponder whether or not it's a good idea for us to dance, before she shrugs and says, "Okay."

Slipping my hands around her waist, I draw her into me, moving closer, until every inch of our bodies—from foreheads to toes—are touching. Our free hands instantly meet, each of our fingers lacing together.

"You smell so fucking good." I inhale the familiar scent of berries and vanilla, letting it flood my senses. "Good enough to eat."

"Eat." The word slips from her mouth.

"Every inch," I confirm in a gravel voice. One of her feet rolls over mine at the same time her fingers dig into the cotton fabric of my shirt. Holy fuck . . . I think she likes the idea of my tongue in and around her pussy.

Well, she's not alone. I want to feast on her for a long time with varying speeds, pressures, and tongue patterns until she begs for me to stop. Unable to resist, I lower my lips to her bare shoulder and graze her skin with my lips.

She sucks in a breath.

"Delicious," I mutter.

"You think I'm delicious?"

"Just like salted caramel."

174

A low laugh escapes her throat. The music spins around us, lifting away gravity. Together, we dance in silent harmony, our feet in perfect sync to the beating of my heart.

Cori leans a little more against me, her hand moves from my chest to the nape of my neck. "I can't believe I stepped on your foot."

"It's fine." My lips, the ones that are aching to kiss her tonight, creep into a grin. The music continues to vibrate around us. We move to the rhythm, chest to chest, thighs to thighs . . . and everything in between mashed up against each other.

Lowering my mouth close enough that my lips are brushing her ear, I sing along with Dean Martin. I'm holding her so tight, I can feel the shiver wracking her body before she steps on my foot again.

She laughs lightly, then leans her head on my chest, right where my heart is banging away like a mad man. "That's very amateur."

"Considering we've danced a million times before," I tease. But there is nothing friendly about the way we are moving. This is fucking sexy as hell. "Unless—" I step back enough to spin her in a circle, then pull her back to me— "You're still thinking about the kiss." I gauge her reaction before diving in.

"I'd be lying if I said it hasn't crossed my mind."

Her admission sends a heated charge through me. My arms encircle her waist. Our steps slow to barely moving, no longer dancing, our bodies glued together.

Our eyes lock before hers slide to my mouth. As far as signs go, this is a positive one. She's ruminating about my mouth on hers. Which seems only fair, since I've given a lot of thought to the same thing and more.

"Dean," her voice is tiny, filled with lust that burns into my bones.

"Hold that thought." Releasing my grip on her, I head over to the door and lock it. My feet move swiftly across the floor, closing the space between us. Cori meets me halfway, and my heart does that little kick which has become associated with this woman standing in front of me. "You were saying."

"I keep telling myself, we're friends."

I nod. We've lightly brushed on the fact that we've kissed, but this is the first time we're really talking about this shift in our friendship or the possibility of ... whatever that's developing between us.

"I shouldn't want . . . you."

Wait. What? Cori wants me? My heart nearly leaps out of my chest. I will myself to stay calm. "Tell me that's not what you want, and I'll never bring it up again." A heavy silence falls between us. I run my palms over her arms, up the nape of her neck, sending electricity straight to my heart. "Cori?"

The tip of her tongue runs over her lower lip, drawing my attention to her mouth, tempting me with erotic suggestions. When she meets my gaze, her eyes are smoldering with lust.

"I haven't been able to stop thinking about kissing you again," she confesses.

My heart gallops. Need courses through my veins. I cup her face and gently tilt her chin, until we are staring at each other. Our breaths mingle. And then we're kissing again. Tongues sliding, lips melding, as though we can't get enough of each other. Her hands move over me—my face, shoulders, melting me away.

She grips the front of my shirt, her fingertips curling around a button, until I hear the faint ping as it hits the wood floor. Then her hand is on my skin, heating me everywhere, and it feels good.

I touch her too. Everywhere and with hunger. I cup her breast over the material and squeeze. When a soft mewling sound escapes her throat, I swear in frustration. Desperation. "I need to feel all of you," I say against her lips.

"Yes. Please," she says between ragged breaths.

Cori is begging me to touch her. My racing pulse is throbbing so loudly in my ears, at first, I don't think I heard right. I'm convinced my ears are deceiving me, until she whispers, "Touch me."

A groan rips from my throat. The divide between the desires of my heart and the restlessness of my mind crumbles. This is the moment I haven't been able to stop fantasizing about since we kissed, and I don't want it to end—not ever.

Somehow, our bodies move across the room, until I'm pushing her against the wall. My hands find hers, lace them together above her head. "I want you." To prove how much, I press my straining erection against her waist. "Tell me you want the same thing."

Her eyes flutter open. They are dark with desire, my own lust reflecting in hers. "I've been thinking about this since we kissed," she admits, her cheeks a little pink.

Coriander Phillips wants me.

She wants me.

I want her.

I'm dizzy with lust.

My cock, hard as a steel pipe in my pants, begs to be set free.

I want to push the hem of Cori's dress up her thighs, tug off her panties, lick her clit, and sink into her heat. But common sense kicks in, grabbing control from my dick. This is Coriander, my best friend. I can't fuck her in my parents' library.

When we do sleep together, I want to savor the moment, every sound, every touch, every kiss, the feel of our bodies together, the look on her face as she screams my name. Yes, I need to remember every detail, so that the memories never leave me.

With all my strength, I take a step back and put a sliver of space between us.

"Dean?" Her eyes search mine, a slight frown on her forehead.

"Not here." I exhale, and run a hand through my hair. "Come home with me after the party."

She reaches for my face and lightly brushes her fingers against my clean-shaven chin. "I didn't know you had it in you, Dean Conrad Morello."

"What's that?" I ask, slightly puzzled.

A faint smile touches the corner of her lips. "To not go for the quick and easy lay."

Ouch, that stings a bit.

Many people believe that men's love for sex makes them incapable of waiting for it. That's not entirely true. This is Coriander we're talking about. Whatever is going on between us will never be classified as a random hook-up in my book. "You'll never be a quick and easy lay, not with me." I take her hands in mine. "Come home with me tonight."

She gives me a long calculating stare. I can feel caution slipping back between us. "Just like that," she says, brows knitted.

"You want me, and I want you. It's as simple as that."

She slips her hands from mine and ambles over to the desk, where she picks up the book, analyzes it, then returns it to the same spot, before turning to face me. "Or as complicated as that."

I hear the hesitation in her voice. She's wrestling with the consequences that come with having sex with me. How that may change our friendship. It's a recipe for disaster or a long, happy . . . something.

Frankly, I don't know how this story will end. I haven't figured out all the details. One thing I know for sure, nowhere in the text will it read, 'Dean gave up.' I've decided, with stone-cold certainty, I want Cori more than I'm afraid of the ramifications of pursuing her.

"A lot of things in life aren't easy, but that doesn't mean we shouldn't give them a try." My voice is surprisingly calm, even though, inside, I'm dying to take her into my arms and kiss her until all of her doubts vanish.

"Most of our mistakes, Dean, are the results of letting our emotions overrule logic." She stares down at her hands clasped together in front of her, before looking back at me. "My current conundrum when it comes to us. Do I give in to my curiosity and risk losing you?"

"You'll never lose me, no matter what."

"How can you be so sure? We have a perfect friendship. What if sex ruins it?"

I brush my thumb over her forehead, relaxing the creases. "Take your art, for instance, not everything you create is perfect," I say gently. "And it really shouldn't be." She smiles at that, and I can't help but do so as well. "Do you know why, Cori?"

She blinks, no answer.

"Because perfect is boring." My gaze drops to the floor where the buttons of my shirt are scattered. A few minutes ago, Cori's fingers had been on me, her lips against mine, begging me to touch her. Taking a step, I close the space between us, but not enough that our bodies are touching. I cup her face. "You're the last person I expected to want like this," I admit in a low voice. "But I do want you, and I don't care how messy and complicated things get between us." My lips descend on hers for one last lingering kiss, before pulling away. I walk over to the door, unlock it, grip the handle, and pull it open. I stop and glance back in the room, where Cori is leaning against the desk. "Just think about this for me."

"What's that?"

"What would you do if you weren't afraid?"

I don't wait for an answer. This time, I'm the one who walks away from us, leaving Cori with complete control to process her options—to step forward into whatever is happening between us, or to step back into safety.

Whatever she decides, nothing will ever be the same between us.

Chapter 19

"We should be lovers, not just friends."

THE USEFULNESS OF MY THOUGHTS evaporated some time ago, yet my mind churns in the darkness like a runaway motor. When I start trying to do math with Haskell Brooks Curry in my head, that's when I know things are bad. This sleeplessness is my torture. While the rest of the world embraces their dreams, their eight hours of rest, I am wide awake, drunk on silence, my thoughts consumed with Cori, dreaming about the things we could be.

I toss and turn, desperately trying to banish the way she felt in my arms, her lips against mine, how perfectly our bodies fit, pressed against one another.

Is she in bed, wide awake, fighting a mental war, as I am?

I want her.

She wants me.

Just not enough. Actually, she's smart. We're a bad idea. I'm well aware of that, except I like bad ideas. Exhaling, I scrub a hand over my face. This unrequited desire needs to be tucked away. I should have put an end to these crazy thoughts from the beginning, but I entertained them . . . like a playful pet. Now, my desire has grown into a ferocious animal.

Acceptance is key here. I need to accept that I'm the *boy* friend, without the perks, and move on. No need for unnecessary tension. Our circle is tight. Attraction, lust, are part of the human flesh. These wild horses of my mind must be tracked down, captured, and tucked away in the *Do-Not-Touch* Cori file.

My dick, the treacherous prick, not ready to surrender so quickly, throbs against the cotton fabric of my sweatpants. The stubborn bastard is aching to get intimately acquainted with Cori.

Porn.

I need a distraction, some form of release. Sliding my hand past the waistband of my sweatpants, I palm my raging erection. A good jerk off session should at least provide temporary relief. Before I can even begin stroking, a visual of Cori's lips on the tip of my shaft flashes in my head.

Great. I can't even fucking jerk off in peace.

Pathetic.

Where are the ménage fantasies when you need them?

I groan out a swear, let go of my throbbing dick, and sit on the edge of the bed. Needing to clear my head, I stare into the night. Outside looks like the gods are having a pillow fight. A cold shiver of disappointment travels through me. I guess, deep down, a part of me was still holding on . . . to what, I'm not sure. Maybe hope that eventually she'd say fuck it, show up at my doorstep, ready to give in to whatever is happening between us.

My lips twitch. Even though I'm an eternal optimist, I know enough to understand that hope is not always a bright star in an infinitely dark universe.

Cori hadn't taken the bait. It's one thing to be tempted and another to fall. In the end, she left my parents' house one hour before I did, with a simple goodnight and barely making any eye contact. Almost as if she regretted what had transpired between us in the library. The idea that she might think that way makes my stomach hurt and feel empty.

I need to speak to her, send her a text. Anything to get communication going. I grab my phone from the nightstand. It's four in the morning. Chances are, she's fast asleep. Every fiber of my rational mind knows I should wait until the morning.

That's my common sense talking. It's been irrational.

Coming to my feet, I grab my green crew neck sweater, casually thrown on the weathered leather armchair in the corner, and pull it over my head. My brainpower is moving faster than Lucas' five-year-old daughter can speak, as if it's stuck on fast-forward, and the volume is jammed right up. I want to wash my brain in cold water, chill the whole thing right out, but I can't, not until Cori and I talk. I need to see her and wrest back control of my mind. Sitting there, pining away for someone, has never been my thing. Not even if that woman happens to be my best friend. The fact that she's not here pretty much cements her choice.

I don't agree with her decision, and no, my ego is not bruised. My dick is awesome. I'm the epitome of tall, dark, and handsome. Even at my worst, I'm fucking incredible.

Okay, maybe my ego is a little bruised. But the bastard will rebound. This isn't about my need for Cori and I to roll naked together. We are much more than that. At the end of the day, my priority is our friendship. We need to go back to the way we were, no tension, back in the friend zone.

The only way to ensure that is to talk.

A quick glance outside confirms the blinding snowstorm has not subsided. A ten minute-drive may turn into forty minutes, but it's totally worth it. I slip on my boots and stride from my bedroom, grab my peacoat and keys along the way. I swing open the door and come to a screeching halt.

Chapter 20

"Sex just makes the friendship more intense."

THE SIGHT OF CORI AT my door in the wee hours has knocked every wisp of air from my lungs.

She stands before my eyes, bundled inside a knee-length, puffy, black coat with the oversized, fur-trimmed hood covering her head and obscuring her face. Only the tip of her nose and nude full lips are exposed, but I recognize her. I've always been aware of her presence, but lately, the feeling has amplified.

"Hi." A wobbly uncertain smile touches her lips.

Every muscle in my body is frozen. As the realization that she's come to me bounces inside my skull, I stand in silence, with an expression of stunned surprise. She's rarely impulsive and hates driving in the snow, even though she drives a badass black Jeep.

This means . . . she wants us, to be with me.

I am rejuvenated by adrenaline.

It's as if someone poured kerosene on my spark of wonder. Nothing I'm showing on the outside can adequately reflect what I feel inside; it's like every neuron in my brain is trying to fire in both directions at once—the best kind of paralysis.

"You're going out?" She bites her lower lip and buries her hands inside her pocket. The only sound between us is the soft murmuring of the snow as it falls. "I should go."

It takes a second or two for her words to sink in. She thinks I'm going over to some chick's house for sex. "Cori." My voice is low and rough. Suddenly, my body is off pause-mode. I catch her wrist and stop her from turning away. My other hand reaches up and sweeps the hood down her head, giving me a full view of her face. Her brows are creased, her face tense. "I was coming to you."

Her eyes widen as the word 'oh' slips between her lips. I pull her gently inside the house, into me, as I kick the door closed behind us.

In the seconds that follow, we're kissing, deep and hard. There's a fire in our kiss. A promise. This is the moment we're going the distance.

My heart is beating rapidly. A thrill races through me as I fight to get closer to Cori. My nimble fingers find the buttons of her coat and flick them open. Impatiently, I slide the thick fabric down her shoulders to the hardwood floor, freeing her slender form, and press her curves against me.

She's soft, lightly fragranced, and feels so good in my arms. Oh, the things I want to do to that sweet body of hers, starting with licking her from chin to that sweet spot between her thighs. Just thinking about it has my thoughts scattering with a myriad of crazy emotions—giddy with joy, a little

187

nervous. The magic of the moment is no longer a flight of my imagination.

I moan against her lips while our mouths continue to tango, wanting nothing more than to feel her skin, her tits pressing against my chest with no barrier, or bend her over by the sofa and mount her from behind.

Must. Take. This. Slow.

Slow and steady, logic tries to persuade me, but my dick, hard as wood, pokes against my sweats, begging to be let loose. I grab the hem of her T-shirt, ready to pull it over her head, when she sets her hands on my chest.

There's hesitation in her touch. A flurry of nerves accosts my senses. I drag my lips away and search her face for answers.

"We should talk," she says. "I mean . . . we should establish—"

"I'm not into anal," I say breathlessly against her lips, "not my thing."

She laughs. "Good to know, but I meant talk about us, make sure we're on the same page."

"We're on the same page." Whatever she wants, I'm game. Anal may not be one of my kinks, but that doesn't mean I'm not into crazy, nasty fun. Bring on sex toys, some crazy role playing, or some weird fantasy, and I'm your man.

An image of Cori, tied to my bedposts with nothing on as I have my way with her, blazes my brain. Yeah, we're definitely on the same page. And to prove it, I let one of my hands slide up to sink into her hair, the other on her lower back, nudging her even closer.

The problem is, I'm a smart guy, my brain is always on, even during sex or the potential of sex. Something is telling me she's not referring to how she'd like to be fucked. As much as I want to be with Cori, there can't be any doubt on her part. "Tell me one thing, you want this."

I wait, throat parched. Unless she's one hundred percent sure, nothing is happening.

"I want this," she confesses.

My heart trips as relief floods through me. "And no regrets."

She smiles. "That's two things."

This time, I'm the one smiling.

"I'm sure." She slides a hand through my hair. "No regrets."

And then I kiss her, deep and wet. When her eager hands strip my coat off me, I nip at her lower lip. A pleased whimper leaks from her mouth as she opens for me, giving me full access. My senses spin as my tongue slips in, licking hers, plunging as I fall into the kiss.

In one move, I sweep her off her feet into my arms, my lips never leaving hers, until she tilts her head back in laughter.

"You're a romantic, Dean Morello."

I've never been called a romantic in my life. Outside of a few times I've picked up Cori while goofing around, I've never carried a woman anywhere, especially to my bedroom. I guess there's a first time for everything. "There's a lot you don't know about me."

She wraps her arms around my neck, her crescent shaped eyebrows inclined slightly as she meets my gaze. "Do tell."

"I'd much rather show." I'm kissing her again and don't put her down until we are in my bedroom. Holding her hand in mine, I reach over and turn on the light on my nightstand to a dimmed glow, then meet her questioning gaze. "I need to see all of you."

She's changed her outfit from earlier. She's wearing an oversized red Henley, which appears to be something designed for sleeping, and black yoga pants tucked into calf-length, Adirondack boots. An outfit thrown together in a rush. A smile touches the corner of my mouth. If I were a gambling man, which I am, I'd be willing to bet she'd been tossing and turning in bed as I have. "Couldn't sleep?"

A blush creeps onto her cheeks, but she doesn't look away, or hide the hunger and desire reflecting in her eyes. "Not a wink."

Lust stirs deep in the pit of my stomach. "I can help with that."

"I'm a little nervous. I mean, it's been awhile."

I know exactly how long it's been since she was with someone, fourteen months to be exact. Now, butterflies bounce around inside me with anticipation. After a little over a year, I'm going to be the first man to see, touch, feel, and kiss every inch of her sweet body. I get to take her there, and experience all of her.

Yes, as a guy, that is a major ego stroke. And I want to make this special for her, for me, so we are permanently tattooed in each other's heart.

My body is buzzing everywhere. Since our first kiss two weeks ago, I've dreamed of this moment. And now she's here, in my house, my bedroom.

"It's like riding a bike."

This garners a laugh from her. "I hope you have a helmet for us."

I chuckle. "Don't worry, I have us covered." My fingers trace the black lace of her bra strap that peeks from underneath her shirt. Slowly, I pull the soft cotton material over her head. Little sparks of static dance along my skin. I'm not sure whether they're from her shirt or from my hands skimming her flesh. Either way, it's a magical feeling that causes my body to heat in complete pleasure and ecstasy.

"Dean." She lowers my head to her chest. "Touch me."

My lips brush her shoulder as I kiss her neck. I unhook her bra and let it fall away, leaving me face-to-face with firm, round, and deliciously feminine breasts. "Fuck, Cori."

She smiles wickedly. "I was hoping for a little foreplay first."

I cup her breasts in my hands. "Foreplay, uh?" Flicking my tongue over one luscious peak, I then suck it deep into my mouth. I could caress her silken skin forever.

She draws a breath. One of her hands digs into my hair and grabs a handful, while I lick, then gently catch the pink tip between my teeth, and bite lightly.

191

"So good." Her words are music to my ears.

After kissing, sucking, and squeezing one soft breast, I take the other tit in my mouth and give that beauty the same kind of attention. Then, my hands are on the waistband of her yoga pants, and I'm rolling them, along with her panties, past her ass, down her thighs, until I'm on my knees unlacing her boots. After removing her socks, she steps from the pants. And I come face-to-face with her snatch.

My heart races like a nerd on his way to get the new issue of *Dr. Who Space Time Continuum* magazine.

Holy. Mother. of. God.

She's fucking bare. Nothing turns me on more than a shaved pussy. And no, it's not because I'm some pervert with prepubescent fantasies. When a woman is bald, or nearly bald there, it makes it easier to admire, to fuck with my tongue, and it's just . . . naughty good.

I run the pad of my thumb on the skin surrounding her flesh, before pressing my face against the junction of her thighs and inhaling. No trace of soap, chemicals, or other extraneous substances.

For the record, men like a pussy to smell like a pussy. The natural aroma and flavor is the best part. Cori's scent engulfs me and sends me into a heady trance, one that won't end until our bodies are as close as two souls can be.

"I want to eat you like you've never been eaten before."

She moans.

"Is that something you want, Moonchild?"

"Yes," she confesses, voice low. "Fuck me with your mouth, Dean."

She's a talker. A dirty talker at that. I've fucking hit the jackpot.

Wildfire shoots through my veins. My heart is a train pounding down the tracks. My pulse is a racecar. I'm excited, pumped with sexual energy.

Sliding one hand between her thighs, I drape one of her legs over my shoulder and place a kiss on the delicate spot. Her hips arch up to greet my mouth. Famished, I open her a little farther, lick a little a deeper, and groan with regret as I gently plant her leg back on the floor.

The truth is, I can feast on Cori's pussy all night, but fucking her with my tongue, while I'm on my knees, will blow my mind. Control is a must. Slowly, I rise to my full height, take her hand in mine, and lay her on the bed. In a few smooth, economical movements, I strip to nothing.

Her eyes rake every hard inch of me, from my face, to my chest, to my full-on erection, before meeting my eyes.

"Wow." Her voice is husky. "You're beautiful, much more than I've imagined."

Actually, she's the beautiful one. My eyes drink in the sensuality of Cori lying on my bed. Passion-red cheeks. Perfectly swollen lips. Long, black hair tumbling over her shoulders. Dark, feral eyes. The body of a goddess. If the gods are real, then Cori is their masterpiece.

I lower myself beside her, nip her lower lip, and then crawl south, kissing every inch as I go.

Nudging her legs wider, I settle in and kiss her inner thighs, taking my time as I make my way to her tasty delight. When I stroke my finger over her core, she moans and arches her back. Then I spread her wider, before putting my mouth on her most sensitive spot.

"Oh, God." She fists a handful of my hair. Anchoring her hips , I hold her immobile as I eat her from end to end with a doggedly patient precision, until she cries out, "Oh, my God."

"Not God, baby. Dean," I say, my face still buried between her thighs. She's dripping wet. Her sweet, delicious cream coats my tongue, exciting me, making me crave more. "So fucking delicious." Shifting gears, I capture her swollen clit in my mouth and suck as I slip two fingers inside her.

Her hips shoot up, and strong runner's thighs squeeze the side of my neck. "Dean." My name trembles on her lips. "I can't think."

That makes two of us.

My fingers move faster, in time with my tongue. I want to make her lose all inhibition, to feel wild and utterly out of control. I need to drive her to the edge, even past it, enough that she hovers over the cliff, in that stomach-clenching heartbeat immediately before the free fall. "Come for me, Cori."

"God . . . Dean." She writhes against my face with a groan, her fingers yanking my hair. "I'm coming." I move my fingers faster, lick her deeper, faster, and look up, needing to watch as waves of orgasms overtake her body, gushing her juices over my tongue, down my throat.

This is how I've pictured her in the forbidden spots of my mind—lying on my bed in the throes of passion, fingers wound around my hair, strangled cries leaving her throat—as her body rockets with pleasure.

When she collapses, I catch her, until I feel her limbs relax on the bed. Then I wipe my face with my hand and lie next to her. "You okay?" As much as I want to slide my hard, swollen cock into her wet pussy, I'm willing to wait if she needs more time.

"Yeah." Her expression indicates full-blown ecstasy. "I've never come that way before and so quick."

This news surprises me. I'm not one of those guys who ever felt the need to be a woman's first in anything. In fact, the more experience, the better for me. But knowing that I'm Cori's first at something . . . Well, I can't help but feel a bit smug.

"Have you ever had back to back orgasms?"

Biting her lower lip, she asks, "On one night?"

I nod.

She's quiet for a beat. As she seems to consider my question, her hands move over my chest and down the ridged muscles of my abs, which makes me quiver with need. Then her hand ventures south to the promised land. She palms my cock and strokes.

I shiver, let out a low, guttural sound of appreciation, and thrust in her hand. "What's the answer?"

"No," she whispers. "I've never had two back-to-back orgasms in one night."

195

The Boy Friend by Mika Jolie

"Then you're in for a treat." I grab a condom from the drawer and tear it open with my teeth. I'm rolling the rubber onto my dick, when I catch her watching me. "Help me put it on." I take her hand and guide it, along with the condom, down my length.

After she sheathes me, I roll over her and nestle between her thighs. "I need to be inside you."

"Fuck me."

That invisible line between us, the veil, is overthrown by the plea in her voice. Slowly, I push my way past slick, tight muscles, filling her inch by inch, until I'm snug against her, completely surrounded by her in the best possible way.

The connection robs me of air.

Fuck. I'm inside Cori. Deep inside her, and it feels incredible.

Our bodies fit together as if we were made just for this, to fall into one another, to feel this natural rhythm.

When she begins writhing under me, I let out a tortured groan. "Not yet." Otherwise, I might blow a load right away. "You feel so fucking good."

"So do you." She holds my gaze. The current of gold and amber in her eyes reminds me of a well-aged whiskey. "I've dreamt about us like this."

Electrical sparks of pleasure crackle through my body. I imagine this is what a drug user feels when abusing their drug of choice. Everything in my life falls to the wayside, and I'm only here in the moment with Cori.

"Me, too," I confess. Slowly, I begin pumping in and out with long, thick, smooth strokes. Weight braced on my forearms, I can't take my eyes off her. She's mesmerizing . . . hypnotic, sensual, erotic, and sexual.

My heart trips and a moan of pleasure escapes my throat. Gritting my teeth, I slide almost all the way out, and then drive deep inside her.

"Oh, Dean, do that again."

I obey, give her what she wants by repeating the motion, and watch her eyes threatening to roll back in her head. "Like this?"

"Yes." Her mouth lets out a moan of ecstasy as I thrust into her again, fucking her slowly, sensually, deeply. "Harder," she begs. Her fingernails dig into my skin. "Faster, please."

"Not yet." Slow and steady. This time, I'm in control. I want to fuck her long, hard, hot, and dirty. I need to drive her crazy, take her to the precipice, then stop. And do it all over again, until she begs me to finish this. Even then, I won't, not until I do every naughty thing to her, until her mind and body explode. "Look down at us."

She does as I instruct and watches my cock—long, thick, and hard—glistening with her sweet juices, stretching her, reaching deeper with each stroke.

We are moving like partners in a dance that is written in our DNA. Our bodies, melding from bellies to thighs, fit together as if we are made just for this, to fall into one another, to feel this natural rhythm.

She hisses and scrapes her nails down my back. When she looks at me, I see my own heavy-lidded expression reflecting in her eyes.

"We look—"

"Hot." My voice is gruff as I continue pumping in and out of her slick, wet pussy.

"Perfect." She arches up, seating me even deeper inside her. The way she's biting her lower lip is an indication I am hurting her so good.

A rough groan leaves my throat. My mouth crushes hers, kissing her hard, and I ram into her as our bodies move together. When I feel her walls clench around my cock, I hold her head between my hands and hold her gaze. "I need to remember this."

"Forever," she whispers.

There's a vulnerability in her voice. It makes my heart rattle on a seismic scale. "Forever, Coriander. Forever."

"Dean." My name trembles out of her lips.

Her pussy is tight around me, getting hotter, more juicy. Needing to catalog this moment, I straighten my arms on either side of her head so I can watch the pleasure that flickers across her face, how I'm impacting her. Every movement, every desperate little whimper she makes, gives my heart an instant jolt. The joy of knowing I make her feel things that she craves and wants is . . . magical.

Our bodies are slapping together, over and over, hard and quick. I'm caught between the intoxication of the climax and extending a moment I never want to end. "Cori," I mutter her name, quickly losing all self-control. "I can't hold back anymore."

But then she cries my name as the pleasure takes her, muscles squeezing me in erotic, sensual waves as she skitters over the cliff.

I thrust faster, harsher, expanding her walls with brutal strength and urgency, until I growl out, "Oh, fuck," and unravel, coming with her, face-to-face, my eyes holding hers through the most intense orgasm of my life.

My arms collapse, and my full weight falls on her, breath ragged, muscles trembling, hearts pounding against each other.

I'm not sure for how long I stay with her, on top of her, buried deep, leaving no part of us untouched, cocooned in her arms. I am immersed in fields of sensation and feeling. It is pure, sumptuous, delicious, exhilarating freedom. When I finally steady my breathing, I shift my weight to my arms, she opens her eyes and gazes at me, and I can't look away.

Cori appears soft under me, feminine, trusting.

She has never been more beautiful.

Something in my heart shifts. But I don't dwell on it. With my free hand, I brush damp hair away from her face and place a kiss on her lips.

"Wow," she whispers on a smile. "That was—"

"Incredibly perfect."

The Boy Friend by Mika Jolie

Chapter 21

"Blur the lines between friends by knocking boots."

WHEN I FINALLY PEEL MYSELF away from Cori, and roll off the bed, I feel as if I'm missing a limb. Usually, after sex, I want to eat, urinate, go home, and sleep. Not with Cori. I want to prolong the connection as long as possible.

"Be right back." On my feet, I take one more glance of Cori on my bed. In her blissed-out, post-coital state, she looks mellow and rumpled, like a sated goddess. My heart skips a beat, and I feel a silly smile spread over my face. I've never been this excited about sleeping with a woman . . . giddy with joy, and the butterflies . . . forget the butterflies, the whole damn zoo is trampling inside me. "Have I ever told you that you're beautiful?"

She rolls on her stomach, her tight ass in full view for me to admire. "Yes." Her lips curv up. "But I don't mind hearing it again."

I lean in and give her a kiss then whisper, "You're fucking stunning." I disappear into the bathroom, and after discarding the condom, I wet a wash cloth with warm water. Re-entering the bedroom, I move straight to Cori's side of the bed, and when I try to wipe her clean, she puts a gentle hand over mine.

"I'll do it." With a smile, she takes the towel from my hand.

In the past, after sex, the woman always disappeared into the bathroom and did her business. Afterward I'd do mine. The exchange never bothered me before. Yet, as I watch Cori cleaning herself, gingerly wiping away any evidence of us, this feeling of longing settles in my chest.

For some unknown reason, I'm a tad disappointed. Not sure why. There's a level of intimacy when a man cleans a woman after sex, something I've never done before. Once again, I remind myself, this is Cori. What we shared goes beyond the physical act. We are friends. Emotionally, we are connected on some kind of level. Of course, it's normal for me to want to share more with her.

Not wanting to dwell on it, I focus my attention elsewhere. Aside from the Yin-Yang framed poster hanging over my bed— a gift from Cori—the walls are bare. My bedroom is large, simple, uncluttered, and classically decorated with limited décor—black headboard, white sheets and comforter, dark charcoal walls.

When I feel the weight of the mattress shift under us, and her thighs brushing against mine, my gaze follows Cori. She's on her feet, gathering her clothes.

"What are you doing?"

"Going home." Her voice is very matter of fact, no hint of remorse or regret.

I glance at the window. The soft snow is still falling. "It's snowing out." Lamest excuse ever. It's not like there's a blizzard outside. Additionally, Cori drives a badass Jeep. The kind with tires that can handle a freaking tsunami.

She picks up her bra, analyzes the black lacy material for a long moment before meeting my stare. "You don't do sleepovers."

My eyes stay on her breasts for a minute, fascinated by the movement of her adjusting her tits behind the lacy material before clasping the back.

It's true; I've never spent the night at a woman's house. Going away with someone for a weekend at a hotel is one thing, sleeping at their house or mine is a definite no—too intimate. But I don't want Coriander to leave. If anything, I want to make love to her again and again, until we're both exhausted, then I want to hold her in my arms and fall asleep together.

"Some rules are meant to be broken."

In her naked glory, she turns in a slow circle, clearly looking for the rest of her clothes, until she finds her panties and slides them on. My eyes follow the whole act, and I must say, it's a fucking turn on.

"I can't be your downfall," she says, not looking at me.

To my surprise, the idea of something greater between us makes me feel high as a kite. A dizzying effect for a guy who prides himself on being the perpetual bachelor. "What's wrong with you being my downfall?"

Her shoulders tense. She stops and looks at me for a long beat, then shakes her head. "Dean, I don't want us to have any regrets."

"How can I regret something that feels so right?"

Her silence sends impending doom to my gut. "Cori," I say, my voice low and controlled. "Do you regret what happened?"

Her gaze flies to my face. She opens her mouth, then closes it to bite her lower lip in what could be indecision or excitement. Obviously, I'm hoping for the latter.

"No."

Her answer makes my heart nearly pound out of my chest. I roll off the bed to my feet and close the space between us. Cupping the sides of her head, I thread my fingers into her hair and stroke her cheeks with my thumbs. "I want to make love to you again, rough and dirty, sweet and tender." I kiss her hand, needing her to understand that, whatever is happening to me, between us, is much more than sex. And although I have no idea how to process it at the moment, I don't want to let her go. "I don't want you to leave." Not now. Possibly not ever.

Silence clings to the room, making my blood as cold as the winter air. I can feel the need and hunger rolling through her, but there's hesitation in her eyes. As my friend, she knows my ways. In passing, I've shared stories about how the need for women to cuddle after sex is the last thing a man wants. She knows I don't ever bring a woman to my house, that I'm not ready to settle down.

Why should she be any different?

I can see the doubt creeping its way across her gorgeous face.

"Coriander, this will sound a bit cliché." I take her hand in mine, holding her stare. "Nothing about you is like any other woman." Exhaling, I force myself to ask the most important question. "Was one time enough for you?"

"Not even close," she says with a smile.

Her admission sends my mind in a pure sexual frenzy. I take her hand and wrap it around my erection. The worry in her gaze turns into a spark of excitement. Her palm clasps around my dick and begins stroking up and down my length.

"What about you, Dean. Was one time enough?" She's back to the sexy, teasing Cori.

"Not even close." The words barely leave my mouth when I pull her into me. Within seconds, we are kissing again, our hands moving over each other, exploring, familiarizing.

Her lips move to my neck, down to my chest. "My turn for control."

My body vibrates with pleasure. I pull back and meet her gaze. "How much control do you want?"

"Full control." Her lips twitch with naughtiness. "I want to taste you."

"Coriander," I grunt, because I have a pretty good guess what she means by those words. Something tells me, the minute her lips are on my dick, I'll explode.

She leans into me. Quickly, we are tangled in a kissing, touching war, until we tumble on the bed, side by side, mouths fused together.

Slowly, she works her way down my body. Her breath is hot on my chest as she kisses and licks everything along the way—nipples, abdomen, and continues farther south over the narrow, happy trail, letting me know exactly where she is going with those lips, but not necessarily racing to get there.

She flips her hair away from her face, lifts her chin, and smiles at me. Her lips are full, sensual, and they're about to cover me—a fulfillment of my fantasies.

My muscles flex with anticipation.

"My turn to make you come with my mouth."

Before I can speak, her fingers creep south, past my navel, and encircle my rigid erection. I groan in pleasure as she tightens her grip and strokes.

I'm a dead man.

She continues to touch me without hesitation, owning me. When her mouth grazes my inner thigh, I prop my weight on my elbows and freeze, anticipating the brush of her lips, the softness of her mouth as it engulfs me.

"Cori, I need to be in your mouth." At this point, my heart is hammering in my chest.

"Like this?" The rosy tip of her tongue sweeps over the throbbing head of my swollen dick and licks away a bead of liquid.

I hiss and grit my teeth. I grow stiffer. Larger. "Fuck, Cori."

"Later."

Now that she's reached her destination, she doesn't appear in a rush, but ready to explore. She releases my dick and spends some time licking and sucking my balls . . . And fucking Christ, I'm in heaven. When she lets them fall from her lips, I contemplate begging for more, but after a long, slow lick from the base to the head, she resumes her appreciation for my cock. Wrapping her lips around, she uses enough suction to make me groan. I watch as her small mouth expands over the length of my dick, until I hit the back of her throat.

"Holy shit, Cori."

She looks up.

Eyes innocent and wild smile at me.

Pleasure, awareness, spreads through my body. "You're killing me, Moonchild."

"You're so delicious, Dean. Come for me."

Oh, fuck yeah. From deep in my throat rumbles a low, rough noise. A helpless sound.

Her mouth is on my dick again, working me over and over. Hot, molten desire shoots through me. With each brush of her lips, I take a step closer toward madness. My head falls back in resignation, accepting the torturous pleasure as she explores every throbbing pulse, building me up.

And it feels unreal.

My hands flex and fist in her hair, not to guide her, but to connect in any way. Needing to capture this moment, I force my eyes open and fix them on her lips, sliding up and down over my engorged flesh.

Every nerve in my body is responding to her touch.

The pressure builds.

My leg muscles grow warm, fresh air enters my lungs, and blood flows into all my limbs.

Her head bobs faster and faster.

With each stroke, she preys on me a little more, takes me a little deeper, mauling me with her tongue, while her fingers fondle my thighs and everything in between.

My hips buck, control slipping.

I climb higher and higher. Panting. Grunting. Unleashing. Release is so close, I am practically vibrating with pleasure. "Coriander. I can't hold back."

A wild groan slips from her throat. She squeezes my dick in her hand, increasing the pace of each stroke and sucking. She's ready for all I've got, and I'm ready to subside.

My thigh muscles twitch.

My gut tightens.

My vision blurs.

After three hard, deep thrusts, all the air whooshes from my lungs as I come, hard and longer than I ever thought possible.

For a stunningly breathless moment, my heart stops. Then my body collapses onto the bed, and I shiver. I haul her against my body, her breasts melting against my chest. "Give me ten minutes."

"How was it?"

Is she fucking kidding me? That was the best blowjob ever. As an answer, I kiss her long and deep. I'm not one of those guys who's sketchy about tasting myself in a woman's mouth. The warmth, the salty flavor is strangely . . . satisfying. When I finally break for air, I ask, "Did I answer your question?"

"I think so." She laughs, a soft, melodious sound. "Is it strange that I want to be the best you've ever had?"

My heart stumbles, before finding its rhythm once again. I shift my head a few inches away from hers and stare at Cori with a kind of wonder. "Everything about the two of us and tonight is bigger and better than how I've ever imagined it'd be between us."

"Are you sure?" she asks, her fingers smoothing along my chest.

"One hundred percent."

LESS THAN TEN MINUTES LATER, we are, once again, seeking each other like wild creatures. We kiss each other's face, mouth, throat, any piece of flesh we can find, until Cori rolls over me, straddling me, with my hard length thick between us.

Our eyes meet, and hers look wild, reflecting the hunger burning within me.

"My turn to make you come again." My voice shakes with raw desire.

"How about we come together?"

"I love that idea." Grabbing her waist, I place her warm entrance on the tip of my erection. "Ride me," I say, and then I lower her until I'm buried deep inside her. Skin on skin.

We both gasp, then she begins moving on me. The feel of her clenched muscles gripping me like a vise magnifies the exquisite friction of the direct contact. We're like fireworks and symphonies exploding in the sky.

This is so fucking good.

It's unlike anything I've ever experienced.

I am flooded with pleasure.

Mind in a haze, I let the significance of the action run through my veins.

I thrust up into her, driving deeper, and watch as the pleasure mounts, until her breathing grows shallow, the speed of her movement increases, and cries of ecstasy fill the room.

A little while later, I pull the white comforter over us, roll to my side, and press Cori's back against my chest. Warmth and darkness envelopes us, along with a comfortable silence. And that's how we fall asleep.

"Is the old adage 'friends make the best lovers' true?"

WAKING UP NEXT TO CORI is possibly the best feeling I've experienced. Seriously, it's out-of-this-world amazing. Don't get me wrong, I'm not talking shit about the sex. That was incredible, like, fingernails down the back, can't feel my legs, neighbors wonder if somebody is getting killed great. I've never had better sex with anybody, so don't think I'm somehow dissatisfied. I don't even know how to describe what we shared last night.

The closest I can compare sex with Cori is perhaps being in the front row of a Mumford and Sons concert, while everyone else watches the performance on YouTube. The video is fantastic, until you've experienced the real deal. And although the English rock band is easily one of my top go-to chill mode bands, comparing Cori to them doesn't do her justice. She's not a random hook-up, the kind when I'm eager to leave as soon as the buzz wears off.

No, I want to stay right here, in the spooning position, Cori's back plastered to my front like a second skin.

I run my hand over her arm, my fingertips gently grazing her skin. In response, to my delight, she writhes against my morning wood.

See what I mean.

This is fucking heaven.

Groaning quietly into her neck, I inhale the scent of her hair, before it's washed, when it smells like *Cori*, not the shampoo that reminds me of her.

"Awake?" I ask against the softness of her skin as I leave a trail of kisses on her shoulder.

"Barely."

Even her sleepy voice—sounding cute and cuddly—is a turn on.

"I see you are." She laughs into my arms, then turns her body toward mine as I roll onto my back. Her head is on my chest, one slender arm around me, our hands interlocked.

"How are you feeling?"

"Great."

"Sore?"

"A little bit."

I brush my lips against the top of her head. "We can take it easy."

"You can't help your size." She tilts her head, half-asleep, a smile on her face, and says, "I'm not complaining."

Phew! Relief washes over me. Not that I was worried about the machinery, but let's be honest, it's a few inches above the average size and doesn't lack in girth. I'm glad Coriander likes it. "Well, shit, in that case," I say, feigning rolling over her.

She laughs. "But this is nice."

"Beyond nice." Life simply can't get any better. This is the money shot. We're talking like lovers, laughing like friends. My body is thrumming with emotions I've neither expected nor sought.

Desire.

Need.

And something else. A new and unfamiliar feeling for me, nothing I can even begin to explain.

"What did you love most last night? Which position I mean?" she asks.

The answer comes to me without hesitation. *You.*

I clamp my mouth shut.

Holy shit! I'm in love with Coriander.

This revelation hits me like a meteor crashing into earth, disrupting the composition of my mind, leaving me dazed by the powerful force.

This feeling is strange—frightening even. It stretches throughout my whole body. It's overwhelming, yet makes me feel complete. It has no bound, nor length, nor depth.

It's as if I'm in a dangerous fire; yet I'm safe at the same time.

I feel light, on top of the world, yet my heart is constricting, pleading for oxygen.

It's just . . . absolute.

"Dean?"

Clearing my throat, I say, "Yeah."

"What's wrong?"

"Nothing." Remember, I analyze shit for a living. This love thing is new to me, a path untrodden, twisting out of sight. Before I proclaim my undying love, I need to make sure this isn't my dick ruling my heart because it had the best sex of its life. *Fucking bastard.* Until then, the greedy SOB is ready to go, and frankly, I desperately need the physical escape. After brushing my lips on Cori's forehead, I lower them toward hers, but she quickly covers her mouth, blocking the kiss. "You're not a fan of my kisses?"

"Morning breath," she muffles behind her hand.

"Do you care?"

"Not with you."

That makes two of us. Gently, I remove her hand over her mouth. "Neither do I." Within seconds, Cori is on her knees, her tight round ass perked up in the air. For a split second, I think about grabbing a condom, but now that I've experienced that skin on skin friction, sex with Cori with a rubber is going to feel like showering in a plastic jumpsuit. I spread her legs, run two fingers over her sleek mound, and then I thrust forward, burying myself inside Cori in one rough stroke before the world catches up with us.

EVENTUALLY, I DRAG MYSELF out of bed to clear off Cori's car, then I park her Jeep in my garage next to my shiny baby. About thirty minutes later, I enter the bedroom and find the bed empty, the bathroom door slightly open. I can hear the shower running.

My initial thought is to speak to Cori about us—our feelings toward each other. What's next for *Cori and Dean.* But that conversation can wait. Cori is in my shower, in her naked glory, using my soap, rubbing her hands over her body.

Sue me, I'm a guy. I think with my dick . . . a lot.

Besides, we have all day.

I strip off my sweater and damp jeans, push the door open and step inside. Steam rolls over me as the water beats against the tile floor. For the briefest moment, I stop and take in the faint outline of her body, before sliding the glass door open. Her hands are moving along her shoulders, her breasts.

Desire flares.

Initially, I assumed one night with Cori would satisfy this craving. Obviously, I was wrong, and now, there's the whole I've-fallen-in-love-with-my-best-friend complication.

What if she doesn't love me back?

Shit! I've never thought of that possibility. My cocky ass automatically assumed she feels the same way.

She has to, right?

I mean, she did drive here in a snowstorm . . . it couldn't be just for the sex, could it?

Shaking off the doubts, I slide the door open and ask, "Mind if I join you?"

"I think there's room for the two of us." She steps aside to make space for my large frame.

"Let me do that." I take the soap from her and rub it between my large hands long enough to build some suds.

"Thanks for cleaning my car. I could have done it myself."

"Yeah, I know. But I love doing it. The same way I'm enjoying doing this." I drag the soap over her body, letting it caress her skin as if it is my kisses, down to the softness of her flat stomach, and freeze. I stand absolutely still, silent and rigid, as if my brain has short-circuited and needs to be rebooted. My heart is racing, possibly right out of my chest, but not in a good way. This is a pure fucking panic attack.

Last night, we didn't use a condom when Cori rode me like a porn star. The first time is easy to dismiss as being caught up in the moment. But a few minutes ago, when I plunged inside her while she was on her knees, that'd been a conscious decision. I wanted to feel and take all of her.

In my thirty years, I've never gone bareback with a broad, not even when I was a horny teenager controlled by my penis. The idea of a limp dick because of carelessness has never been my thing. From my end, I'm as clean as fresh laundry. There's no concern about Cori's lifestyle. I know who she's been with and like me, she's a stickler for the old rubber.

But there are other consequences with having unprotected sex. Babies are also made that way.

A heavy weight settles in my gut. I'm not ready for a baby. Nervous energy fills my chest.

"You're okay?" She drags her fingers through my wet hair, her brown eyes searching mine.

My thoughts fumble, panic attacks like a bird of prey. I give myself a mental shake then say, "Yeah, I'm fine."

But inside my head is a mental war. Cori openly admitted to wanting to start a family. Sure, I love her. In some way, I probably always have. But that doesn't mean I'm ready to go buy a ring, take the walk down the aisle, the two point five kids, and the picket fence. Honestly, I was going to propose we start dating, see where things go . . . which includes lots of sex, by the way. Now, there's a possibility of a baby. I exhale. Everything is changing too fast. I feel drawn in, and that makes me want to pull back.

She takes the soap from my hand. "My turn."

"Why don't you rinse off," I suggest, my head still spinning at the transition from friends, to lovers, to what-the-fuck.

We know what makes each other tick. She holds me in a stare down for a beat, then she nods and says, "Sure."

A vicious silence hangs over us. The water continues to beat on the tile. Cori and I need to connect through the familiar and lead the conversation in a new direction. Quickly, I search my brain for a topic of discussion that will vault over the awkward pause and fill it with common ground. Instead, my mind comes up blank. I stand, muted, rooted to the spot, and watch her rinse the suds off her body.

When she finishes, she flashes a smile that doesn't quite reach her eyes. "I should get dressed."

I nod. "I'll be out shortly."

After the door closes, an empty sensation takes root in my chest. I turn the knob to the hottest temperature my skin can handle. Leaning my hands against the warm tiles, I close my eyes, lower my head, and let the steamy rivulets beat over my back and soak into my skin.

When I enter the bedroom, Cori is fully dressed in the same outfit from last night. After putting on her boots, she rises to her feet.

"Cori, we should talk."

Her brown eyes roam over me, my face, chest, the towel wrapped around my narrow waist. When she meets my gaze again, her facial expression is closed.

"Moonchild," I say her name in a low tortured voice.

Her chin trembles. She sucks in a breath, closes her eyes for a moment before opening them. "Don't say anything, Dean."

Silence, stifling and itchy as a wool blanket, hovers over the room. She's shutting me out. I can make this . . . *us* . . . better.

"Please look at me." I've never begged a woman in my life. I've never fucked without a condom. I've never brought a woman to my house or spent the night with anyone. I've never fallen in love before, either. Welcome to the 'firsts' in Dean Conrad Morello's life.

The guilt sits on my chest, my heart sags under the weight of being responsible.

"I panicked earlier." Again, my stomach lurches and gurgles. There are two Deans inside me. The one who desperately wants to be with Cori, and the one who's not ready to have a high chair in the middle of my dining room.

Roadblocks I should have thought of before.

I run a hand through my wet hair. "We didn't use a condom."

Cori's eyes have their own vocabulary and always show the antiquity of her soul. When I stare into them, there's no hint of the fun-loving artist I adore. Instead, hurt and sadness looks back at me.

She crosses her arms over her chest. "I'm on the pill, Dean."

A wave of disappointment sweeps over me. *Why the fuck am I disappointed?*

"I thought you wanted a baby."

"I also want love."

Silence falls between us, not the good kind either. *You love her. Tell her, you dimwit.* For a talker, I'm speechless, completely unable to find the right words.

"Don't worry." Cori keeps her eyes steady, resting on my face like I'm her home, but just briefly, before glancing away. She walks past me with long fluid steps, and pulls out her keys from her pocket. "I didn't expect anything to come of us."

"Why not?" I ask in a gravelly voice, my heart struggling to keep a steady beat.

"Because one of us will get hurt." A hint of a smile forms on her lips. "Most likely me."

With a few quick strides, I'm by her side. I cup her face and tilt it up so that we're staring at each other. "I'd never hurt you."

"Promise me something."

"Anything." I'm willing to give her the world, if that's what it takes to make her smile again, to look at me without pain.

"Let's not let last night change our friendship."

Too late for that. Everything has changed between us. We connected on a different level last night, this morning. Even now, I am seeing a part of her soul she never lets out of the bag. When we touched, I saw her reaction, beautiful and raw. "But—"

She steps from my reach. "I should go."

Every nerve in my body wants to stop her, but I don't. Instead, I stand in the middle of the room and watch her walk over to my dresser, where a few of my knickknacks sit on display. She grabs her cell phone and stuffs it in her coat pocket.

As she makes her way to the door, she stops, leans into me, and places a kiss on the corner of my lips. "See you Friday."

I want to remind her about our weekly dinner date. Instead, I say, "Yeah. Text me when you get home." Having Cori text me when she gets home, especially after we've hung out, is a ritual between us, a way for me to make sure she's safe.

She nods. Then she walks away, closing the bedroom door behind her, leaving me standing in my room. Alone.

Go after her, my conscience tries to persuade me. Only, I'm dazed, confused, and presently experiencing life at a rate of what-the-fuck just happened. Slowly, I lumber over to the bed and drop my weight on the mattress. On my back, I stare at the ceiling, questions spinning in my head.

Is it really possible to go back to being just friends?

Is that really what I want?

The answer is a resounding no to both of those questions.

But I still freaked out over the possibility I might have impregnated her.

Yeah, I'm officially the biggest douchebag.

My panic attack hurt her. Now everything has changed between us.

Nausea swirls unrestrained in my empty stomach. My head swims with half-formed regrets. I don't know how long I lay on the bed staring blankly at the ceiling, wishing I can turn back time.

When my phone beeps on the nightstand, I sit up and read Cori's message.

I'm home.

I text her back.

Glad you're safe.

My fingers clasp around the device, as if letting it go would be, in a way, releasing Cori. A few minutes pass before it vibrates again with another text from her.

Dean . . . you're my best friend.

Five little words. They tear me up and remind me, once again, I've hurt her. My fingers hover over the keyboard. I want to apologize. I want to tell her I've fallen in love with her. After the longest minute, I type back a one-word response.

Ditto.

Afterward, I throw the phone on the bed and flop on my back. Something tells me Coriander and I have just become strangers who know each other too well.

Chapter 23

"Sometimes a heart cannot afford to be just friends."

HOURS AFTER CORI LEAVES, and feeling like shit, I tell myself this is a momentary setback in our relationship . . . whatever it is at the moment. But for now, a little time to clear our heads will do both of us good. So here I am, on a date. An actual fucking date.

Dating is crappy.

I look at my watch for the fifth time as the pretty blonde goes on and on about . . . whatever. I'm not listening.

Lorraine and I are in Times Square at a fancy five-star restaurant, on a date. Candles are flickering on the tables, and the lights are nicely dim. The ambiance is quiet, romantic even. Across from me, Lorraine is eating silently. She's model hot. Under any other circumstances, we'd be naked, shaking the sheets.

In the past, I never had the need to wine and dine a woman, but for once, I thought it'd be a nice change to actually go on a 'date'. Bad idea. The problem is, I don't care how sexy Lorraine's cleavage looks in that little green dress. I don't want to be here. My lackluster mood is obvious, but I can't fake what I'm feeling.

I can't remember the last time I took a woman out to dinner. Cori. I've taken her out to dinner numerous times, whether to a fancy night out in the city or grabbing a bite at a diner. Our dates have always been fun, effortless.

Dates.

The times we've gone to the movies together, bowling, accompanying each other to some event, the night we karaoked and sang "You're The One That I Want" at the karaoke bar. That night we shared our first kiss.

Every significant time I've spent with a woman comes back to Cori.

After each of these occasions, I've gone home feeling euphoric, alive, as happy as a dog at a dinosaur dig.

Were all of these times spent together dates?

I've loved her for over twenty years as a friend, but things have changed. Can I really 'love' love her?

Is that what happened?

How the fuck do I know for sure?

I've never analyzed or even made much of those moments. They've always been effortless. And yet, these series of events have defined my life, unapologetically stole my heart.

Were we ever strangers? I'm not sure we were. That day I first saw her in the schoolyard, there was something even then, though I didn't know what. But I was hers then. I've been hers since the second we met.

And although I've never given it much thought, she's my happy.

She never leaves my mind. She's always there—mentally, if not physically. She's the sky and the clouds, the gentle river and the birds that sing, my medicine. I've fallen in love with Cori, can't fall any further. I'm already on the ground. And I have a feeling that I slipped my heart into her pocket some time ago.

This morning, when we woke up naked next to each other, I'd been fine, happy. Now, the world is monotonous, my energy leaving me like an ink stain bleeding into blotting paper.

"What do you think of the view?" Lorraine asks after taking a sip of her white wine. Cori likes red or an old fashioned.

My girl.

My heart rattles.

I glance at the majestic view of the skyline. Lights glitter everywhere. Rows of towering skyscrapers and small buildings collide in a mixture of shadow and geometry. It's a gorgeous view. One I should be enjoying. Instead, my mind is conjuring an escape strategy. Maybe when she makes her customary trip to the restroom, I can tiptoe from the restaurant like The Pink Panther.

Of course, I'd pay the bill first.

"It's a great view." My voice is flat. I'm struggling to feel with anemic emotions that have no substance.

"I'm glad we're here."

My gaze rests on her matted cherry-red lips. For a split second, I imagine her mouth wrapped around my dick.

Nothing. Not even a tingle or a hint of a bulge. I sampled the goodies, now the bastard that is my dick is addicted. It's a sad situation when my dick has decided to go on strike. On top of that, waves of nausea, for allowing my imagination to think of another woman, adds to my misery. I feel sick, dirty, guilty.

"What do you think?" Lorraine asks with enthusiasm.

"About?"

"A nightcap at your place."

I take a swallow of my scotch, needing a moment to come up with an answer that will not make me look like the complete asshole that I am. "Lorraine." Shit, already her face is crestfallen. "I'm sorry, but it's not happening."

"Why?" She laughs nervously. "I thought we had fun the other day."

Honestly, our fucking session is a fog in my memory bank. "We did." Not entirely a lie. I vaguely recall banging her on the floor of her house. "But—"

"You're one of those guys."

I sit a little straighter. "What kind of guy?"

"The ones who are afraid of commitment and don't bring women to their house." She places her fork down and holds my gaze in a stare. "Do you even want to be here? You can't stop checking your watch."

Okay, let's back up. Why am I here? It's obvious this is the last place I want to be.

Well, after Cori left, I spent most of the day wallowing in my sorrow. My phone pinged with message after message, none of them from Cori—hers has a special ring, "We Go Together".

See the trend here? Moonchild loves the movie *Grease*.

Anyway, eventually, when Lorraine texted, checking to see if I was around, I decided that feelings are like temperatures. Attraction is warm. Curiosity is warmer. Anger is boiling. Hate can torch, but it can also freeze. Love . . . Well, that's a temperature best left under neutral.

So, here I am.

Only I'm not stuck on neutral. I want to be wrapped in a pretzel position with Cori, with the soft feel of her breath on my neck. I want to fall asleep to the sound of her heartbeat beating against mine.

Elbows on the table, I take Lorraine's hands. This isn't her fault. She doesn't deserve this treatment. "I'm sorry," I apologize. "I'm being a dick."

"It's okay," she says with a smile. "Who's the lucky girl?"

For the first time tonight, I smile. "Her name is Coriander."

"Strange name." One perfectly arched eyebrow rises. "A hippie."

Cori doesn't like to be labeled. Call her a hippie, and she'll tell you categorical labeling is a tool that humans use to resolve the impossible complexity of the environments we grapple to comprehend. Like so many human faculties, it's adaptive and miraculous, but it also contributes to some of the deepest problems that face our society.

She's so fucking sexy when she's spitting knowledge.

Love it.

I laugh partly to myself, some of the tension slowly leaving my body. "A little bit."

"Does she know you're in love with her?"

"No."

"Then how will you get the girl if you don't tell her how you feel?"

I sit back in my chair. "Good question."

She takes another sip of her wine then says, "If you love the girl, tell her. Forget about the rules or your fears." Her green eyes study me. "I have a feeling you have a lot of fears, but she'll understand."

It's as if I'm seeing Lorraine for the first time. Conversing with her is actually . . . nice.

Beyond her physical attributes, there's substance there. In the past, I've never allowed myself the opportunity to get to know a woman. Now that we know sex is not on the menu, I find she's easy to talk to. Maybe it's because I'm depressed as hell and need to be on a sofa crying to a fucking therapist.

"Still interested in having dinner with me?"

She shrugs. "We're here, and I have a hot dress on, so yeah."

I laugh again. "Perfect. By the way, you look hot as fuck." She does. It's just, there isn't going to be any fucking.

TWO DAYS LATER, MY mind's a mess, and my heart's a wreck. Every piece of me wants to call Coriander, just to hear her voice. At the same time, I tell myself, a couple of days not speaking will do us good. We need the distance. At least, I know I do—to clear my head.

After eyeing the phone for several seconds, I grab it, thumb my code, and bring up my contact list. When I reach C, my thumb stops scrolling. My finger taps on Coriander Moonchild.

Hey, how's things?

Scratch that. Too casual. That's not who we are.

Uhm. Hi? Remember me? We used to be best friends?

Too desperate. I type another short text. This one is better.

Wanna hang tonight?

Nope. Now that we've had sex, those are words for a booty call.

What are you wearing?

A little stalkerish? The black leather chair creaks as I shift my weight. Yup. My balls are still there, intact.

We need to talk. I love you. I miss you. Marry me.

Slow down, lover boy. Way too desperate and needy. Plugging my earphones to my cell phone, I fit them in my ears and crank some music. For the next thirty minutes, I'm able to bury myself in my work and wade through the mountain piling at my desk, until Michael Stipe's voice is interrupted by a ding. I glance at the screen and notice Red's text.

I'll be home at 10. See you tonight.

Without thinking, I start answering.

Not tonight. I have a . . .

What exactly do I have? A thing? A headache? Sorry, I can't fuck you today, because my sister's friend's mother's grandpa's brother's grandson's fish died, and yes, it's tragic.

Pathetic. I know.

With a quick tap, I delete my original response.

Maybe a distraction is just what I need.

My dick, flaccid, hangs his head. The bastard is sulking, furious with me.

Believe it or not, our dicks don't control every breath we take . . . well, not usually. I did say before that every second was a slight exaggeration. Anyhow, my dick has gladly put itself on hiatus. When it comes to a woman, it only wants Cori.

The truth is, so do I.

I'm in love with Cori.

She's my heart. This isn't a small, almost imperceivable event in my life.

My everything.

So fucking sappy. Seriously, a part of me wants to puke right now.

Quickly, I compose a text.

Need a raincheck.

Her response comes quick.

See you Friday.

Shit! I've forgotten about Red coming on the ski trip.

Shit.

Shit.

Shit.

I exhale, then massage my temples to suppress the bitch of a headache I feel coming on.

"Yo man, we're hungry. You coming?"

I look up at Cam standing in the doorway of my office. "Yeah."

"PMS'ing?" Cam casually asks.

I groan.

"Yeah, definitely time of the month." He chuckles. "What's eating you up, Gilbert?"

I swivel in the leather chair and stare at my diploma. It offers nothing. LeBron, my man, help a guy, will you? *Niente.* What am I supposed to say? I'm in love with Cori, but I'm gutless and freaked over the idea of impregnating her?

"Nothing." I lock my computer and join Cam. We stop in front of Nora's desk, and I hand her a folder. "Can you make sure Donner's wife gets these first thing tomorrow?" The jackass is begging for his wife to take him back. She's playing hardball. Good for her.

Nora studies me with a frown. "You look like you lost your best friend."

My gaze shifts to the red exit sign. This is Cori's grandmother. I can't let her know what's going on between Cori and me. Swallowing the lump of guilt in my throat, I say, "I'm glad this Donner situation is coming to a close. It's tiring."

She nods in agreement and changes the conversation. As I start to walk away, Nora says, "Just remember, true friends are forever."

I nod, stuff my hands in my pocket. "Thanks, Nora."

"So, did you lose your best friend?" Cam asks as we continue towards Lucas' office. He's silent for a minute as we pass a few people chitchatting in the busy hallway. "And I don't mean Lucas and me."

The thing about friendship, even between guys, we don't say much to each other, yet we still know when something is bothering one of us.

"I don't want to talk about it."

"Have you told Cori about Red coming to New Hampshire with you this weekend?"

"No."

From the corner of my eye, I see Cam shaking his head.

"Dude." Cam claps my shoulder. "Someone is going to get hurt. And I bet my money it's gonna be you."

Me. I thought he was going to say Cori. "I'll be fine. There's nothing going on between Cori and me."

"Yeah, and bringing someone you're hooking up with will pretty much seal the deal."

We stop in front of Lucas' office. To our surprise, the door is locked, something that rarely happens. The dude takes the 'my door is always open' motto a bit literally.

Before we can knock, the door swings open, and Lucas' ex-wife, Lucille, storms out, almost crashing into Cam. Her blue eyes sweep over us, disdain on her gorgeous face. During the two years they were married, she bitched every time Lucas hung out with the guys. Not that we'd ever steer a married guy wrong. Seriously, I believe in the sanctity of marriage. My parents, remember? I admire and respect their union.

"Which one of you is he fucking?"

The question comes out with pure venom in her delicious French voice. Cam and I cough, but it's me who finds the strength to say, "How are you, Lucille?"

"He won't fuck me," she spits. Her French accent thicker than usual.

I glance over her shoulder at Lucas, who only shrugs.

"You're divorced." Cam is the one who speaks, his voice surprisingly warm. "Even made a cute little baby girl together."

"What's your problem?" she snaps at Lucas. The man is pure steel when necessary. He just stands there, arms folded across his chest. With a flip of her dark hair, a scowl still on her face, she hisses. "Just remember, I can make your life a living hell." Then she elbows her way between Cam and I.

"Oh." She pauses by the door. "I hate all of you." Then the door slams behind her.

"What was that about?" I ask after a long silence.

Lucas walks back to his desk. "Her typical threats to take Emma back to France."

"What are you going to do?"

"Call my lawyer." His fingers are hitting the keyboard with efficient speed for a minute before he looks up at us. "But first, I need food." He grabs his jacket. "By the way, who were you with on Sunday? We texted you to hang."

"Yeah, I was busy."

"Right," Lucas says dryly.

Cam and Lucas study me through assessing eyes. I square my shoulders a little bit more and meet their stares. Male friendship is built on a solid foundation of testosterone, sarcasm, inappropriateness, shenanigans, and the weirdest porn we've ever seen. Please don't downplay the complexity of the way we bond. We have feelings and emotions; we just display them differently. We can spend hours talking about sports, food, and sex. If the Giants beat The Cowboys, that's worth a lengthy conversation. If a random hookup turns out to be the best sex of our life, we share it with each other.

Except when the act is with someone we care about.

Then we zip our lips. Which is what I'm doing now. What Cori and I shared went beyond a hook-up. Don't get me wrong. Had things turned out differently— you know—if Cori and I were still banging, I'd be standing here with pride, announcing my days as a bachelor are over and the pathetic bastards were now on their own.

Unfortunately, or fortunately—depends on the perspective—I'm still free as a bird. Which means, I can sleep with any woman out there, on any given day, without any remorse.

Somehow, that thought fails to cheer me up. If anything, loneliness squeezes my heart.

"Are we eating or what?" Turning on my heels, I start walking ahead of them out of Lucas' office.

"Cranky, much," Lucas says as they catch up with me. "Time of the month?"

"According to a report done back in 2004, a quarter of men confessed to having man period," Cam adds.

"I don't fall in the quarter."

Cam snorts. "So you say."

Lucas stops midstride, examines my face. "Is this related to Cori?"

"Oh, about that, he still hasn't told Cori about Red."

"Jesus." I scratch my left brow. "Stop talking as if I'm not right here."

"Our trip is—" Lucas taps his temple—"oh, three days away. Just tell her, you fucking idiot."

"What does it matter?" I push the door open to the lounge and press the down arrow elevator button. "We're friends. Nothing more."

"Is that what you want?" Cam asks, surprisingly serious.

No, that's not what I want. But marriage . . . A knot twists in my gut. "Yes."

This is what I call coping. The process of turning shit into sunshine.

Chapter 24

"Friends. Lovers. Or Nothing."

HALFWAY THROUGH THE WEEK, I break down and call Cori. The phone rings. I drum my fingers on the table. My stomach is filled with butterflies of nervousness as I wait for her to answer. After three rings, I am ready to hang up, when she answers.

"Hey," she says, out of breath. "Good to hear from you."

Just hearing her voice makes me feel giddy, blissful, like a kid in a candy store. "Can you meet for lunch?"

"Oh," she says after a slight hesitation.

I can see her chewing on her lower lip.

"I'm on my way out," she says softly on the other end.

Hope dashes.

There's a moment of silence on the line before she adds, "Meeting with a friend."

Code word for a date.

"Brandon." His name slips out of my mouth before I can stop myself. A tinge of the green-eyed monster creeps up on

239

me over the thought he's still in the picture. Believe it or not, engaging in lovemaking with your sexy best friend makes some people feel territorial. I'm officially the jealous friend, ex—something.

Jealousy sucks. Period.

"Yes," she confirms.

My heart smashes and splinters into a million pieces, each one cutting my chest and right through my body. Numb. I close my eyes for a moment, count to three hundred, then say with as much indifference as I can muster, "Alright, I'll let you go then."

"Dean."

"Yeah." I am officially dead inside.

"Is there something you wanted to talk about?"

"No," I lie. After a few days of back and forth, last night I woke the fuck up and realized Lorraine was right; I need to let Cori know how I feel, and today was going to be the day I put myself out there. Joke's on me. No need to unpack my emotions. Brandon is still in her life—a clear indication we're not compatible. "See you on Friday."

"SOMEHOW, I'VE ALWAYS pictured you owning a two-seater convertible," Red is saying as we're driving down I-95. The road ahead of us is covered in a thick layer of snow.

"Not a truck, huh?" I ask over the tires rumbling on the road.

"Nope."

"You're right, this is my parents'." Due to the weather conditions, I had to borrow my parents' truck for the weekend. One bad thing about a sleek sports car, they're shit in bad weather. "But why do you peg me as a two-seater car owner?" This is my attempt at small talk with Red during this long-ass drive. I'm well aware of all the stereotypes. I'm sure you've read or heard them as well. You know, the bullshit about guys with flashy sports cars are overcompensating for other, uh, shortcomings in their lives. "And don't say, owning a sporty vehicle of choice is really just a rolling phallic symbol that screams, 'Please, please notice me!'"

She lets out a low laugh. "We both know you're not lacking."

I stay quiet. Whatever I say will not be received well. We're two hours into our drive to New Hampshire. For the most part, the drive has been decent.

Except, everything tells me we're approaching dangerous territory.

"Speaking of not lacking." She shifts her body and leans towards me. Her greedy fingers are already on my thigh heading straight for my crotch.

I take one of my hands from the steering wheel, catch hers and place it back on her lap.

"Wow, talk about a rejection."

In case you're wondering, my dick is still sulking. Last night, I jacked off thinking about Cori—that had made the bastard happy. "Sorry about that," I say sincerely, because I've realized that I've hurt her. Call me an asshole all you want, but I don't enjoy hurting anyone.

"Is it because of her?"

"Her?" I ask, hands clenched tight around the wheel.

"Your friend, Coriander."

Regardless of what I want, Cori's place in my life is a hybrid of bestie, ex, and one-night stand. "I just want to ski." My melancholy mood continues to hang over me like a black cloud, raining my personal sorrow down on me wherever I go. Taking my eyes off the road for a brief moment, I glance over at Red. Her head is turning toward the road.

Another woman I've hurt.

My heart constricts as realization punches me in the gut.

I'm using her for my own selfish need to get through the weekend. This isn't about sex. That was never my intent, even before Cori and I had sex. But taking her with me is bringing an innocent party into my chaos.

When did I become such a self-centered asshole?

I should have come forward and canceled with Red.

Nothing good is going to come from two days under the same roof with a woman whose name I don't even know and the woman I love.

Chapter 25

"Oh, him? We're just friends."

A LITTLE OVER FOUR HOURS later, I park the truck in front of the cabin, next to Lucas' SUV. Red is on her cell in a conversation with one of her colleagues about work. I signal to her that I'll get our bags, then swing the door open.

An icy blast of late February air slaps my face. My boots sink in the soft powdery snow as I trudge over to the trunk. This is the type of snow we skiers thrive for. Typically, I am filled with excitement, a rush to conquer the mountains. However, today, my body is overwhelmed with a cold, prickly, burning sensation. I am a puddle of nerves about this visit. In a few seconds, Cori and I will come face-to-face again after a week of barely talking to each other.

A part of me is saying, fuck it, get back in the truck, turn that shit around, and go home. In this weather, driving back isn't an option. Ignoring the pinch in my gut, I shake my head, disallowing my second thoughts to get the better of me. I sling Red's overnight bag over my shoulder and open her door. "Ready?"

She raises a finger. "Just need a few minutes to finish this call."

I nod. "Okay. Let me bring the bags in. Take your time."

"Be there in five."

Bags in hand, I head to the cabin. As the door stands towering above me, I gleam over the naked, winter trees, twisting and turning. My stomach twirls and twines with them. I let out a shaky breath, closing my weary eyes for a couple of seconds.

White knuckles grip the doorknob, the cold metal sending a shiver up my already quivering arm. Deep breaths. Almost mindlessly, I turn the handle, opening the door to the fate that awaits.

I pause at the doorway, letting my eyes roam the room before anyone notices we've arrived. At least this way, my mind has a few more minutes longer to prepare.

Kate and Lucas are sitting on the floor by the fireplace, engrossed in a game with his daughter, Emma. Cam is lounging on the sofa, flipping the channels of the television, before settling on a college basketball game.

No sign of Cori.

She's here. I know that, because she drove with Kate. Then a possibility I never entertained entered my thoughts. Brandon. What if she came here with Brandon?

I swallow the bitter tang from my mouth. Yes, that's pretty ballsy and completely selfish of me to worry about coming face-to-face with Brandon when I have Red with me. Even though there's zero possibility of sleeping with her, I still brought her along.

So yeah, I get it. I'm a douche.

Don't worry, I'm sick of myself, sick of who I am as well.

My mind is still reeling with all sorts of inane possibilities, when I catch the legs of Cori's jeans rushing down the stairs. She stops and meets my gaze, her eyes sparkling with delight. Before I can say anything, she's in my arms, greeting me with a hug that can melt the snow outside.

Warmth radiates through my body.

"I've missed you." Her words are soft vibrations of verbal melody. Her warm breath caresses my neck. Goosebumps bloom along my skin. My heart ricochets, bouncing off the walls of my rib cage.

"Ditto, Moonchild."

The bags fall on the floor by my feet. I let my eyes close for a moment as I wrap my arms around her soft curves, clinging to her as if she's my lifeline, letting her seep through my bones.

She feels so good in my arms.

And then it happens.

My short-lived moment of happiness slips out of my hands like an eel.

Cori's body grows tense.

A bad feeling slithers up the back of my neck. I hold on to her, wishing time would freeze.

Gently, but with firmness, her palms press against the sleeve of my puffer jacket. Corded muscles of my biceps bunch as she pulls out of my arms. Her gaze slips to Red standing next to me. And all I can do is watch Cori's rigid posture as the shine dims from her eyes.

"Cori, this is . . ." my voice trails because I don't even know the name of this woman standing beside me. A stab of self-loathing tears off little chunks of my heart and soul.

"Hi," Cori interrupts me, her attention on Red. "I'm Coriander."

I realize what she's doing. She knows I don't know my companion's name.

Way to go, Dean! Give the man the Douche of the Year Award.

"Meredith." The two women shake hands.

Meredith. I store her name away in my mental file.

"You're as beautiful as I've imagined," Meredith adds.

"Thank you." A faint, genuine smile appears on Cori's lips. I wait for her to glance my way, but she doesn't look at me.

A wave of nausea rises and falls in my stomach. But I don't have time to react, because Cam is on his feet. He drops the remote on the sofa, arches a brow in my direction, silently letting me know I'm a complete dick.

Duly noted.

"Just gonna stand there, or coming in?" he asks, voice dry.

Lucas and Kate slowly rise to their feet, along with Emma. Their gazes swivel from Meredith to me. Lucas' expression is blank. For a brief moment, I catch my sister's eyes widen in surprise, before replacing it with a polite smile.

"Uncle Dean!" The hushed atmosphere is punctured by Emma's enthusiastic greeting.

I manage a short laugh, crouch down to my knees and open my arms for her hug. "Hey. Good to see you. Did you get taller?" I ask once she's out of my arms, and I'm back on my feet.

"Daddy said I grew an inch." I hear the pride in Emma's voice.

"Stop growing. I'm not ready to deal with you as a tween yet." Even though my attention is on Emma, I am aware of Cori's every move. From the pasted-on smile, to the way she scrapes a hand through her hair.

Emma laughs. "What's a tween?"

"Well, that's the stage before becoming a teenager," Red says next to me.

Shit, I've completely forgotten about her.

"Oh, thank you." Emma smiles then turns her brilliant green eyes on me. "Are you a friend of Uncle Dean?" she asks innocently.

"Yes, sort of," Red answers with a warm smile. "And you are?"

"Emma. My dad—" She looks over her shoulder at Lucas, who is now standing behind her, along with Kate. "—and Uncle Dean are best friends."

I take off my black puffer jacket and hang it on the hook by the door, then my gaze zones in on Cori. Last time we saw each other was almost a week ago, and I can't take my eyes off her.

I slowly appraise her disheveled appearance—the faded jeans containing a few paint spots from her days in the studio, the mismatched socks I gave her as a stocking stuffer for Christmas, the beige, oversized sweater that buries her slim frame, her unruly mess of dark hair that my fingers are aching to be burrowed in.

"Well, nice to meet you, Emma." Meredith's voice snaps me out of my stupor. "I love your name."

Lucas, Kate, and Cam introduce themselves. Afterward, Cam returns his attention to the basketball game.

"Thank you." Emma whips her head of dark hair in Cori's direction. "I thought you were Uncle Dean's girlfriend."

A dead, cold silence hovers over the room. Everything seems to go in slow motion, spinning like a top as everyone gazes at me, their blurred bodies creating waves on my vision.

"No, honey," Cori's voice slices through the silence. "Dean and I aren't boyfriend and girlfriend."

"Oh." Emma tilts her head to look at Cori. "Then what are you guys?"

"Oh, we're just friends," Cori answers.

Her words, though somewhat truthful, are too indifferent. They seep into me, turning my emotions jagged, my insides tight.

"Hey." Lucas glances at his watch then lowers his gaze at Emma. "Why don't we have a tea party in the kitchen and give Uncle Dean and Meredith some time to settle?"

"Oh, yes!" Emma's upturned face is beaming. Her attention now fully on her tea party with her father.

Kate laughs. "Can I come?"

Emma slips one tiny hand in Kate's. "Of course." She hesitates for a moment and looks at her dad. "Is that okay, Dad? I mean it's usually just the two of us, but I think Kate will have fun."

Lucas chuckles. "Of course. Let's go." They head for the kitchen, stop. "Come on, Cam." Lucas says over his shoulder. "Come drink imaginary tea with us."

Cam groans. "I thought we were heading out for real drinks."

"In a minute," Lucas says, voice firm. "Let's go."

Cam clicks the television off, then disappears, along with everyone else, leaving me alone with Cori and Meredith.

"Um." Cori is the first to speak. "I'm going to join them." She turns on her heels, stops, and fixes her eyes on Meredith. "Welcome, Meredith." Briefly she glances in my direction. "We're heading out for dinner. Joining us?"

This is where I should claim fatigue, fake a headache or another malady, rather than put the three of us through any more hell. Instead I hear myself answer, "Yeah, give us ten minutes."

"A broken friendship can be a comma, or a full stop."

THE BEER BOTTLE DANGLES BETWEEN my fingers. I'm sandwiched between Red . . . Meredith, and my sister. I sit in silence, taking in the scene. The local restaurant is fairly dark, but in a cozy, homey sort of way. The conversation around the table changes from one subject to another, quick as the movement of some wild animal.

Everyone is having a good time, even Meredith. The tension from earlier seems to have melted away. Yet, I feel painfully out of place, like a pepperoni that had mistakenly made its way onto a vegetarian pizza.

"Do you still have friends in California?" Meredith asks Cam, after he finishes a story about his former life back in San Francisco.

"A few." Cam answers. "One of my good friends still lives there."

"Reagan." Lucas drapes one arm over the back of Kate's chair, who is holding a sleeping Emma. "Your college sweetheart."

"For the, oh I don't know, millionth time, we're friends," Cam says good-naturedly. Nothing ruffles Cam's feathers; the guy is always cool as a cucumber. Must be the surfing lifestyle he embodies so well.

Reagan's role in Cam's life is an on-going debate between my two friends. Lucas thinks Cam secretly wants her. Cam disagrees. Once in a while, I join in the torture for the kick of watching Cam squirm. Truthfully, I do think the dude has it bad for his friend, but what does it matter? They are thousands of miles away. And based on the last update, she's in a serious relationship with an actor. One of those that's not quite an A list, but well on his way.

"She's hot as sin," Lucas continues, pushing our friend's buttons. "I have a trip to San Francisco in a few weeks. Why don't you give me her info? I'll take her out to dinner."

"Have you forgotten she's in a relationship?"

Lucas shrugs. "No, but I can make her forget."

Kate elbows Lucas. Cam flips him the bird.

Satisfied, Lucas laughs then says, "Men and women can't be friends."

"We're friends," Kate points out.

"You're also one of my best friends' sister. That makes you completely untouchable."

"Actually, I agree with you, Lucas," Meredith adds, "attraction eventually gets the better of any straight male and female friends."

Lucas nods. "Sex gets in the way."

I roll the beer bottle between my fingers, listening. When it comes to this burning topic, everybody's got an opinion and an anecdote to share.

"Cori and Dean are friends." Cam tips his chin in my direction. "What do you guys think?"

My gaze zones in on Cori, giving her an opportunity to speak first. She remains as quiet and expressionless as a nun's face.

"Friendship between men and women is not impossible," I say, one of the few times I've spoken tonight.

"As long as there are caveats," Cori adds.

A hush falls over the table, everyone on standby. You'd think *When Harry Met Sally* would have already settled this question a quarter century ago, but you'd be wrong. The debate continues to come up again and again.

"Caveats?" I ask quietly, almost to myself.

"Yes." Cori leans forward, elbows on the table. "Don't cross the friend zone." Staring straight at me, she adds, "Ever."

My mind whirls as emotions thrash through me. Regret. Guilt. An indisputable sense of sadness, because a once-strong friendship has disintegrated. After taking a long sip of courage from my beer, I say, "I disagree."

Cori tucks a handful of hair behind her ear. Lucas taps his fingers on the table.

"If two people are attracted to each other," I continue, "there's nothing wrong with exploring it."

Cam lifts a brow. On my left, Meredith takes a sip of her wine. Kate slides me a pained look. As if she senses that Cori and I have crossed the line, and shit hit the fan, she sits a little straighter. Lucas gives my sister's shoulder a light squeeze.

Cori shakes her head. "The friendship will never recover. It's not worth it."

My heart sinks. "If the foundation of the friendship is solid, it won't crumble, even if two friends choose to step out of the friend zone."

Our friends' gazes ping-pong between Cori and I.

"Only if both sides are honest going into the FF zone," Meredith adds.

"FF?" Kate asks quietly.

"Fuck friends," Lucas says with a smile.

"Then both will know that it's solely about sex," Cori says.

For the record, sex with Cori was never only about satisfying a physical need.

Cam rubs his chin. "So, you're saying the two parties involved should be sure they are on the same page if they choose to step out of the friend zone?"

"Absolutely," Cori answers. "I'm not saying they need to have a contract, but they should at least have a loose discussion about what it is they're doing, and what they're committed to going forward."

The night when she came over, she attempted to initiate a conversation. But I had been so eager to be with her, I never gave her a chance to voice her thoughts. Was that what she was trying to do? Establish boundaries, expectations?

"Then neither party can accuse the other of using each other," Cori adds in a low voice.

Is that what she thinks? That I used her to satisfy some sick fantasy of two friends getting it on? The thick silence continues, chilling me.

"Otherwise." Cori tilts her chin up, meeting my eyes. "There will be emotional fallout, and then the friendship is doomed."

Regret washes over me in long, slow waves. Each one is icy cold and sends shivers down my spine. "Is that how you feel?"

"Absolutely," she answers without a beat.

Her words hang in the air like an eagle floating on the wind. Our gazes meet and hold for two to three seconds. An odd feeling cranks over my chest. Exasperation, I decide, and look down at my beer bottle.

No one speaks, everyone's waiting for my rebuttal. But I stay quiet. This isn't the time or place for me to convince Cori how her presence in my life—even as only a friend—is a fundamental piece of who I am.

After a long, awkward moment, I down my drink, throw a couple of bills on the table, push my chair back, and rise to my feet. "See you guys back at the house."

The worst feeling I'll ever know is sitting next to the person who means the world to me, and I can't touch her. Trying to spend time with Cori is like playing scratch off. We're under the same roof, at times in the same proximity, but never close enough, never alone. All day today, Cori and I have managed to co-exist in the house. She speaks to me when necessary. For the most part, she's managed to avoid being alone with me, giving us zero opportunity to speak about the big elephant in the room.

Us.

Hence, the reason why, when Cam asks Red to go on a few runs with him, I leave the slope early and return to the cabin. This morning, Cori volunteered to babysit Emma after her ski lesson ended. Which means, we're alone. For the most part.

A chill runs up my spine. Not from the cold outside, but the truth that waits for me inside. I exhale a heavy breath, then open the door.

My eyes are on Cori. She's lying on her stomach on the floor, her dark hair is loose and spills over her shoulders, legs crisscrossed in the air, deep in a conversation with Emma. Whatever the little girl said made her laugh. The sound of her laughter enthralls me.

A vision of Cori as a mother unfolds before me.

My heart rate kicks up a notch at the thought of Cori holding a baby, soothing her with lullabies, while stroking her tiny back and soft hair.

Our baby.

And that's when everything hits me, the full reality of my feelings for Cori. When she gives birth, I want it to be my baby, no one else's.

Holy shit! She's the one.

My soulmate.

My forever.

My heart stops, then pounds excitedly against my rib cage.

I stand, mesmerized, in a trance, until Emma says, "Auntie Cori, Uncle Dean is back."

I notice when Cori's shoulders go rigid. After a long stretch, she rolls to her side, tilts her head toward the door. "You're back early."

Her voice is filled with discomfort. She doesn't want to be alone with me. This truth makes my stomach roll.

"Yeah." Removing my wet gloves, I set them on the table by the window, then close the door behind me.

"Emma and I were in the middle of an intense game of Candyland."

We look at each other for a beat, then our gazes slide rapidly away from each other. Hers falls on the board game on the rust colored rug.

I snap my ski boots open, kick them off, and leave them next to the pile of shoes. Then I pad across the floor to where Cori and Emma are sitting. "Hey, Em, I need to speak to Auntie Cori."

"We're in the middle—" Cori starts, but Emma is already on her feet. I fucking love that little girl.

"Sure." She looks us over with all the innocence of a five-year-old. "Are you two fighting like mommy and daddy used to do?"

For a split second, Cori's eyes widen, then she takes Emma's tiny hands in hers. "Dean and I aren't fighting, sweetheart."

"Okay. I don't want you to stop loving each other." Emma smiles, all trace of concern no longer evident. "I'll be in my room." She starts to leave then stops. "Oh." Her green eyes rest on the board game on the floor. "Should I clean up now?"

"Don't worry about it," Cori answers, "I'll clean up."

"Okay."

Once Emma's footsteps disappear, I take off my black puffer jacket and hang it on the hook by the door, then I face Cori. This is our first time alone since . . . our night together. I want to touch her. Kiss her. Bury myself inside her.

"I better clean up," she says in a low voice.

Drawing on my fine command of the English language, I say nothing. We stand in the heavy silence, staring at each other, awkward as strangers. We always have something to talk about—city or state politics, a novel we've read, a movie we've seen. Conversations between Cori and I have always been easy, never forced. Even the quiet moments are always comfortable, never strained.

I stand, rooted to the spot, heart in my mouth.

Nothing is happening.

Everything is happening.

Our unsettled eyes glance unceremoniously around and try to avoid catching each other.

Tension coils deep inside my gut.

I shift my weight from foot to foot, hoping the blaring quiet will come to an end.

"You went on a date with Brandon?" My voice slices through the silence.

She blows out a breath. "I met with Brandon to let him know we weren't going to work."

Hope flutters in my stomach. "Why?"

"There was no chemistry."

Another lapse of silence sweeps the space. My gaze follows as Cori rearranges the pillows on the sofa. The lack of any audible sound continues to echo in the room. When she starts folding the plaid comforter, I say, "You can leave that there."

She stops, looks at it, then back at me.

"I slept there last night, and I will tonight," I say, because it's important for her to know there's nothing going on between Meredith and me.

Her gaze roams over my large frame then back to the sofa. "Aren't you uncomfortable?"

258

My heart squeezes at her concern. Couches don't make the best sleeping surfaces, not for a guy with my build. This morning, I woke up with a crick in my neck, and my spine out of alignment, after spending the night on the sofa. I frown. "I'll survive one more night."

She nods. Not what I was hoping for, but at least she's aware I'm not shacking up with Meredith. The discussion suddenly turned to silence, dark and heavy, reminding me of a hovering storm cloud.

"Meredith is nice," she says quietly.

I nod, not sure where she's going with this. But she's right, Meredith is doing her best, considering how I selfishly threw her in a hostile environment. After the initial shock, everyone has warmed up to her, even Cori. "Yes, she is."

"I should put this away." She lowers herself to her knees in front of the board game.

I'm quick by her side, squatting in front of her. "I got it."

"No," she says a little too quickly. "It's okay. I got it."

We reach for the pieces of Candyland together. Our hands touch. My heart rattles. I hold on to her fingers for a second before she pulls away.

"Cori."

"Dean," her voice cracks on my name. She closes her eyes temporarily and inhales. Slowly she rises to her feet.

I follow. "We need to talk."

"About what, exactly? The fact that you freaked out after we had sex, because you thought I wanted more?"

259

"No." I rake a hand through my hair. Every muscle in her face is tense, and without a word, she communicates intense mistrust, anger, and hurt. "Yes," I admit in a rough voice. "I got scared about the baby thing."

"And you brought Meredith here."

"I'm an asshole."

The conversation collapses like a depressed concertina. Cori's chin trembles, her eyes brimmed with tears threatening to spill. My heart deflates. I wish I could wipe away all the sadness etched on her face.

I know that's a selfish want.

How can I take away her sorrow, when I'm the reason behind her grief?

She didn't ask for my stupidity. It arrived like the gift she never wanted.

"Remember that night at *Une Pression?*"

With a slight nod, I acknowledge the night Cori revealed she wanted to settle down.

"I said to you, if I ever walk away from you, it'll be because you hand me the scissors to cut the string." Her voice is strained, empty.

My heart drops. No. Our friendship can't end like this. "Cori, let me explain." I take a step toward her. She steps back, standing, arms crossed, as fragile as a spider's web.

"Do you know what hurts?"

The fire snaps and pops, flinging sparks. The air is full of unspoken words, unformulated guilt. I wait, sick of myself, sick of who I am.

"You're the person who always used to make me feel special."

The hurt in her voice layered with absolute steel stabs me to the heart. I drag a hand through my hair. "That's because you are and will always be."

"Then how can you make me feel so unwanted?" Her voice cracks again. She lowers her head for a long minute, hiding behind a curtain of rich brown hair. With a heavy breath, she lifts her lashes and meets my gaze. Her expression is dialed to an unbearable sadness that I can't take.

Sadness because of me.

"Let me explain."

"Please go." Her voice is full of decision, a finality.

The temperature in the room sinks, and my heart hitches a ride. All my instincts urge me to cry out to her, I love you. Come sit with me; hold my hand. Eat chips with me. Call me friend. Look into my eyes, connect, because I've fallen for you.

The idea we can never be together as lovers or as friends is too much of a strain. When she turns, at last, to face me, there are no trace of tears. Her eyes are narrowed, rigid, cold, hard. In that moment, I know I've lost her.

We stare at each other for a long minute as her words seep into my blood, paralyzing my brain. In her eyes, I see she's speaking her truth, the whole truth, naked, cold, and fatal as a patriot's blade.

During our friendship, she's cried on my shoulder countless times. I've been her anchor, the one who heals her.

The fact that I've continued to hurt her slices through me.

What am I supposed to do now?

I've always been the one to stop her pain; now I'm the one inflicting it.

The one who breaks her.

I nod, accepting her decision. In love or not, I can't hurt her anymore.

And this is our time keeper with a passion for repercussion, because we acted on our emotions and blurred the lines. For over two decades, we've been inseparable, stuck together like glue. And poof, just like that, Cori and I are no more.

This is our end.

Cold air washes over the room. Everyone is back from today's ski adventure. "Everything's good?" Lucas ask from the door.

"Yeah." I shove a hand through my hair and nod. "Meredith and I are leaving first thing in the morning."

Chapter 27

"My guy best friends know my feelings."

TECHNICALLY, LAST WEEK WAS the start of Cori's absence. But today, my first day back from our disastrous ski trip, is the first full day without her in my life.

The desire to talk to her is on high.

Whatever I do, she's on my mind. In fact, I find pieces of her in everything I do.

10:00 AM

I stop at our favorite coffee shop and order our usual bulletproof coffee. I should click a selfie with her favorite beverage and send it to her.

Oops! You are not with me right now. I Miss U.

12:00 PM

I have just finished pizza with our favorite topping—anchovies. This topping is the real original topping that came out of Naples. Salty, delicious, perhaps a controversial choice for some, but always a winner for Cori and I.

As I get up to leave, I stop and wait for you.

Oops! You are not with me right now. I Miss U.

2:10 PM

Since I can't focus on work, I'm reading an article on Simple Things about *inding hygge*. I find it very interesting and decide to take a pic of the important points. I take a screen shot and scroll to your name. After a long pause, I set the phone back on my desk.

Shit. We're no longer on speaking terms. What the fuck!

2:20 PM

Rarely do I lose my cool, but today, I almost shouted at Cam when he plopped on my couch with a bag of chips, chewing loudly as fuck.

Fuck! You are not with me right now. My mood is off. I miss U again.

4:00 PM

I am struggling to remember one of my friends' cell numbers. I realize that I remember about six phone numbers from my long contact list. Yours is one of them.

Why aren't we talking again? I Miss U.

4:40 PM

My Google search history of today is *recipes with coriander*. Countless tabs are open. I want to discuss all the one hundred and twenty recipes that came up on my search.

I shouldn't have freaked out about getting you pregnant. I shouldn't have brought Meredith to New Hampshire. Let me love you. I Miss U.

CAM PASSES THE BALL INBOUNDS to me. I make a fast break down the court and pass the ball to Lucas for a wide-open layup.

We take a two point lead.

"Hit the gym, your game is weak," Lucas says over my shoulder, already in defensive mode.

This is day two sans Coriander. We're at the local Y in downtown Princeton, engaged in an intense three-on-three basketball game with the Serrano brothers. Cam became buddies with them after he worked with the older brother, Rafa, on the financial part of a pipeline effort to bring clean water to Haiti.

We're playing the third game of best of three. Each team has taken one game. The losing team picks up the tab at Winberries afterward. My adrenaline is pumped. Cori is not on my mind. This is just what I needed, a physical challenge to release my pent-up energy.

That's a lie. Cori is right there, front and center in my mind, my heart. She owns me. I wish she was here, sitting on the bleachers, cheering me on, just like Zander's fiancée, Colbie is cheering her man on.

Cam steals the ball from Max, the younger of the Serrano brothers. He passes the ball to me. I give myself a mental shake, and release a fade away shot. The ball turns repeatedly

265

around the edge of the basket, until it veers away from the net. The sound of rubber hits the polished, wooden floor.

The Serrano brothers have the ball. As they run their offense, we play tough defense and give up nothing. Well, Cam and Lucas are playing tough defense. My body has no spring, no vibrancy. I wipe the sweat sliding down my forehead. My legs are heavy and weak. I'm guarding Zander, the former Navy Seal, who got his leg blown off in Iraq. He's in a wheelchair, so I have to respect the imaginary cylinder that marks his available space.

Don't let the wheelchair fool you. The guy is a beast and takes no prisoners. He wheels the chair and bounces the ball simultaneously as he makes a fast break down the court and scores. His two brothers give the usual congratulatory high-five.

"Dude, you're so slow. If you move any slower, time will stop," Zander says as he wheels past me.

The trash talking continues for the next twenty minutes. The lead shifts from team to team. Cam attempts a shot and misses. I go for the ball, but Rafa cuts under the net and snatches the rebound. He slows the game down, passing and passing, until the right moment comes. Then, the asshole releases a high-arching jump shot and hollers, "Nothing but net."

Swish!

Game over.

After the game, Zander leaves with Colbie. Since I drove with Cam and Lucas, I have no choice but to hang out. We eat lots of wings, drink beer, and talk a lot about nothing. Oh, yeah, I watch the guys flirt with a few women. I make no effort to join in the fun.

This is no longer about my dick sulking. The bastard is still pissed off, but there's no fun in the game for me anymore. My heart has found its home in Cori.

"YOUR GAME WAS OFF tonight," Lucas says next to me over The Roots on the radio. We're on the Palisades Interstate Parkway heading back to Alpine. Roads are sparsely illuminated. Traffic is light.

"A bit." My attention stays on the road, but I can feel Lucas' brown eyes studying me.

"You slept with her, didn't you?"

My jaw clenches. From the corner of my eye, I notice Lucas rake a hand through his dark hair. I tap the up arrow on the steering wheel and fill the space with the sound of Otis Reading.

"Time to confess, bro," Cam says from the backseat.

From the rearview mirror, I cast a glance at Cam's face, buried in his phone as he types away. "What are you doing?"

"Right now, I just finished kicking Reagan's ass in a Scrabble game." He looks up from his phone, a satisfied grin on his face. "So how did you fuck it up?"

"Don't want to talk about it."

Cam scoffs. "I wrote a poem last night, want to hear it?"

"Do I have a choice?"

"Roses are red, shit is brown—"

"Shut the fuck up, I'm in a bad mood," I finish.

"Yeah." Cam places one of his large hands my shoulders. "But we don't care about you."

"Answer Cam's question," Lucas presses. "How did you fuck it up?"

"What do you want me to tell you?"

"Tell us you're an idiot for letting your other head ruin a twenty-year friendship," Lucas answers in a voice laced with disappointment.

Get in line, buddy.

Someone, please put a muzzle on both of them. Then again, if I can't talk to these two knuckleheads, my male best friends, who the hell can I talk to?

Cori.

Except, we're no longer on speaking terms.

And so, I tell them the whole story, minus the graphic details. But my brain burns with the memory. How perfectly fit we were together. After I finish, I exhale, flick the signal, and turn left to Lucas' house.

Cam extends his hand toward Lucas. "Pay up."

Lucas groans, reaches in a pocket for a bill, and slaps it in Cam's hand. "You fucked up," he says directly at me.

"No shit, Sherlock." My brows raise. "Were you betting on when I'd sleep with Cori?"

Cam shakes his head. "Nope. Just that you were with her that Sunday when you went AWOL."

Fuckers.

Lucas leans forward and locks me in a serious stare. "You give a fuck, right?"

Of course I give a fuck. When it comes to Cori, I give lots of fuck. As a matter of fact, I'm a fucking prostitute of feelings.

"You're in love with her, right?" Lucas continues, his eyes never wavering from me. "Otherwise, we're boys and all, but I just might beat the shit out of you, because you know . . . Cori is part of the clique."

"Of course I'm in love with her."

"Have you told her?" Cam asks.

I shake my head. "Never had a chance."

"You know where she lives, where she works. You have her phone number, probably even know her daily routine like a true boyfriend." Lucas claps my shoulder. "You have all the opportunities you need. If you want to be together you have to. get. her."

Lucas' words are on replay in my head. Inside my house, I go straight to my bedroom, strip off my clothes and shower. After that, I pick up my phone and scroll to Cori's name. Ignoring the little voice of doubt whispering to let her be, I quickly type a text and press SEND:

Hey! I miss you. Let's talk. Coffee?

I wait.

My textpectation makes me antsy. The anticipation. I check my phone several times. No answer.

Two hours later. Zilch.

It's three in the morning. And still nothing.

Silence is an answer, too.

Have you ever been punched in the stomach by Muhammad Ali? Me, either. But now, I know what it feels like. The blow-off knocks every wisp of air from my lungs. In the dark, I lay on my bed, flat on my back, staring at the ceiling with my arms crossed under my head.

Cori is out of my life. No amount of pain has ever felt so agonizing or concentrated. It's like a giant hole has pummeled into my chest, with no hope of repair. Tears start to cloud my vision, and a single stream falls down my face.

Before we start with the name calling such as 'you're weak, a pussy,' let's get a few things straight.

Number one: I have the utmost respect for the pussy.

Number two: Men hate to cry. They rarely ever do. When a man cries over a woman, I guarantee you, he loves her, because men only cry when they lose something, or when they are afraid of losing something that they love as much—or more—than they love themselves.

Number three: I did say tears were shed. Why does it always have to be the woman shedding the tears?

"Every girl needs a guy friend to help her laugh when she thinks she'll never smile again."

DAY 2:

Dear Life,

Whatever, motherfucker. Whatever.

My three moods today:

I'm empty, sober, and joyless, like a sheet of paper.

That evening, I get sloshed. Alone. At a bar in New York. Then I catch the path and Uber my ass home.

Pathetic.

DAY 3:

Waking up after a night of drinking with a hammering headache and a stomach rolling around like a sneaker in a washing machine is not as fun as it used to be in college. I drag my ass to the kitchen and grab an isotonic sports drink to rehydrate myself for some much-needed energy.

Later in the day, Lucas stops by my office on his way out. "Cam and I are heading to the city. You joining us?"

271

"No," I answer, eyes on my computer. "Need to work." Total bullshit. The truth is, I don't want to do much. My mind's a mess. My life's a wreck.

When I finally make it home, I watch Netflix until I've seen every documentary my subscription has to offer, and yet, nothing seems to smooth my heartbreak or soothe the longing I feel.

True Story: Breakups are a bitch, and heartbreak is a bigger bitch than fucking karma.

DAY 4:

I'm a smart guy. I can compartmentalize my feelings. Emotions this strong for another person should be considered suspicious anyway. I also have bigger priorities to think about—like the pile of work on my desk—than the health of my heart and mind.

I think I can say, with pretty solid confidence, most people would rather get smacked in the face with a metal pole than get their hearts broken. It's why we try to avoid it.

This is too consuming. Time to wash all those lovey-dovey chemicals out of my system and bring the old Dean back.

My head says, "Time heals all wounds. Who cares if Cori is out of my life?"

My heart says, "You do, dumb fuck."

DAY 5:

My week continues its downward spiral. All the butterflies in my stomach have died. Stuck between mourning and longing, I'm wrestling with the urge to text, or call Cori again.

Just when I'm ready to succumb to my heart, I tell myself if she wants to talk to me, she'd reach out to me.

But this self-scolding doesn't exterminate the heartache.

P.S. I wonder if life smokes after it fucks you?

DAY 6:

Dear Cori,

My heart is a blender of amplified emotions. It has taken a beating lately. Right now, I am angry, confused, sad, happy, scared, lost.

More importantly, my heart is hurting. This heartache of mine is like the music of a great orchestra. At some times, it is quiet and allows me to function; at other times, the violins play, and I'm morose. And then, it rises to a crescendo, and the anger bursts from my chest in a vicious shout of anguish. At this point, there is a flute playing, and I am able to remember you with fondness. I enjoy this moment.

Many more emotions have been added to the mix, but these are the primary ingredients.

Need.

Desire.

Lust.

Love.

I want you to feel me deep inside you. I want to hear you moan my name. I want to hear the sound of your voice as you go over the edge. I want to hear you beg me to fuck you harder. I want to make you smile. I want to be your anchor. I want you, all of you.

I am lost in the torrid vortex of the moment.

I need you.

I want you.

I love you.

I feel it all.

Chapter 29

"We'll always be best friends, because I love you too much."

SUFFERING. THAT'S HOW I can describe the last few days. Although, I believe it's much more than just 'suffering'. It's a plethora of shattered bones, burning flesh, and cracked skulls.

In other words, I miss Coriander. Badly. Almost two weeks later, the smell of her perfume is still stuck in my bedroom, on my clothes.

No, it's not about dipping my stick in the pool one more time. Well, that would be nice, too, but this hollow feeling inside me runs deeper than that.

Memories of her continues to tip-toe their way into my dreams. I miss Cori's laugh. Her pale pink lips that remind me of a perfect rose bud. How many times have I stared at them when she bites her pencil in concentration, drinks from her mug, or applies lip balm to keep them soft?

I want to feel her lips against mine.

A week since we've last talked. Two weeks since she's lain in my arms . . . an eternity in my world. There's a void in my heart that only Cori's presence can eradicate. We've gone from seeing each other at least twice a week, calling and texting every day, to nothing.

Since my last text attempt, I haven't reached out to her. Not because I don't want to, but I'm stuck in uncertainty lane, unsure about where to go from here. Every day is agony. The line between friendship and whatever-the-fuck we are now has become blurred. Relating, and communicating, and so many other facets of us have become ambiguous.

"Oh, Dean," my mother is saying, "the cleaning crew found these buttons in your father's library." She places three light-blue buttons on the table in front of me. "Figure they're yours since you changed your shirt the other night."

"Yeah, thanks." The events of the night flip through my brain like a slide show—Cori and I dancing. The way she stepped on my feet. The sound of her voice as she begged me to touch her.

Just thinking about that scene has my heart thumping harder, my dick straining against my zipper. Since I have no desire to sport a boner during a family dinner, I manage to shove those thoughts to the back of my head.

I take the buttons and stuff them into my jeans pocket. From across the table, my sister is assessing me. I'm ignoring her. Not up for her interrogation. We're at our parents having dinner. Truthfully, I'd like to be home on my bed, wallowing in my sadness. Watching more documentaries on Netflix.

Needless to say, I've been in a funk. Some might even call it heartbroken.

"Darling, what's bothering you?"

I meet my mother's worried eyes. "Nothing," I lie. For the most part, I've managed to hold shit together and bury myself in my work. At night is when I fall apart, as my mind grapples with questions.

What the fuck happened?

Did I really think we could become the next Harry and Sally, Dylan and Jamie?

The romantic comedy section of Netflix might say yes, but we all know reality is a little more complex and totally unscripted.

How can I make her forgive me?

Being an idiot is part of a man's genetic makeup. Cori's smart, she should understand that.

"You don't look well," my mother continues.

My sister snorts.

Ignoring her, I say, "I'm fine." But my voice is sullen. How can I explain my emotional turmoil? Even to me, it doesn't make sense. One minute I'm swallowed by sadness, which makes me mad. Madness takes over, making me angry. Anger then consumes me, making me mad. The cycle continues.

"Word on the street is, you've been staying late in the office," my father says.

His source is none other than our office manager and Cori's grandmother. I've been avoiding the woman like the plague. Out of guilt. "Lots of work lately."

"Yeah, but don't use work to escape whatever is bothering you."

I nod. My dad is one of those guys who believes in life-work balance. He and his partners have no problem shutting the office down once in a while for a surprise company picnic or giving their employees a day to themselves.

"Did Cori turn you down for one of those—" My grandmother waves her hands, the tiny wrinkles on her forehead scrunching together. She snaps and smiles. "—hipsters. That's the word."

I smile and shake my head. "Grandma, there's nothing going on between Cori and me." *But I wish there were.* While we're on Cori's type, she's not into hipsters.

I take a forkful of the braised short ribs Dad prepared earlier, with black truffle potato puree, wilted swiss chard, and port glaze on the side. I told you, the man is a master in the kitchen.

"You should write a cookbook," I say to Dad. "I need the recipe for this one."

My dad laughs, takes Mom's hand in his, and brings it to his lips. The dude is a romantic. "Son," he says, his voice filled with admiration for his blushing wife. "I'll give you the recipe when you find that special woman."

"He has a special woman," says my seventy-year-old, nosy grandmother. "Cori. He's in love with Cori. Give him the recipe."

Jesus!

"Are you and Cori together?" my dad asks.

"We're . . ." My voice trails. Cori and I are neither on good terms or bad terms. We are no longer anything. "It's complicated."

"Then no recipe," Dad gloats. "Let me know when the status changes, and I'll gladly take you shopping for the ingredients."

My parents look at each other and smile. Kate continues eating. Her silence makes me wary. When my sister has nothing to say, be prepared to feel her wrath.

A FUNDAMENTAL THING I'VE LEARNED the last few weeks is that emotional pain has a biological purpose: to teach, to educate us away from unhealthy patterns and relationships. I want Cori back in my life, not only as a friend, but as her boyfriend. There's only one problem.

I haven't figured out how to get my girl back. I know the beginning and the middle of the story, as most fools do. It's the end I fear.

The cogs in my head are still turning when my office door opens. My sister strolls in, looking pissed as hell. Without even a glance in my direction, she struts straight to the framed, autographed, LeBron James poster and removes it from the hooks where it hangs beautifully on the wall.

What the fuck!

My breath hitches. Surely she's on crack for even touching such a treasure? This isn't only about the King of basketball. It's about the moment captured in time. I was there, in the overheated arena, full of excited and red-faced fans, when one of the hottest players in the NBA made a breakaway, jumping high in the air, right at the basketball, stuffing the ball for the winning score, and clinching their spot as NBA Champs.

Cautiously, I ask, "What are you doing?"

"Give me one reason why I shouldn't destroy your most prized possession?"

Uh. "Because it's LeBron fucking James." Carefully, I walk over and remove the framed poster from her clenched fingers, then restore it to its rightful place. "What's the problem?"

The way her eyes squint when she glares at me reminds me of a pit viper's slit-like pupils. I release a deep breath. A burning animosity is in her brown orbs, and I can tell I'm the root cause of the problem.

"Cori and I had lunch today."

My ears perk. Shoving my hands in my black slacks, I ask, "How is she?"

"Fine." Kate eyes me up and down before settling on my face. "What's going on between you two?"

"Why do you ask?"

"Because she looks like shit."

This makes me happy. Cori never looks like shit. Even when sick with the flu, she manages to look adorable. If, indeed, what Kate is saying is true, that only means she misses me.

Yes. A burst of hope rises in me.

Don't even start with the eye roll. For the sake of my shattered and broken heart, I, also, look like shit. Look at me. Three days' scruff. Bagged eyes. And the messy hair, it's not because I'm trendy and going for the just-rolled-out-of-bed look.

Exactly. I look like shit. I'm heartbroken. Destroyed.

"Also, when I brought up your name, she started acting weird."

"Define weird?"

"Oh, I don't know, try bawling her eyes out." Kate stares at me, hands on hips. "So, what gives?"

I release a deep breath, but say nothing.

"You slept with her?" Kate's voice is low, anger thick on every word.

"I sleep with a lot of women. You have to be more specific." Yeah, I'm stalling.

"Coriander Phillips." She jabs a finger into my chest. "You slept with Cori, my best friend, Dean." Her nail pokes the fabric of my shirt. I'd be surprised if I'm not bleeding at this point. "She's a sister to me." Another finger jab. "To us."

I hold her hand then step out of her reach. "First of all, I've never viewed Cori as a sister. Friend, yes, but never a sister."

"You're not denying the two of you had sex."

281

A long weighted silence hangs over the room. I drag a hand through my hair. "What is this about, Kate?" Notice how I avoided discussing whatever happened between Coriander and me?

"She's supposed to be untouchable. The same way I'm untouchable to your friends."

My eyes narrow. The other night, she was at Lucas' house, hanging out with him and Emma, like a big happy fucking family. "Which one of those assholes is sweet talking you?"

"No way, don't try to change the topic." She huffs and crosses her arms over her chest. "This is about Cori and the fact that you hurt her."

"She's not talking to me, Kate."

"Can you blame her?" She shakes her head. "You slept with her, then brought a woman with you to our yearly getaway, and rubbed it in her face. God, Dean, how can you be such an asshole?

I release a deep breath and drag a hand through my hair. Truth is, I am an asshole. "I'm not sleeping with Cori." Not anymore. For fuck's sake, we slept together one night. Okay we had sex all night and had the best morning sex of my life. My dick twitches. Mention Cori, and the asshole comes to life. "And her name is Meredith. She's not a bimbo." Angry maybe. The 'go fuck yourself' text I received a little while after I dropped her home pretty much sealed the deal of ever salvaging a friendship. Can't blame the woman.

"So, Cori was a one-time screw?"

"Of course not." Jesus H. Christ. My head hurts. I rub my eyes, suppressing the headache coming on. "Why are you so upset?"

"Other than the fact that now, there's tension between my brother and a woman I consider a sister." She looks me up and down, disgust in her brown eyes. "Cori is in love with you. Do you know that? She's always been." Another frustrated sigh leaves her mouth. "God knows, I don't know why."

Kate is still talking, but I've stopped listening since the Cori-is-in-love-with-you bit. "What did you say?" I ask, needing confirmation that the words I heard were not a figment of my imagination.

"You're an inconsiderate asshole."

Inconsiderate asshole. Check. Got it. "Before that."

"You brought one of your bimbos on our ski trip, even though you're sleeping with Cori, which makes you an inconsiderate asshole."

Technically Cori and I were not sleeping together, but that's neither here nor there. I shake my head impatiently. "Before that."

Kate's brows knit together. "She's in love with you. Does that make you happy?"

Yes! My heart leaps. "Actually, it does." I lean into my sister and place a kiss on her forehead. "I'll see you later."

"Where are you going?"

I lock my laptop and head to the door. "You're smart, figure it out."

"Dean." She's quick by my side. One of her hands on my arm, silently pleading for me to keep my distance.

Not gonna happen.

Time to get my friend, my girl, back. "Cori and I need to talk."

"Cori isn't her parents. She needs a foundation, a home." Kate's voice is laced with love, concern. I've always admired their friendship.

"I'm aware of that."

"If you can't love her back, don't mess with her head."

I nod. "You have my word."

Chapter 30

"Friendship may, and often, does grow into love."

A LITTLE OVER AN HOUR later, I enter Cori's studio. A dozen needles are dancing their way across my forehead. Cori is nowhere to be found, but she's here. I can feel her.

Other than the Callum Scott version of "Dancing on My Own" playing in the surround system, the large space is quiet. The lyrics fill the air without effort, giving me chills. In this tale of heartache, the singer is watching the woman he loves dancing with another man, while she is unaware of his presence on the dance floor. I remember the jealousy that coursed through my veins that night at the club while watching Cori dancing with Brandon. My mind replays the scene in agonizing detail. The way her body swayed to the music. The smile on her face as she looked up at him.

The green-eyed monster stabs me again. I shake the image out of my head.

Let it go, bro. You're here to get your girl back.

Wait. Was she ever mine?

For a fleeting moment, she was.

Nerves, mingled with excitement, tap-dance in my belly. I quickly remove my coat and drop it on the green velvet lounge chair. And although I've been here a million times before, I give the room a cursory glance. Lots of storage space that is miraculously well-organized. Exposed wooden beams with visible pipes. Ancient mullioned windows casting squares of brilliant noon sunlight onto the wooden walnut floor. Shelves filled with color-coded paint tubes, books, vintage pottery jugs with art brushes, other materials and supplies, anything an artist could want in one place.

A wave of emotions sweep over me. I am surrounded by Cori. Her essence.

With my heart suddenly feeling too big to fit inside my rib cage, I take a few steps across the room. My pace slows as I stop to examine one of Cori's latest art works. The colors are bold and painted with such precise lines that are curved, yet sharply defined, giving a stable appearance. Only the long, narrow lines tumble at the same time into a mosaic. Like me, I think, stable but in an emotional free-fall inside.

I'm still examining the painting, when the double doors at the back of the studio are pushed open. Cori emerges, wearing a 'Let it Gogh' teal T-shirt and black skinny jeans, both covered with patches of paint. Her hair is bunched in a messy bun. A dry art brush is tucked behind her ear, two rolls of paper towels in one arm, and a gallon of paint in the other.

My heart does that funny little thing saved just for Cori.

I'm so happy to see her.

But the slight pause in her steps is a clear indication the feeling is not mutual. Let's be blunt, she doesn't look happy to see me.

"Hi," she greets in a low voice. "Sorry, you caught me off guard." Her lips crack into a smile that never makes it to her eyes. I return a similar pained expression. "To what do I owe this surprise?"

My first instinct is to run to her and pull her into my arms, tell her how much I've missed her, her voice, her smile, her scent, her ... everything.

So many words to say, but I can't find a way to say them. My gaze lowers to my shoes for a moment. I give myself a silent pep-talk. All things break. All things can be mended. Time to fix Cori and Dean.

Meeting Cori's gaze, I search her face and have to watch, in silence, as she closes herself off, right before my very eyes.

Okay. Okay. I can do this. Stay focused. I'm on a mission to win Cori back.

In the space of a heartbeat, I'm standing in front of her. Now that I'm closer, I notice her face is a bit puffy, her eyes red.

She's hurting.

I'm the culprit.

My heart sinks to my stomach. Not wanting to dwell on my past actions, and how much I've hurt her, I take the paint and the paper towels from her hand. Our fingers touch, and I swear, her breath hitches. Ignoring the temptation to drop everything on the floor, cup her face, and brush my lips

287

against hers, I cross the room and place her supplies on the counter top, next to the deep stainless steel sink.

Although my purpose for my visit here is clear, for a minute, I'm not sure how to proceed. My thoughts are scattered, too edgy to think straight. After a long stare, she flashes a smile, then heads over to her desk. Neither of us speak, yet the room is filled with noise—the ripping sound of tape, a sheet of paper towel tearing away from the roll, drafting paper being balled up and tossed in a wastebasket, the clink of brushes bumping against each other as Cori sorts through a jar for the right one.

"You never answered my text." My voice slices through the silence. It's surprisingly controlled.

She glances at me with a puzzled frown. "You texted me?"

I nod. "Last week."

Her index finger taps her cell phone on her desk. She lowers her head, seeming to read through her messages, then shakes her head. "I'm sorry, Dean. I don't see a text from you."

Pulling out my phone, I check the message status. The word *delivered* at the bottom indicates my text has yet to be read.

"I had a phone mishap Monday night."

On a few occasions while working, she's dropped her phone in paint or whatever is near. Many times, we were able to salvage the device. The other times, the phone had to be replaced.

"I accidentally dropped it in a bucket of water," she explains with a sheepish smile, and I can't help but smile too.

288

"Did you have to get a new phone?"

"Yeah," she says, blushing.

"So you didn't just blow me off?" I ask, while rubbing the back of my neck.

She laughs. "Of course not."

The knot of worry in my chest loosens.

She moves farther into the room, grabs a paint-splattered board, and sets it near the floor-to-ceiling window, on an old ladder that now serves as an easel. Once done, she saunters over to the shelves. After scanning the paint tubes, she grabs a few and heads toward where her easel stands.

Since I know her routine, I hustle over to the closet, grab a paint-stained sheet, and place it on the floor in front of the easel. Then I carry her stool to where she'll be sitting.

"Thank you," she mouths.

"Figured I could put my muscles to work."

She smiles, the kind of smile that paints a ray of sunshine all over her face.

I made her smile.

Pleasure spreads inside my chest. My fingers are aching with a need to touch her. I want to feel her lips against mine, feel their softness, passion, and the promise of the sweetness she's given so freely to me before.

My dick stirs for the first time in a long time. Can't blame the shameless fucker. We're in the same room with our Moonchild, standing inches away from her.

"So, what brought you here?" she finally asks, leafing through a book.

"I want to apologize."

A sigh slips through her lips. Her shoulders go rigid.

"I can't move on, Cori," I say, ready to grovel until she sees I'm human. A flesh and blood man who is capable of making mistakes like everyone else.

Nothing but a loaded silence.

A few quick strides bring me by her side. I take the book from her hand, put it on the desk, and gather her hands in mine. "I'm sorry I've hurt you."

"I'm not mad, Dean. I'm hurt. There's a difference."

I rub the pad of my thumbs over the chalk and pastel grease on her skin. "How can I make us better?"

She closes her eyes, her lips pressing together in a slight grimace. "Don't do this."

"The morning in the shower, I completely messed up," I say, revisiting the hurdles leading up to where we are now. "I wish I could take back my reaction." A deep breath slips out of my mouth. "But I can't."

Her chin trembles. Shit, she's going to cry again. My doing. I don't want to torment her any more than I already have. But I need to get everything off my chest.

"And I had no right bringing Meredith to New Hampshire."

"Why did you?"

I've wracked my mind for all possible reasons, and only came up with one. I was hurt. "When I first asked her, you had just started dating again. After the night you and I shared, I should have rescinded my offer, but the way you left made me think you didn't want a relationship. And then I thought you were still seeing Brandon."

She lets out a breath, her eyes filled with raw emotion. "So an eye for an eye."

No. Never. Not with Cori. She means too much to me.

"No."

Slowly, she releases her hands from mine and ambles over to her stool. "Then why?"

"I didn't think what we'd shared mattered to you."

She sends me a long, pained look then breaks eye contact.

"Cori." I take a step forward then stop. "You need to know I never want to be the one to hurt you."

"But you've already hurt me, Dean." Her voice is filled with the pain of my betrayal.

"I know."

Silence lingers.

She removes the paint brush tucked behind her ear, examines it as if she'd forgotten it was ever there. Then she rises to her feet, walks over to one of the shelves, and sticks it into one of the vintage pottery jugs filled with other brushes. "Brandon and I went on a couple of dates. But he wasn't the one."

I say absolutely nothing, because I'm too fucking scared to ask if I'm the one. What if she says no?

"You've been on my mind," she says, while she wipes her hands on a rag.

My heart kicks up a notch. I blink twice. No, make that at least six times. If I knew for sure I wouldn't come across as a little on the pathetic side, I'd pinch myself.

She's been thinking about me.

That means . . . Hope leaps wildly and ricochets off my chest. My heart has been sitting heavy in my gut for the last two weeks. Slowly, I feel it go back to its designated spot, now that Cori and I are standing face-to-face.

Fighting the urge to pull her into my arms, throw her on that desk, and make sweet, passionate love to her, I stuff my hands in my pockets. "I miss you."

Red leaks into her cheeks as a small smile plays on her lips.

I take a couple of steps forward, closing the space between us. "Coriander."

"I'm angry and confused." Emotional pain seeps out of her words. She lowers her gaze to the small towel in her hand. A long beat of silence fills the room.

"Cori," I say her name, my voice as rough as gravel, filled with panic and fear.

Chin up, she meets my gaze. "Let's start over."

Holy shit!

Holy shit!

She's giving me a second chance. My breath catches. I'm happy as a pig in shit. A grin creeps onto my face, and it soon stretches from one side to the other, showing every single tooth. "I like the sound of that."

"We can be friends," she continues.

"Friends," I say the word as if it's foreign to me. No. No. I can't go back to being the *boy* friend. Not with all of these emotions pouring out of me. "What's the alternative?"

She shrugs.

Wait. That's it? Friends. Or nothing.

Out of desperation, I want to accept her offer, comply with all the rules that come with it. Friendship is better than nothing at all, right? I mean, friendship is a precious gift. Cori doesn't owe me sexual or romantic interactions. Just respect her, and the relationship I already have with her, right?

A convincing *fuck no* comes from my heart.

It's the whole package or nothing. But I'm skating on thin ice, a new territory between us. "Is that what you want?"

"The last two weeks taught me something."

"What's that?" I try to ignore the tightness in my chest.

"I'd rather have you in my life as my friend than nothing at all." She smiles and squares her shoulders.

"Do you want more?"

Her head shakes. Whether in answer to my question, or because, whatever is on her mind sums up too abstruse to understand, I have no idea. Turning her to me, I watch as her long lashes sweep upward, whiskey eyes pummeling me with a one-two gut punch.

"Too much at risk," she says. "Our friendship is more important to me than testing the waters to see if we'd work."

In my heart of hearts, I know Cori is the one for me, but, in her eyes, I can see the doubt and the desire to have me back in her life. I don't want to admit it, but she has a point. There's no guarantee we'll work, but I want to at least try. "Okay, we can go back to being just friends . . . on one condition."

She shakes her head again. "You have that look in your eyes."

"I want a date with you first."

Cori stands as still as statue. "What?"

"One date."

Her brows rise in curiosity. "Like a 'date' date?"

I nod, brushing the pad of my thumb over the corner of her lip. "A man and a woman date, where I kiss you at the end, or we make love."

Her breath catches in her throat. Her eyes darken with unmistakable desire.

"However you want it to end."

"But—"

"Say 'Yes Dean, I'd love to go on a date with you'."

Crossing her arms over her chest, she pins me with a stare. "Why?"

But I'm not afraid anymore to let her know how I feel. My muscles are relaxed. There's a lightness in my chest. I move closer, to erase the distance between us, facing Cori straight on. Clasping my hand around the back of her neck, I tilt my head down and kiss her. Her lips immediately part, welcoming me. Shivers run down my spine, and I cling to her like a life line, until we break for air.

"I want to be your boyfriend," I say in a low voice, my lips a fraction away from hers.

"What?" she says on a nervous laugh.

Stroking her cheek with the pad of my thumb, I say, "Give me one date to show you I can be a great boyfriend."

"One date," she repeats, eyes locked on mine.

Hope burns in my heart; mentally, I will myself to stay calm. "Is that a yes?"

Her head tilts back just enough for her gaze to meet mine. I can see the flecks of doubt swirling in her eyes. There's an emotional war going on. The part of her that wants me, then the cautious Coriander.

After the longest pause, she finally says, "Okay, Dean. One date."

Waves of relief ripple down my spine. And I'm the happiest man in the world.

Chapter 31

"One day, love and friendship met."

I HAVE A LITTLE SECRET. One I'm trying to mask as I consider my appearance in my bathroom mirror.

I'm nervous as hell.

On the outside, nothing gives a hint of the grapefruit-sized knot in my stomach. Dark-brown hair, slightly tousled on the top. Clean-shaven chiseled jaw. Button-down white oxford shirt. Dark wash jeans.

Casual, but not in the I-don't-give-a-fuck-how-I-look way.

In less than a half-hour, Cori will be arriving for our date. My job tonight is to impress her. Convince her I'm the one. Her lobster. If I do that well, I'll achieve my ultimate goal, which is becoming her boyfriend, and so-on.

Hence, my pre-date jitters.

My footsteps move swiftly into my bedroom. A quick time check tells me that, in about forty minutes, the braised short ribs will be ready. Which is perfect, gives us time to talk, have a glass a wine.

Picking up the two top pillows, I fluff them before setting them back on the bed. Then I skim the bedroom. The last few days, I've been on the sloppy side. And since my cleaning crew isn't due until next week, I left work early to tidy the house as much as I could.

Not that I'm expecting Cori and I to end up in bed . . . okay, I want us to end up in bed, wrapped together in a pretzel position or something. I haven't been able to think about anything else.

But if that doesn't happen, that's fine too. That's not the reason I asked Cori to have dinner with me.

My main objective is to get my girl back. Sex is icing on the cake.

Grabbing my phone, I swipe the screen, scroll to my dad's contact, and press TALK. He answers right away.

"Did you follow the directions step by step?"

"To a tee," I answer while padding down the hall. Right after Cori agreed to our date, I reached out to Dad for that recipe. The one he promised to give me when I found that special woman. Well, I gave him the very short version of how I fell for Cori. After I finished, not only did he gladly share it, the man spent about two hours shopping with me for all the ingredients.

"I have a confession," Dad is saying on the other end of the line.

"You botched the recipe on purpose." I enter the kitchen. The sweet aroma of onions, carrots, and celery tease my nostrils.

Dad laughs. "Secretly, your mom and I always wished you and Cori would become more."

The worst kept secret ever. "You don't say."

"So, Coriander, huh?"

I smile at the excitement in my dad's voice. "Yeah."

"Do we need to talk about the birds and the bees again?" he asks, clearly amused.

I shake my head emphatically, to no one in particular, since I'm alone in my house. When I was fourteen, my dad sat on the edge of my bed and said to me: *Always think with your head, not the one in your pants. And always wear a condom. Otherwise, you'll walk around with a head that's out of commission. You don't want a head that's out of commission, and you don't want babies until you know love.*

"No need," I answer. "You did a great job the first time."

"Son, your mom and I are happy it's Cori." I know he means it wholeheartedly. "Have fun tonight."

After we hang up, I head over to the living room.

Last night, Lucas had a late meeting, and since his babysitter wasn't available for a last-minute emergency, Emma and I spent some time together. For me, it's not babysitting. I love that little girl. I pick up a few pieces of LEGO, fragments of fraying string, and tiny triangles of construction paper from the mosaic project we worked on together, then place them inside the art project container I keep just for when Uncle Dean comes to the rescue.

I light a match and burn a few candles. So, I like candles. They make my place smell like an adult lives here, not some lazy-ass college kid. It's a dude candle, okay? This scent, in particular, gives you the smell of pine burning in the distance, tea, and even a little leather.

Picking up the remote, I click off the television playing in the background and replace it with Vampire Weekend, feel good music to help me get ready. Just what I need to take all the insane pressure off wooing a girl.

Not just any girl. Coriander. The girl who stole my heart over twenty years ago.

And just maybe, she'll forgive all of my stupidity and give me a second chance.

After arranging the white dinner plates on the table, I head to the bar and pour myself a glass of whiskey. When the ding-dong of the doorbell announces Cori's arrival. I give the room a once-over. Wide open space. Dark colors. Taupe sofa. Diplomat vintage leather chair. Clean, masculine lines, rough-hewn logs. My house screams a bachelor's home.

But today, it reflects romance. Two dozen pink carnations are striking against the backdrop of the stone wall. One of Cori's favorites, "La Traviata," now plays softly on the sound system. The burning candles light the room.

I take a deep breath to calm my jangled nerves. Anxious thoughts breed anxious thoughts. Time to break the cycle. She said yes to a date. Now she's here. This means she's open to the idea of us, right?

Not giving myself time to think, I open the door, and there stands Cori.

My heart about stops for a minute, until I give myself a mental shake and help her out of her long, wool coat to reveal a navy, halter jumpsuit.

When she walks past me to enter the house, I get an eye-catching view of her jumpsuit. The back is cut low and covered by the thick layers of her halter neck tie closure. I fight the urge to tug on the ties, releasing them for my pleasure.

She stands in the middle of my living room, body language unsure, lips painted red, hair pulled back from her face in a slight updo style that makes her look like a beauty queen. Wait—red lips. That has to be a good sign. Brandon didn't get red lipstick.

"What have you done here?" She snaps me back to reality.

I watch her scanning the room. "You don't like?"

She turns to me, her whiskey eyes roaming over me from head to toe, until her gaze rests on my face. See the slight shimmer, the hesitation. I can detect lust warring with caution, and when caution wins, I take it as a good sign. She wants me. But her dilemma is evident. By the way her hands are clasped together, she's still a bit guarded.

Patience has never been my virtue. But I'm in love.

A changed man.

Strong enough to chance being broken again. Preferably not. But willing to take the risk.

Because of that, I ask, instead, "Wine?" and walk past her down the hall into the kitchen, slow enough for her to join me. Which she does. For a moment, we walk in silence. Our footsteps in synchronized beat. "You look gorgeous, Coriander."

"Thanks." She smooths her hands over the front of her pantsuit, then her eyes scan up and down my frame. "So do you. Then again, you're quite easy on the eyes."

The compliment makes me smile. "You think I'm easy on the eyes?"

She nods.

"How come you never told me?"

"You already have a mammoth ego."

I laugh. "I prefer to say I never went through the phase where I questioned my self-esteem." We enter the kitchen together. I check the timer, then grab her favorite Pinot Noir. As I unscrew it, she inhales the aroma of the braised ribs. I swear, I heard her stomach growl.

"That smells delicious, Dean."

"Thanks. I've been cooking for the last two and half hours."

"Wow. I feel special."

Our gazes lock and hold for several heartbeats. I'm sure, on the surface, I appear calm and unflappable, but there's an underlying tension in my body. "Let's get one thing out of the way," I say in a husky voice.

"What's that?"

She licks her bottom lip. My heart trips. As much as I'm dying to kiss her, I refrain. Instead, I caress a strand of loose hair from her temple, tucking it behind her ear. Eyes still locked on hers, I say, "I'm in love with you."

Silence ensues. Cori's facial expression is closed.

Not what I expected. "Say something, Moonchild."

"You don't know what love is."

"Maybe not fully," I admit, holding her gaze. "But I know it's messy, scary, and the most wonderful fucking feeling I've ever felt in my life."

"The tug and pull game has never been my thing," she says after a long minute.

I trail a finger down the curve of her face, down her throat, to her bare shoulder, feeling her shiver under my touch. "This isn't a game."

Rich, golden brown eyes appraise my face for a long moment. When she finally speaks, her voice is accusing. "You flaked on me . . . twice."

"I'm an idiot." There's an awkward silence I have no idea how to broach. "This is where you're supposed to say, but also caring," I joke.

She smiles at me, and then drags her teeth over her lower lip as she appears to contemplate my words.

Fuck. I want to do that. And much more.

"You are caring, but" –she steps out of my grasp– "Dean, I don't know."

As she walks past me, I reach for her hand, lace our fingers together, and stop her mid-stride. "Do you trust me?"

"I'm here."

True. But she didn't answer the question. I've learned a few things in my thirty years. One of them is that forgiving isn't the hard part, trusting again is the challenge. "I need you to trust me again."

After the longest minute, she says, "I trust you."

"Can you keep an open mind?"

"About?"

"Us." The timer dings. Neither of us move. "I need to know you'll do that."

Finally, she nods and whispers, "Okay." A wave of relief washes over me, until she says, "But—"

"No buts," I say, half-teasing.

She lets out a sigh. "Our friendship . . ."

Bringing her hand to my mouth, I brush my lips against the back of it. "This is where our friendship and our love meet, Coriander."

She shakes her head as if to clear it from any temptation to let go her reservations. "Let me decide how to proceed." She pauses. The silence stretches, until she speaks. "If I want more, I'll initiate. You need to give me that, because you and I are greater than everything else around us."

"Alright." I nod, understanding the significance of her statement. We've known each other all of our lives. Our worlds are forever connected by family and friends. She owns my heart. "Ball's in your court. It's your move to make."

Chapter 32

"Love is friendship set on fire."

PART WAY INTO THE EVENING, we're in the dining room, eating dinner. The mood is relaxed. Conversation is easy. There's a battle inside me. I want to kiss Cori, but I don't want to come off as pushy or overbearing. Also, I don't want to ruin the atmosphere.

"Remember when you stood in as my model?" she asks after a taking a sip of her wine.

"When I was made to feel cheap?"

She grins. "You loved it."

"Confession time."

She arches a brow. "Should I be scared?"

"I kept looking at your ass the whole time," I admit. "I had to keep reciting the periodic table."

She laughs and it makes my heart smile.

"Did it work?"

I shrug. "Thank goodness I still have a love-hate relationship with the periodic table." I take a forkful of the truffle fries I made, just for her, and place them in her mouth. After she swallows, she releases a satisfying sigh. My dick stirs. I shift in my chair.

The periodic table contains one hundred and eighteen elements of chemistry. Chemical element: Actinium. Symbol: AC: Atomic number eighty-nine.

There. Much better.

If anything is going to happen, she has to make the move. By the way, I can probably list all the elements in alphabetical order. Not showing off. I just really hated chemistry.

"You were saying about my modeling days?" I ask Cori.

"Well, you were a hit. Some of the women have asked if you'll stand in again."

"If you ever need me for a night, just say the word." Her eyes drop to my lips and linger a minute, before she reaches for her wineglass. Immediately, I grab the bottle and refill her glass. "That was not meant the way it came out. I'm trying to behave."

"I know." She takes a sip of her wine, then gives me one of those smiles that make my heart trip. "So, what is it you want from me, now that you've confessed your love?"

"Are we discussing us?" I ask, needing to be sure she's ready to explore us as a couple.

She appears to consider my question before saying, "The possibility, anyway."

"I want the whole thing with you. A relationship." I don't look away as I say this. "The boyfriend and girlfriend kind, where we snugglefuck."

She clears her throat. "Snugglefuck?"

"Napping, snuggling, followed by passionate or rough sex," I explain.

She purses her lips, drawing my attention to them, all shiny and glossy with a dash of red.

"Basically, I want to always be by your side, or under you, or on top of you."

"I think I got the picture," she says and brushes a swath of hair from her forehead.

But I don't think she does. This isn't about only sex . . . although it might sound that way. It's just the way my mind works. Elbows on the table, I lean forward, holding her gaze. "I want you to move in with me."

"That's a lot." Her brows are furrowed as she pushes her fork around her plate. "And fast."

A note of pain peppers her voice. I engage her eyes with mine, forcing her to see everything that's inside me. "Cori," I start, volumes of regret making my voice hoarse. "I know what I want, and it's you."

Nothing but a loaded silence.

Earlier, I promised I wouldn't push. Willing to give her all the time in the world . . . Well, tonight anyway. If my attempt fails, I am willing to wait for her for as long as forever, even though I hate waiting. But this is Cori we're talking about.

306

My forever.

My best friend.

I have the rest of my life to prove my love. "How're your students?" I ask, changing the subject to something safer. For the rest of the meal, our conversation flows with ease.

After dinner, and a bottle of wine later, we move to the living room. Other than the sound system playing softly in the background, the room is quiet. My head is filled with questions. Is she nervous? Strung out? Bored? Why won't she look at me?

Then something occurs to me. Her online profile. What if she met some douche during the last few weeks?

"How's the online dating going?" I ask and hold my breath.

"I took down my profile." Cori walks over to the carnations and runs her fingers along the petals. "Carnations are my favorite."

"I know. These are for you."

She spins to face me. For the briefest second, her gaze meets mine. Her eyes are sparkling with a million small fires. Then she breaks the contact and focuses her attention on my collection of books in the black salvaged-wood cabinet. A way to shut me out. Too late. I caught the carnal desire burning in her eyes.

She wants me.

"There are at least two dozen carnations," she notes.

"All yours."

She looks at me, shakes her head, but I can tell she's smiling on the inside.

"Let's talk about your online dating."

"Okay."

"Why did you close your account?" I ask, pulse racing.

"I don't think I'll find my lobster online."

Hope beats in my chest like a heartbeat. "No?"

"No," she confirms.

My heart pumps a little faster. I am flying high in the sky, devoid of problems and able to leap small buildings in a single bound . . . no, wait, that is Superman. Must stay focused. "I hear lobsters mate for life."

This makes her smile. "I hear female lobsters are very aggressive."

Need and hunger rolls through me. The way her eyes have darkened tells me the same need is racing through her. "Are you having fun with me tonight?"

"I always have a good time with you."

"Tonight is different."

She doesn't answer, but the silence between us is easy. "Those Magic Changes" starts playing. Three long strides bring me in front of her. I run my finger along the curve of her cheekbone. "Dance with me."

"Last time we danced, your feet were my stomping ground."

"I love being your stomping ground."

She laughs, and I can feel whatever reservations she has leave with the rolling of her shoulders. The muscles around my heart relax. I croon along, but in my Danny Zuko voice. A slow smile creeps across her face. My hand drifts to her hip, settling there, and pulling her closer. She inhales sharply as her arm reaches up and tangles around my neck. Then she's against my chest, chiseled to perfection.

For the next two minutes, we dance. Her face buries in my neck so deep that her lips brush against my skin. A faint inhale fills my senses with her essence—lavender and seashells. It's erotic and comforting at the same time. I close my eyes and let the tempo of our bodies fall into a trance.

"Dean." She runs her fingers down my spine, pulling me closer, until there's no space left between us, and I can feel the beating of her heart against my chest.

My dick immediately stands at attention, poking her through my jeans. I want to kiss her bare shoulders, touch her, feel her. But I can't. She has to initiate. I gave her my word. Brushing my thumb on the exposed skin of her back, I say, "Ignore that tent in my pants."

"Hard to ignore." Her voice is soft and warm against my neck.

"Did you know I can recite the periodic table in alphabetical order?" She tips her chin up to meet my gaze. I soak in her beauty, the slight tilt of her nose, the fullness of her lips. Damn it. Control is slipping. "Cori," I warn, voice low.

"Do you feel that?" she asks, and my heart somersaults, because I'm feeling too much.

"Other than what's poking you through my jeans?"

"Yes," she says, cheeks flushed.

"What are you feeling, Cori?" I'm dying here. This is not merely a dance. Her body firmly pressing against mine is communicating my deepest feelings, wordlessly telling me she wants me. She wants *us*.

"I feel that you and I can be good together."

Butterflies go crazy, low in my stomach, and my heartbeat rages out of control. "What else are you feeling?"

"Well." Her lips curve into a mischievous smile. "You're definitely poking my stomach."

"What else?"

She circles one of my shirt buttons with her finger. Around and around, over and over, slow and steady, and my heart loses its rhythm again. About the time normal cadence returns, she works the button in and out of its hole.

With a tilt of her head, our eyes lock, hers serious. "I want us."

The words barely leave Cori's lips, when my mouth crushes down on hers, kissing her like we've never kissed before. In that embrace, my worries lose their sting, and optimism raises its head from the dirt. Perhaps, the hope had been there all along, but without me taking control of my destiny, it was trapped, like crystals in a stone.

When we break apart for air, I rest my forehead against hers and gather some much-needed oxygen. "I've missed you."

She splays her hands on my chest and slowly brushes my shirt off my shoulders. Then her lips are on my skin, trailing delicate kisses on the black ink on my chest. "Show me," she whispers.

Oh, hell yeah. With fucking pleasure. I'd like to say I have willpower and that our lovemaking will be slow. But Cori is in my arms. God . . . I can barely breathe. My brain is on fire and the warmth spreads throughout my entire body.

I am addicted.

The last two weeks were torture. Having her here, now, in my house, telling me she wants me, her kisses . . . this is my salvation.

My hand raises to her hair, and I tangle my fingers in it. My other hand drags along her bronzed shoulders, finds to the knot behind her neck and loosens the strap of her halter top. Leaning in, I kiss along her jaw, down her throat, and then against the hollow of her collarbone, as I unzip the bottom piece of her jumpsuit.

Then I gently push the material down her shoulders, and she steps from the jumpsuit as it falls onto the floor. As flawless as the heart of a diamond, she stands before me in skimpy, black lace panties. Her skin, soft and sun kissed, shimmers golden in the soft light. The moon, in its full splendor, slants in through the window and lights up the room, illuminating every curve of her body in blue radiance—her upward nipples, the contour of her hips.

"Fucking Christ."

"I was hoping we'd end up starting over." She meets my gaze, her eyes hooded with desire and something else that I recognize. It matches all the deep-seated emotions stirring inside me. "As boyfriend and girlfriend."

I pull her against me a little rougher than intended. When our bare chests crush together, I let out a guttural groan. The softness of her skin against the hardness of mine. *Fuck me.* My mind is blown. I love this woman so much. Her confidence. Her sensuality. She's kissing me, hard and full of heat, making my pulse soar.

We're staggering like drunks down the hall, until I scoop her in my arms and carry her up the stairs to my bedroom. We are feasting on each other like starving animals. Our tongues continue to tangle in a hot duet. Teeth, mouths, and hands are everywhere, until I place her on my bed and step back, pulling her panties from her hips as I go.

She meets my gaze with lust-filled eyes. "We're okay?"

"I owe you at least three more orgasms tonight," I say, as I strip off the rest of my clothes in nanosecond speed.

"Why three?"

I sink on the bed next to her. "Because this one is a quickie."

"I love quickies." Her face changes into a vision of relaxed joy. "Especially when I get three orgasms later."

Laughing, I roll over her and adjust her under me. In response, she arches her back, wraps her arms around my neck and her legs around my waist. Seeking me. Giving me full access to her sweet opening. Promising so much pleasure pressing against the tip of my erection, inviting me to penetrate her walls.

"I love you, Dean." She smiles at me with a love so intense, it warms my soul like a fireplace on a cold winter's night.

The emotions spill onto me, making me feel and want things I never thought I would. When I kiss her, it's hungry and soul-searching. I'm consumed by the woman beneath me. Our bodies are aligned—lips to lips, heart to heart.

"So fucking good," I mutter.

She shifts her hips and locks her legs around my ass, drawing me deeper. "Faster. Please, Dean. Faster. I need fast," she urges.

My heart is a train pounding the tracks. Linking our fingers together, I capitulate and give her what she asks. She meets my every move. Each thrust becomes more fervent. Compared to the first time we slept together, which had been intense, this is different. We are connected—spirit, body, and soul.

Love merges with lust as we fuck faster and faster.

EPILOGUE

"Friends yesterday, lovers today, soulmates tomorrow."

ONE MONTH INTO OUR RELATIONSHIP, my feelings for Cori have not waned. On the contrary, every day, I fall deeper. The more love I give her, the more I have bursting inside of me . . . crazy, huh?

We're on our way home from celebrating her twenty-eighth birthday with the rest of the crew in the city. We karaoked, ate and drank too much. Not me though, I'm the driver.

My attention is on the road. Other than the monotonous sound of raindrops beating the roof of my car, blending in with the occasional splash of tires through scattered puddles, there is a comfortable silence around us.

"Tonight was fun," Cori says as we cruise down the freeway back to Alpine.

My lips curve into a smile. "I'm glad you had a good time."

"Thanks for organizing everything."

"Anything for you, Moonchild." We've been living together for a month now. And I couldn't be happier. Let's not even talk about my cock; the one-eyed lizard is over the moon.

"I'm sorry I brought Brandon to your birthday gathering."

I reach for her hand and bring it to my lips. "Now, when we tell our kids about my fateful thirtieth birthday party, I can say we celebrated with the four most important people in my life . . . and Mommy's date."

Cori shakes her head. "You're never going to let me live this one down, are you?"

I laugh. "For you? I'll make an exception."

Leaning into me, she places a kiss on my cheek. "You're the best boyfriend."

"Ever?"

Cori chuckles. "Ever."

"Hey, do you think I need to speak to Kate?" I ask, switching the subject. Don't worry, I'm not hung up on Abercrombie & Fitch dude. I'm over the whole Brandon fiasco. Trust me.

"About?"

"Picnic at Central Park with Emma and Lucas." I shrug. "I don't know." Don't get me wrong, I think Lucas and Cam are both great catches and all, but I've also seen them in action. Most importantly, Lucas has done the relationship thing, even been married and divorced. Settling down is the last thing on his mind.

"Would it be so terrible if something were to develop between them?"

"Well, yeah." I can feel Cori's eyes on me. Taking my attention off the road for a second, I meet her amused gaze.

Allow me to say, I don't share her humor. "Lucas and I exchange stories."

She arches a brow. "About me, too?"

Remember, we don't talk about the women we care about. "Never." My voice is full of conviction as I return my attention to the road. The rain continues to fall in heavy sheets across the roadway, slapping harder and faster than my windshield wipers can clear it away, and creating foggy smudges over the glass.

"Good to know." Cori laughs, not sounding one bit concerned. "Anyway, there's nothing to worry about. Lucas and Kate are just friends."

"So were we," I point out.

"We still are." From her seat, she leans into me and nuzzles against my neck. "I'm lucky. I'm in love with my best friend."

We're still adjusting to living together and learning a few things about each other that twenty-one years of friendship couldn't teach us. For one, she's extremely sensitive to much more than I thought. The woman cries every time we watch *The Notebook*. My opinion? That's the cheesiest movie ever made. But I watch it with her, over and over, because, one, it makes her happy in a sad way, and two, I get to hold her against me.

Another thing, she's passionate about the earth. She also gets annoyed when I leave the toilet seat up. We've even had a few disagreements. But just because we argue, doesn't mean I will stop loving her. Side note, makeup sex is fucking out of this world.

Oh, my time with Cam and Lucas has declined a little, but it's not due to Cori's demands. I'd actually rather be home with my girl than watch Cam and Lucas pick up random strangers.

You think I'm full of shit. Kid you not. We've woven a basket of delicate textures—friendship, trust, lust, and love. I want nothing more than to be with my girl today, tomorrow, forever.

I flick the signal and make a left, opposite of the direction of our house.

"That's not the way home."

Home. I love the sound of that word. "The night is not over yet."

"But it's raining," she purrs, "and I was thinking we could cuddle."

Shifting gears, I pull the car into park, reach over Cori into the glove compartment. As I do so, my arm brushes over the leg of her jeans. "We can cuddle later." I retrieve a navy silk scarf we used as a blindfold last night. "I have a surprise for you."

"A repeat of last night, here." Her eyes sparkle with mirth. "Your car is a bit small. I mean, we get a little crazy . . . but—"

I smile, in spite of the nervous knot in my stomach. "We're not going to do it in my car."

"Too bad."

For a second, I'm tempted to alter my plans and bang Cori in the car. But I refrain. Believe me, that took all of my strength. Trust me when I say this, sex with the right person is addictive as fuck.

"Do you trust me?"

"Always," she says, holding my gaze.

"Then let me blindfold you."

Without hesitation, she unbuckles her seat belt, turns her back to me. I gently cover her eyes and tie the scarf into a knot. "Can you see?" I ask in a rough voice.

"Not a thing," she answers while clipping her seat belt back on.

I rev up the engine and turn on the radio. The Black Keys blasts out of the speakers, the beat pulsing in tune with my racing heart and the rain on the windows.

Less than two minutes later, I let out a long breath as I park. "Don't move."

"Not moving."

I get out of the car and come around for Cori. After unbuckling her, I warn, "I'm going to pick you up." And scoop her into my embrace. She laughs as her arms loop around my neck.

After kicking the door closed, I move swiftly and carry her to our destination. Rain lashes down on us in cold, icy pellets, biting into our skin. Wet grass and dirt mush under my shoes. Focusing on my mission, I quicken my pace. "Still with me?"

"As long as you want me."

Slowly, I release her. My gut tightens as I loosen the handkerchief. She blinks, then her eyes adjust to her surroundings. Our elementary school playground, where Cori punched me in the gut a little over two decades ago. The many trees around us. The playing area with the swings and slides for the smaller children.

"How about forever?" My voice is rough, filled with emotions.

She looks at one oak tree in front of her. We've spent countless hours sitting and talking under that tree. Cori turns and stares at me for a beat before her gaze swivels back to the tree, then back to me. Looking shaky, she whispers in a cracked voice, "Dean."

"I figure, this is the perfect place to ask you to marry me."

Her eyes lower to the little black velvet box in my hands, and she gasps. "Oh."

"You and I are intertwined. It's been this way . . . a long time. Except, for the longest time, I was just the boy friend. I don't want to be only your best friend and boyfriend anymore." I drop down to one knee in front of her, right into a puddle of cold rain. But I don't care. "We're best friends, and lovers, and now, I want to be your forever." With butterflies in my stomach and my head buzzing with possibilities, I ask Cori the most important question of our life. "Will you marry me?

I flip open the box and present the round, brilliant diamond engagement ring I had designed especially with Cori in mind. It's graceful, refined, and feminine, with a whimsical feel. Just like my girl.

Except for the huge raindrops splattering with charged energy, there is absolute silence. My heart thuds in my chest. "Say something, Moonchild."

"Dean." She chokes out my name. It's hard to tell when she starts crying, and even more difficult to discern between her tears and the rain as she turns her face to the sky above.

"Don't cry. Just say yes. Lucas and Cam are betting against me," I tease.

She laughs, takes my hands in hers and brings me back to my feet. "You're soaking wet."

I smile. "So are you, but I—" She cups my face and kisses me hard on the lips. With a groan, I pull a fraction away. "Is that a yes?"

With a quick brush of her hand, she brushes matted hair away from her eyes. "God, yes. I'll be your wife."

My heart rolls over, flips like a somersault. I'm an overflowing bottle of bubbling joy. "I love you, Coriander Phillips."

"I love you, Dean Conrad Morello."

And there you have it. It's official like a referee with a whistle, I'm going to marry my best friend. Ever since Cori and I met over twenty years ago, I knew she was special. I knew what we had was special. Somewhere between all of our laughs, long talks, buzzing texts, even the stupid little arguments, I fell in love.

The End

ACKNOWLEDGMENTS

Big hugs to my beta readers for your patience and your sage words. Thank you to Sarah of Okay Creations for the gorgeous cover! PK Designs Editing and Graphics, and Formatting Done Wright for your brilliance. Huge gratitude to all the bloggers who continue to participate in my journey. Love to all of my readers. Without you, this ride wouldn't be as much fun. A special shout out to my husband, you're sexier than any book boyfriend. Thank you for all of your support and our Happy Chaos.

The Boy Friend by Mika Jolie

OLD-FASHIONED Recipe

Old Fashioned Recipe – Coriander's drink of choice

Old Fashioned recipe

rating

2 oz. bourbon whiskey

2 dashes Angostura® bitters

1 splash water

1 tsp sugar

1 maraschino cherry

1 orange wedge

Mix sugar, water and angostura bitters in an old-fashioned glass. Drop in a cherry and an orange wedge. Muddle into a paste using a muddler or the back end of a spoon. Pour in bourbon, fill with ice cubes, and stir.

Read more: Old Fashioned recipe
http://www.drinksmixer.com/drink407.html#ixzz4aVpJUNz4

PLAYLIST

https://open.spotify.com/user/mikajb/playlist/5leQ5ruSj
VUvTqph93OEg8

Maneater

Grace Mitchell

Volare

Dean Martin

Don't Let Me Be Misunderstood

Nina Simone

Atlas, Rise!

Metallica

Stairway to Heaven

Led Zeppelin

Dancing on My Own

The Boy Friend by Mika Jolie

Robyn

Oh Girl

The Chi-Lites

Stressed Out

Twenty One Pilots

Work

Rihianna and Drake

Dancing On My Own

Callum Scott

Sway

Dean Martin

La Traviata

Luciano Pavoratti

Say Goodbye

Dave Matthews Band

The Boy Friend by Mika Jolie

Friends
Ed Sheeran

Awake My Soul
Mumford & Sons

You're The One That I Want
John Travolta and Olivia Newton-John

ABOUT *Mika Jolie*

Mika Jolie lives in New Jersey with her Happy Chaos—her husband and their energizer bunnies. A sports fanatic and a wine aficionado, she's determined to balance it all and still write about life experiences and matters of the heart. Let's face it, people are complicated and love can be messy. When she's not weaving life and romance into evocative tales, you can find her on a hiking adventure, apple picking, or whatever her three men can conjure up.

She loves to hear from readers. Connect with Mika on Facebook, Twitter, Goodreads and Amazon.

Facebook:
https://www.facebook.com/mikajolie.author/?ref=hl

Twitter: https://twitter.com/MikaJolie1

Goodreads:
https://www.goodreads.com/author/show/8294433.Mika_Jolie

Amazon: http://amazon.com/author/mikajolie

Instagram: https://www.instagram.com/mika_jolie/

For latest news on her current works-in-progress, interviews with fellow authors, or just to see what she's up to, check out her website: http://www.mikajolie.com or sign up for her newsletter http://mikajolie.us8.list-manage1.com/subscribe?u=031e437e36c82d666bd5f3d46&id=af83626053 where you can hear her latest news and enjoy giveaways.

ALSO BY *Mika Jolie*

Martha's Way Series

The Scale

Need You Now

Tattooed Hearts

Wrapped in Red

Poison & Wine Series

Somewhere to Begin